WILLIAM MANN

Empty Ground

"When the buffalo went away the hearts
of my people fell to the ground, and they
could not lift them up again."

—Plenty Coups, Crow chief

Contents

Author's Note

Empty Ground is a work of fiction. Declan Shea never existed. But the buffalo did. The Crow Nation did. Their destruction did.

Between 1849 and 1883, hide hunters working the northern and southern plains killed somewhere between fifteen and thirty million bison. The herds that had sustained the plains nations for thousands of years—organizing their economies, their calendars, their spiritual lives, their entire relationship to the land—were gone within a generation. The last wild count, in 1889, found 325 animals.

This was not an accident. It was policy. General Philip Sheridan said so himself.

Declan Shea is a fictional man. He is also every man who rode onto the Powder River range with a Sharps rifle and a mule and did the work the continent made available to him. He understood what he was part of. He filed it away. He kept working. That is the most honest thing this novel can say about the men who did what he did—and about the human capacity to understand a thing completely and continue anyway.

Ashkáale is fictional, too. But the Crow women who watched their world come apart were not. The Apsáalooke—the Crow Nation—made a calculation in the nineteenth century that has been misunderstood ever since. They allied with the United States Army against the Lakota, their most immediate existential threat. They were not naive. They were not collaborators. They were a small nation fighting for survival on multiple fronts, making the best decision available with the information they had. That decision saved the Crow reservation—the fifth-largest in the United States—and it cost them everything else.

I am not Crow. I am not Native American. I have no claim to this history except the claim any human being has to the truth: that it happened, that it matters, and that silence about it is its own kind of erasure.

I visited the Crow Reservation, the Little Bighorn Battlefield, the Bighorn Mountains, the Powder River country, the Black Hills, and Deadwood while researching this novel. I stood in the grass above the Little Bighorn, where the Crow scouts watched what they could not stop. I stood at the edge of the Powder River range where the herds ran. The landscape is as described. The history is as recorded.

The Apsáalooke endure. The Crow Nation is still here—still fighting for sovereignty, still fishing and hunting on the ceded lands their negotiators secured in 1868, rights litigated as recently as 2019 in the United States Supreme Court. The historical notes and sources in the appendix are offered for readers who want to follow this story beyond the final page.

This novel is my attempt, imperfect as it is, to contribute to the work of honest remembering.

William Mann, 2026

Buffalo Skull Pile

Buffalo skull pile, Raines, Michigan, circa 1892. In 1849, an estimated sixty million buffalo ranged the North American plains. By 1889, there were 325.

1

Deadwood

Deadwood in the fall of 1884 never quite slept and never quite woke. It went on anyway, noise and mud and the sour stink of ambition, twenty-four hours a day, seven days a week, indifferent to the men it chewed through.

Elias had been there three months.

Long enough to learn its rhythms. Long enough to know the men worth watching, the streets to avoid after dark, the arguments best left alone. Long enough that Hendricks's stable felt like another life, the hay and leather, the children playing with Pup, Mrs. Patterson's quiet gratitude, though it had been only two months since he'd ridden north out of the Black Hills with everything he owned tied behind his saddle.

He'd set up at the edge of town, where the noise finally thinned. A rope corral. A lean-to for gear. Enough grass for the string he'd built, trading up from what Bridger left him. Six horses now. Good animals. He knew each one.

Biter stood apart from the others, as he always did. Mean and magnificent and entirely unconcerned with anyone's opinion of him.

Pup lay near the corral gate. Head on his paws. Watching the street.

He was always watching the street.

The man came up the main thoroughfare on a Tuesday morning, moving through the crowd like water around rocks, not avoiding people, just never quite making contact. Big. Maybe fifty, maybe older. Hard to tell with men who'd lived rough. His face had stopped bothering with expressions years ago. Just flat. Watchful. The eyes taking everything in and giving nothing back.

He wore a buffalo coat, worn thin at the elbows, the hide stiff with old grease and something darker. The coat alone told you something. Buffalo coats were common enough, but this one had the look of a man who'd made it himself, from an animal he'd killed and hadn't cared much about the craftsmanship.

He stopped at the rope corral.

Looked at the horses.

Pup's head came up.

Elias was replacing a shoe on a roan mare at the far end of the corral. He registered the stillness in the dog like you registered weather coming. Didn't look up yet. Just noted it. "You selling?" the man said.

Irish.

The accent worn down by years and distance, but still there underneath, like an old scar under new skin.

Elias set the mare's hoof down and straightened. Wiped his hands on his pants.

The man looked at the horses how a man looks at tools. What can this do for me. How long before it breaks.

"Looking for something specific?" Elias said.

"Trail horse. One that'll cover ground. Don't need it pretty."

"Where you headed?"

"North. Maybe east. Wherever the work is."

Elias looked at his string. Six horses. He knew what each one needed, what each one could give, what kind of man each would tolerate.

He looked at Pup.

The dog was on his feet now. Head level. Eyes on the man. Tail down. Still.

Elias thought of Hendricks. The way the old man would go still when a certain kind of customer stepped through the door. Not tense. Just still. Waiting to see which way it went. And afterward, when the man had gone, Hendricks would go back to his work without comment. Just pick up the hoof again. Keep working. As if some things didn't need explaining.

"I don't think I've got what you need," Elias said.

The man looked at him. Something moved behind the flat eyes. Not anger. Just calculation.

"You've got six horses," he said.

"None of them right for what you're describing."

The man was quiet. His eyes moved slowly across the string. Then they stopped on Biter.

"That gray," he said.

"Not for sale," Elias said.

"Everything's for sale."

"Not that horse."

The man was quiet again. His eyes stayed on Biter. His hand moved, just slightly, toward the rope corral, fingers reaching for the top strand.

The growl came from low and deep, the kind that didn't start in the throat. Pup hadn't moved forward. Just stood there, the sound rolling out of him like something ancient and certain. Ears back, head low.

The man's hand stopped.

He looked at Pup for a long moment. Pup looked back. Neither of them moved.

Something passed across the man's face. Not fear. Just the recognition of a thing that meant what it said.

He let his hand drop.

"Mule man," Elias said. "End of the street. Left side. Mule will serve you better on this ground anyway."

The man looked at Elias. Looked at Pup. Then he turned and walked back into the street. Through the crowd. Water around rocks. Gone.

Pup watched until he was out of sight.

Then he turned and looked at Elias.

"Yeah," Elias said quietly. "I know."

He went back to the roan mare. Picked up her hoof. Kept working.

But he watched the street for the rest of the morning.

* * *

The mule trader's name was Pruitt. A narrow man with a narrow face and the cautious eyes of someone who'd been cheated enough times to be suspicious of everyone, but not quite enough times to be smart about it.

Declan looked at the mules in the pen. Four of them. Two were too old, legs stiffening, the kind of animals that would get you halfway to where you were going and quit. One was young and green and would spend the first month trying to kill you. The fourth was maybe eight years old. Deep chest. Short back. The kind of mule that would work all day and ask for nothing but water and grain.

"That one," Declan said.

Pruitt named a price.

Declan named a lower one.

Pruitt shook his head.

Declan looked at the mule. Looked at Pruitt. Looked at the mule again. He didn't say anything. Just waited with the particular patience of a man who had nowhere else to be and nothing else to want and would stand here all day if that's what it took.

Most men couldn't stand silence. Pruitt was one of them.

He came down five dollars.

Declan paid him, most of it, and led the mule out of the pen. Pruitt was still counting the bills when Declan turned the corner.

He'd short-changed him four dollars.

Pruitt probably wouldn't notice until later. And even if he did, he wouldn't be sure. That was the thing about men like Pruitt. They were never quite sure.

Declan tied the mule to a post outside a saloon and went in.

Not to drink. He didn't drink. Drink made men stupid, and Declan had spent too many years watching what stupid looked like to want any part of it. Just to sit for a moment out of the wind and think about the next thing.

The saloon was the kind of place Deadwood had a hundred of. Low ceiling. Tobacco smoke thick enough to cut. Men hunched over cards or drinks or both. A piano in the corner that someone was playing badly.

He took a table near the wall where he could see the door.

Always near the wall. Always facing the door.

He'd learned that somewhere on the road between New York and here. One of the small lessons the continent had taught him. There were men in the world who would take from you if you let them, and the only way not to let them was to see them coming.

He ordered coffee. Sat with it. Thought about the horse trader.

The man with the wolf dog.

There was something about him that sat wrong with Declan. Not threatening. Not weak. Steady in a way that most men in Deadwood weren't steady. Like he'd seen something that had settled him. Like he knew something Declan didn't.

Declan didn't like men who knew things he didn't.

And the dog.

He'd looked into that dog's eyes and seen something he hadn't seen in an animal in a long time. Maybe ever. Not aggression. Not fear. Just clarity. The dog knew exactly what Declan was. Had looked at him like you looked at a thing you'd already decided about.

Declan finished his coffee. Left a coin on the table. Not enough to cover it.

* * *

He walked out into the street.

Deadwood in the afternoon was noise and mud and the smell of men who hadn't bathed since summer. He moved through the crowd with ease. Watching. Calculating. Reading each face for what it wanted and what it had and whether either of those things was any use to him.

He was passing the row of cribs on the east side of the main street when he saw her.

She was sitting in the open doorway of one of them. Young. Maybe seventeen. Maybe less. Dark hair loose around her shoulders. She wore a dress too thin for the weather and too bright for daylight, and she sat with her hands folded in her lap while a man stood over her talking.

Declan didn't know what the man was saying. Didn't matter. The man's posture said enough. The way he leaned. The way his hand rested on the doorframe above her head.

The girl wasn't looking at him.

She was looking at something else entirely. Something that wasn't the street or the man or the crib or Deadwood or any of it. Her eyes were open, but she was somewhere else. Gone inside herself to a place the man couldn't reach.

Declan had seen that look before.

Once.

On a face he hadn't let himself think about in years.

Maeve at the table in the cottage in Clare while Thomas came through the door. Maeve on the pallet in the room on Mulberry Street when the footsteps came up the stairs. That particular way she had of leaving without moving. Of being somewhere else while her body stayed.

He'd thought it was just Maeve. Something particular to her.

He understood now it wasn't particular to anyone. It was just what happened to people when the world gave them no other way out.

He stood there for a moment.

The man was still talking. The girl was still somewhere else.

Declan's hand moved toward his belt. An old reflex. Then stopped.

Not his business.

Never his business.

He'd learned that too somewhere between New York and here. Getting involved in other people's trouble was how you got trouble of your own. The world was full of girls with that look in their eyes, and there was nothing you could do about any of them, and the ones who tried ended up dead or in jail or just used up.

He turned and walked away.

But the look stayed with him.

Maeve's eyes in a stranger's face.

The brush she'd carried across an ocean.

Her hands, empty on the pallet.

He walked to where the mule was tied. Untied him. Swung up.

The mule moved out steady and indifferent beneath him.

Declan rode to the edge of Deadwood and stopped.

Looked north.

Then east.

Then south toward where the hills flattened into prairie.

Wherever the work is, he'd told the horse trader.

That had always been true. That had been true since the day he walked out of the Five Points with a stolen stake and the continent spread out in front of him like something that didn't know yet what he was going to do to it.

He touched his heels to the mule.

Rode south.

Behind him, Deadwood went on being what it was.

Ahead, the prairie opened up.

And somewhere in the distance between where he was and where he'd come from, the story of how Declan Shea arrived in a place like this was waiting to be told.

2

County Clare

Morning found Declan Shea on the cold floor again, the thatch above him dripping in slow, steady betrayal.

A rat crossed near the far wall. He watched it go. There were always rats. They knew the house as well as he did.

His mother had kept them out once. That was before the cough settled in her chest and refused to leave.

He lay still for a moment, listening. Maeve's breathing, slow and steady from the pallet across the room. The wind off the Atlantic finding every gap in the stone walls. And beneath it, the sound he'd learned to dread, his father's boots on the path outside.

He was up before the door opened.

* * *

Thomas Shea filled the doorframe the way bad weather fills a valley. Big. Wet. Smelling of the docks and something darker underneath. He looked at Declan standing in the middle of the room and said nothing. Just moved past him toward the fire, what was left of it, and held his hands out.

"Where's your mother," he said. Not a question.

"Sleeping," Declan said.

Thomas grunted. Looked toward the curtain that divided the room. Behind it, Eileen would be awake. She was always awake when Thomas came home. But she'd learned, same as Declan had, that sometimes stillness was its own protection.

Maeve appeared at the curtain's edge. Ten years old. Dark-haired like their mother, with the same careful eyes that missed nothing.

"Go back," Declan said.

She looked at her father. Looked at Declan. Went back.

Thomas didn't seem to notice. He'd found the bottle he'd left that morning, checked the level, and sat down in the one chair the cottage had. The chair had been Eileen's father's. She'd brought it from her family's house when she married. Thomas claimed it in the first week and never gave it back.

Declan stood near the door and waited for whatever came next.

Whatever came next was always something.

The good days were the ones when his mother was well enough to sit up.

Not well, she hadn't been well in two years, not since the winter the cough came and stayed, but well enough. Well enough to call Maeve to her, take the brush from the shelf, and work through the tangles in the girl's hair while she talked.

She talked about the old stories mostly. The warriors. The kings. Cú Chulainn defending Ulster alone at the ford. Fionn Mac Cumhaill and the Fianna ranging across the hills. The world as it had been before it got small and wet and hungry.

"Your name," she told Declan once, while Maeve sat still under the brush. "Do you know what it means?"

He shook his head.

"Full of goodness," she said. "That's what I named you. Full of goodness." She looked at him over Maeve's head, her eyes too bright the way they got when the fever was on her. "Don't let anyone take that from you."

He hadn't known what to say to that. Just nodded and looked at the floor.

He was fourteen and already understood that goodness was something the world worked hard to take.

She died in November.

* * *

Not dramatically. Not the way the stories went. Just got quieter and quieter over the course of a week until one morning the quiet didn't stop.

Declan sat with her until the light changed. Maeve pressed against his side, not crying. They'd learned not to cry where Thomas could hear.

His father stood in the doorway for a moment when he came home that evening. Looked at Eileen's still shape under the blanket. Looked at his children sitting beside her.

Then he went and found his bottle.

That was all.

Declan thought he couldn't hate the man more than he already did.

He was wrong.

The months after were the months he didn't think about.

Thomas drank more. Worked less. The money Declan brought home from the docks, loading, unloading, whatever they'd give a fifteen-year-old boy, disappeared into Thomas's pocket and came back as whiskey smell and broken crockery.

Maeve stayed close to Declan. Followed him to the door in the mornings. Waited for him at the path in the evenings. She'd stopped talking much after Eileen died. Just watched. Those careful eyes taking everything in.

It was the watching that saved her, in the end.

Or maybe it was Declan.

He came home late one evening in the depths of winter, later than usual, a coin in his pocket from an extra hour's work. The cottage was dark. No fire. That was wrong, Maeve always kept a fire.

He stood in the doorway.

Heard something.

What happened next, he never spoke of. Not on the ship. Not in New York. Not in forty years of moving west across a continent that didn't care what a man had done before he arrived.

When it was over, Thomas Shea was on the floor, and Declan was standing over him, his hands dark, his breath coming hard, and Maeve was pressed into the corner with her knees pulled up and her eyes on her brother.

"Get up," Declan said. "Get what you can carry."

She got up.

She went to the shelf, lifted their mother's brush, and held it to her chest for a heartbeat. Then she nodded.

They were out the door before the neighbors' fires began to smoke.

3

Mulberry Street

The ship took thirty-one days.

Declan counted them. Had nothing else to do but count and keep Maeve close and make sure no one looked at her too long.

One man did.

He didn't look twice.

They came into New York harbor on a gray morning in October, the water the color of old pewter, the city rising out of the mist like something that hadn't decided yet whether it wanted to be seen. Declan stood at the rail with Maeve pressed against his side and looked at it.

He'd expected something. He didn't know what. Something that looked like the future.

It just looked like more of the same. Stone and smoke and men moving things from one place to another for other men who didn't move anything at all.

"Is that it?" Maeve said.

"That's it," Declan said.

She had the brush in her hand. She'd carried it the whole crossing that way, not in her pocket, not tucked away somewhere safe, just in

13

her hand. Like letting go of it meant letting go of something she wasn't ready to release.

"It's very big," she said.

"Yeah," Declan said. "It is."

He put his arm around her shoulders, and they watched the city come closer.

He didn't tell her what he was thinking. That big meant more people. More people meant more of everything. More opportunity, more danger, more men like Thomas Shea and the man on the ship whose name he never knew and whose face he was already forgetting.

More predators.

He'd have to be faster than all of them.

* * *

Castle Garden smelled like fear and cabbage and too many bodies in too small a space.

They processed through it in a line that moved like cold molasses. Men in uniforms asking questions in English that half the people in line didn't understand. Names written down wrong. Places of origin mangled beyond recognition. A doctor who looked at your eyes and your tongue and your hands and decided in thirty seconds whether you were fit to enter.

The doctor looked at Maeve longer than Declan liked.

"She sick?" the man said.

"No," Declan said.

The doctor looked at him. Looked at Maeve. Stamped the paper.

They walked out into America.

* * *

The Five Points was where you went when you had nothing.

Which meant it was where the Irish went.

Declan found them a room in a tenement on Mulberry Street. Room was a generous word. A space, really. Eight feet by ten. A window that looked onto a shaft between buildings where the light came down gray and thin for maybe two hours a day. A pallet on the floor. A nail in the wall.

Two dollars a month. He didn't have two dollars.

The landlord, a fat man named Coyne who was Irish himself, which made it worse, looked at Declan. Looked at Maeve. Looked at the brush she was still carrying.

"Week by week then," Coyne said. "Fifty cents. In advance."

Declan paid him with money he'd taken from a man's coat pocket on the dock while the man watched his luggage being unloaded.

He wasn't sorry about it.

He wasn't sorry about much anymore.

The Five Points was its own country.

Its own language, its own laws, its own economy of violence and hunger and desperate ingenuity. Men who'd arrived with nothing and built something, even if that something was just a corner they could defend. Women who kept their families alive through sheer force of will. Children who ran errands for the gangs because the gangs fed them.

And underneath all of it, the smell. Garbage and offal and the tanneries along the river and the bodies of animals and sometimes people left too long in the heat.

Declan learned it fast. Had to.

* * *

He found work at a slaughterhouse on the edge of the district. Hard work, filthy work, the kind of work that got into your skin and stayed there. But it paid. Not much. Enough.

He came home every evening with whatever he could manage: bread, a bit of meat, sometimes just a heel of something hard enough to break a tooth on. Maeve never complained. She took what he brought and made something of it the way Eileen had made something of nothing in the cottage in Clare.

At night he sat behind her on the pallet and worked the brush through her hair the way their mother had done. Long, slow strokes. Maeve's eyes closing.

He told her the stories. The warriors. The kings. Cú Chulainn at the ford. Fionn and the Fianna.

He didn't believe any of it anymore. But she did. And that was enough.

"Tell me the one about the name," she said one night.

"You know that one."

"Tell me anyway."

He kept brushing. "Declan means full of goodness," he said. "That's what Mam said."

Maeve was quiet for a moment. "Are you? Full of goodness?"

He thought about the man on the ship. The man on the dock. Thomas Shea on the floor of the cottage with his hands dark.

"Go to sleep, Maeve," he said.

She leaned back against him. The brush moving through her hair.

* * *

Outside, the Five Points went on being what it was.

He was gone longer than usual the day it happened.

A man named Doyle, who ran numbers for one of the gangs, had offered him work. Not gang work, just carrying, delivering, the kind

16

of thing that wasn't quite legal and wasn't quite criminal and paid three times what the slaughterhouse paid. Declan had taken it. They needed the money. Winter was coming, and the room had no heat, and Maeve's cough, not bad, not yet, just a small dry sound she made in the mornings, worried him in a way he didn't examine too closely.

He was gone six hours. Maybe seven.

He came back with bread, a bit of salt pork, and enough money to pay Coyne for the next month and maybe buy Maeve a coat before the cold came in hard.

The door was open.

Not broken. Just open. The manner in which you left a door when you left in a hurry or didn't care who came in after.

Declan stood in the doorway.

Maeve was on the pallet. On her back. Her face turned toward the wall.

He knew before he crossed the room. Knew from the stillness of her. The particular stillness that had no breath in it.

He knelt beside her.

She was gone. Had been gone for a while. The body already cooling.

Her hands were empty. The brush she'd carried across an ocean was gone.

He looked at her face. Tried to understand what had happened. No obvious wound. No blood. But the way she was lying was not the way a person lay down to sleep; there was something wrong in the angle of it, something that said she hadn't chosen this position.

He sat back on his heels.

He sat there for a long time. The light in the shaft outside going from gray to darker gray to black. The sounds of the Five Points coming through the wall. Voices, laughter, someone screaming somewhere, the eternal noise of too many people crammed into too small a space.

He didn't cry.

He'd stopped crying somewhere on the Atlantic.

He just sat with her until the dark was complete.

Then he stood.

Looked at Maeve.

His mother had named him full of goodness.

His mother had been wrong.

He walked out of the room, left the door open behind him, and didn't look back.

He spent three days looking for the brush.

Asked questions how you asked questions in the Five Points, carefully, with your back to the wall, reading every face for the lie in it. A brush. Bone handle. Woman's brush. Belonged to a girl on Mulberry Street.

Nobody knew anything.

Nobody ever knew anything in the Five Points.

On the fourth day he stopped looking.

He took what he needed from a man sleeping drunk in an alley off Baxter Street. Not much. Enough.

Then he went to find out about the West.

4

The Hudson

He'd watched the man for two blocks before making his move.

That was the thing about the Five Points. The neighborhood itself was invisible to men like this one, well-dressed, soft hands, the careful walk of someone moving through territory he considered beneath him but necessary to cross. Men like that didn't see the Five Points. They walked through it, staring at some point in the middle distance, as if focusing on nothing meant none of it could touch them.

It always touched them.

Declan stepped out of the alley when the man passed.

Not fast. Not slow. Just suddenly there. Beside him. The knife low, where only the man could see it.

"Purse," Declan said. Quiet. Conversational. "And the watch."

The man stopped walking.

He was maybe forty. Well fed. The kind of face that had spent its whole life being agreed with. He looked at Declan with an expression that moved through surprise, then fear, and arrived quickly at outrage.

"Do you know who I am?" the man said.

Declan looked at him.

"Purse," he said again. "And the watch."

"I am an associate of Fernando Wood," the man said. His voice had dropped to something urgent and certain. Like the name itself was a weapon. "Fernando Wood. Do you understand what that means?"

Declan saw the man's hand move toward his coat.

He caught the wrist. Squeezed until something shifted in the man's face.

"The purse," Declan said. "Now."

The man gave him the purse.

The watch came next, the chain snapping when Declan pulled it.

He walked away. Not running. Just walking. Back into the Five Points, where men like Fernando Wood's associates didn't follow.

But he heard it behind him. The man's voice finding itself again, climbing toward something.

"Fernando Wood! I work for Fernando Wood! Someone find a constable!"

Declan kept walking.

He knew the name now.

Didn't know what it meant. But the way the man had said it, like a shield, like a threat, like something that should have stopped him, told him enough.

This was the wrong man to rob.

He went back to the room on Baxter Street, where he'd been sleeping since Mulberry Street became impossible. Took what little he had. The knife. A spare shirt. The purse, maybe twelve dollars inside, more than he'd expected. The watch, wrapped in the shirt.

He was out the door before the constables started asking questions.

He didn't look back.

By midnight, he was sleeping in a doorway on Chambers Street, cobblestones cold through his coat, the city dark around him.

His hand went to his pocket before his eyes were fully open.

Still there.

He needed to be north of the city before it woke.

He started walking.

* * *

He walked north through the waking city, keeping to the side streets where the traffic was thin, and the faces were busy with their own morning, not his.

The Five Points fell away behind him. Then the respectable neighborhoods. Then, the ragged northern edge, where the buildings thinned, and the lots between them grew wider. The smell of the river came in stronger.

By the time the sun was fully up, he was above the city.

The road ran along the high ground above the Hudson, the river visible through the trees below, wide and gray and moving with a kind of authority he hadn't seen in a river before. The rivers in Clare were intimate things. They knew their banks. This one didn't care about its banks at all.

He just walked.

The road was busy enough that he didn't stand out. Men with carts heading north. A woman with a basket. Two boys running some errand. Nobody looked at him twice.

Good.

Two hours north of the city, the road dipping down toward the river through a stand of old oak, he saw them.

Three men sat at the edge of the tree line. Not white. Dark hair, dark eyes. A stillness that wasn't laziness but something deliberate. Practiced.

The oldest one sat in the center. Really old. The kind of old that stopped being a number and became something else. He wore a blanket over his shoulders despite the morning warmth, and around his neck hung something, beaded, intricate, the kind of work that took more patience than Declan had ever applied to anything. Beside him on the ground sat a basket, tightly woven, its pattern geometric and precise, clearly the work of someone who knew exactly what they were doing. A clay pipe rested in his hand, carved with figures Declan couldn't make out from the road.

The old man looked at Declan.

Not the cautious look most men gave him. Not the sizing up. Not the calculation of threat. Just looked. Level. Unhurried. The way a man looks when he has been in a place long enough that strangers passing through are just weather. Noted. Not remarkable.

Declan met his eyes.

The old man didn't look away.

Declan did.

He kept walking. Something about it stayed with him. Not the man exactly. The weight of him. Sitting there like he'd been sitting there forever. Like the road had been built around him, not the other way.

Declan didn't know what he was looking at. Didn't know that the beadwork around the old man's neck told a story older than anything in County Clare. Didn't know the basket beside him came from a tradition older than the city Declan had just fled. Didn't know the figures on the pipe were clan markers tying the old man to a lineage older than anything Declan could imagine.

He just saw an old man by the road.

And walked on.

But the old man's eyes stayed on his back until the road curved and the tree line took him.

Declan felt it the whole way.

* * *

The freight boat tied up at Albany on the third day.

Declan had worked the whole way. Loading at stops. Unloading. Moving whatever needed moving without being asked twice. The two freightmen didn't talk much, and neither did he. That suited everyone.

At night, he slept on the deck with his coat pulled over him and watched the stars come out over the river and didn't think about anything at all. Just the water moving under the hull. Just the dark shore sliding past.

He didn't dream.

He hadn't dreamed since Mulberry Street.

Albany was bigger than he'd expected. Not New York, nothing was New York, but a real city. Stone buildings along the river. Warehouses. Commerce moving in every direction. The smell of the river mixed with woodsmoke, horses, and the particular smell of a place where things were bought, sold, and moved on.

He helped unload the last of the barrels and the nearer freight man, the one who'd done most of the talking, which hadn't been much, counted out coins into his palm.

"Fair work," the man said.

Declan pocketed the coins. Said nothing.

He walked up from the docks into the city.

Albany felt different from New York. Less pressed in. Like the buildings had room to breathe. Like the people did too. He moved through it without the constant feeling he was prey, like he had in the Five Points. Who's watching, who's a threat, which way out if something goes wrong. Here, he looked at the people as if they were prey. He liked that better.

* * *

He found a tavern near the waterfront. Ate his first real meal in three days. Salt pork, bread, and something that might have been turnip. He sat with his coffee, looking out the window at the street.

Nobody knew him here.

Nobody knew his name or his face or what he'd done two nights ago in a street near the Five Points.

He was just a young man eating salt pork in Albany.

He could be anyone.

The thought sat with him while he ate. Turned it over. He'd never been anyone before, always Declan Shea from the cottage in Clare, Thomas Shea's son, the boy whose mother died and whose sister…

He stopped that thought.

After he ate, he walked west through the city until the streets thinned and the buildings gave way, and he found himself standing at the edge of something he hadn't seen before.

The canal.

It ran east to west, straight and purposeful, cutting right through the earth as if the land didn't have a say in the matter. The water was flat and brown and busy with boats moving in both directions, mules on the towpath pulling lines, men calling to each other across the water. Lock gates opening and closing with a heavy mechanical certainty.

West of the last lock, the canal disappeared into the distance. Just went. Flat, straight, and seemingly without end.

Declan stood at the edge of the towpath and looked west.

He'd never seen that before. A direction that just kept going. In Clare, the land ran out, into the sea, someone else's field, a wall that told you this far and no further. In New York, every street ended in another street, every block in another block, the city folding back on itself endlessly.

But this.

This just went.

He didn't know what was out there. Buffalo, he'd heard men say on the boat. Land for the taking. Gold maybe. Room enough that a man could disappear into it completely and never be found.

Room enough to become something.

Or nothing.

Either would do.

He stood there until the light started to go. Until the canal traffic thinned and the mule drivers headed for whatever shelter they used at night, and the water went dark and still.

Then he turned and went to find somewhere to sleep.

Tomorrow he'd get on the canal.

Tomorrow, the west would start.

In his coat lining, wrapped in a handkerchief, the watch ticked on.

Steady.

Indifferent.

Like time itself didn't care where he was going.

5

The Salt City

The canal boat tied at Syracuse on a Thursday morning in early spring, the air carrying the smell before the town came into view.

Salt.

Not the clean salt of the ocean that Declan knew from Clare, that cold Atlantic bite that got into everything and meant something. This was different. Heavier. Industrial. The smell of brine being boiled out of the earth in enormous quantities, the steam rising from the works along Onondaga Lake visible before anything else, white columns drifting north in the pale morning air.

He'd heard about the Salt City on the canal. Every boater had something to say about it. A rough town. A working town. Irish labor doing the worst of it as Irish labor did the worst of it everywhere in America. The salt works ate men. The steam, the heat, the brine getting into cuts and staying there. Men worked a few years, and their lungs went, or their hands gave out. They moved on to something else, or they didn't move on at all.

Declan had no intention of working the salt.

He helped unload the boat at the Syracuse basin, where the Erie and Oswego Canals came together in a wide commercial sprawl: boats tied three deep, mules being unhitched from towlines, men moving barrels and crates and sacks in every direction with the purposeful chaos of a place that never quite stopped.

The boatman paid him off without ceremony.

"You going on?" the man asked.

"No," Declan said.

The man shrugged and turned back to his boat.

Declan picked up his bundle, the knife, the spare shirt, the watch still wrapped in its handkerchief, and walked up from the basin into the town.

Clinton Square opened up in front of him.

It was the center of everything. The canals meet here; the commercial buildings ring the square; the weighlock building stands solid at the water's edge, where boats are brought in to be measured and taxed before moving on. Men everywhere. Canal men and salt men and merchants and the particular type of sharp-eyed men who existed wherever commerce existed and money changed hands in volume.

Declan stood at the edge of the square and looked at it.

He'd been moving for months now. Albany. The canal towns: Rome, Utica, places that blurred into each other after a while, lock after lock, the same flat water, the same mule smell, the same men doing the same work. He'd taken what he needed along the way. Small things mostly. A purse here. A wallet there. Once a horse, he'd sold it two towns later for half what he could have gotten for it legitimately.

He was getting better at it.

Not proud of that. Not ashamed either. Just noting it how you noted when a skill was developing. When the gap between what you attempted and what you achieved was closing.

He needed a few days in one place. Needed to eat properly and sleep somewhere that wasn't a boat deck or a barn floor. Needed to let the road settle out of his bones before he pushed on west.

He found a boarding house on a side street off the square. A German woman ran it, solid and efficient. She looked at him with the expression of someone doing a rapid calculation of cost versus benefit.

She named a price.

He named a lower one.

She studied him for a moment. Then nodded.

The room was small. A cot. A window. A nail in the wall.

He'd had worse.

He dropped his bundle on the cot and lay down and stared at the ceiling.

Outside, Syracuse went about its business. The canal. The salt works. The commerce of a town that had figured out what it was good at and committed to it completely.

He closed his eyes.

Didn't sleep. Just rested.

Thought about the west.

Always the west.

He'd heard more about it on the canal. Men talked. Boaters who'd been to Buffalo said the lakes were something to see. Water stretching out like you'd imagine the ocean if you'd never seen the ocean, which most of them hadn't. Beyond the lakes, Ohio. Indiana. Illinois. And beyond that, the plains. Flat and endless and full of buffalo, men said. Millions of them. A man with a rifle and no particular attachment to staying in one place could make real money out there.

A man with a rifle.

He didn't have a rifle.

He'd need one before he got much further.

He opened his eyes.

Looked at the ceiling.

Somewhere in this town, there was a rifle he could afford or acquire.

He'd find it.

He always found what he needed.

He got up. Washed his face in the basin. Ran his hands through his hair.

Picked up the knife.

Went out to see what Syracuse had to offer.

* * *

He heard about the rifle from a man at the canal basin.

A fellow in Geddes, the man said. Salt worker. Selling a Winchester for less than it was worth, needed the money, couldn't afford to keep it. Good rifle. Clean. Declan should go look before someone else does.

Declan went.

The road ran west from Syracuse along the southern shore of Onondaga Lake. He'd seen the lake from a distance since he arrived in the city with the steam rising from the works along its edge, the flat gray water beyond. Up close, it was something else.

The shore was industrialized as far as he could see in both directions. Boiling blocks lined the water's edge, long, low buildings where brine was pumped up from underground springs and boiled in enormous iron vats until the water cooked off and the salt crystallized. The steam rose constantly, white and heavy, drifting north across the lake in long, slow columns.

The smell was everywhere. Not the clean salt of the Atlantic he'd grown up smelling from the cliffs above the shore in Clare. This was different. Heavier. The smell of industry. Of something being extracted.

The hills above the lake had been stripped.

That was the thing that struck him most. In Clare, the hills were bare too, worn down by centuries of grazing, the trees long gone, the land exposed to whatever weather came off the Atlantic. He was used to bare hills. But these were bare in a different way. You could see the stumps. Hundreds of them, thousands maybe, marching up the hillsides in every direction. The forest had been there recently enough that the stumps hadn't rotted yet. The wood still pale where it had been cut.

They'd taken every tree.

And now, where the wood smoke from the boiling blocks should have been rising thin and gray, the smoke was darker. Thicker. A different quality to it entirely.

Coal, he'd heard someone say at the basin. They bring it up from Pennsylvania now. Ran out of wood.

Declan looked at the bare hills, the dark smoke, and the lake, flat and gray below it all.

He didn't think about what it meant.

Just walked.

Geddes sat at the western end of the works, a rough settlement of houses and outbuildings that had grown up around the industry. Quick, functional, and not much concerned with anything beyond the immediate need.

He found the man he was looking for without much trouble. A salt worker named Briggs, broad and red-faced, who met him at the door of a small house and led him around back to a shed.

The rifle was there.

Declan picked it up. Checked the action. Sighted down the barrel.

The rifling inside the barrel was worn smooth where it should have been sharp. A rifle that had been fired too many times without proper cleaning. It would shoot. But not well, not reliably, and not for long.

"How much?" he said.

Briggs named a price.

Declan set the rifle down.

"Not worth it," he said.

Briggs started to argue. Declan walked away.

He was hungry. The walk from Syracuse had taken the better part of two hours. He found the eating house at the edge of the settlement, a low building with smoke coming from the chimney and the smell of something cooking that was better than it had any right to be in a place like this.

He pushed through the door.

And that was where he saw John.

The room was low and warm, a fire going in the corner, rough tables filling the space. A woman behind a counter was ladling stew from a pot that smelled better than the room deserved.

Declan found a seat near the wall.

Facing the door.

Always.

The room was full of salt workers. Irish mostly, he could hear it in the voices, Clare and Galway and Mayo worn thin by America but still there underneath. Men who'd crossed the same ocean he had and ended up here, boiling salt out of the ground on land that wasn't theirs either, breathing coal smoke instead of wood smoke, their hands cracked white at the knuckles.

He ordered the stew. It came hot and thick, more vegetable than meat but substantial. He ate without tasting it and watched the room.

That was when he saw him.

Sitting alone at the far end.

Not Irish. Not German. Dark hair worn long and simply pulled back. His face carried a quality of stillness that Declan had seen once before on a road north of New York City, an old man at the tree line with beadwork around his neck and a carved pipe in his hand. This man was younger. Maybe thirty. His hands were rough from the salt works, the skin cracked at the knuckles, like everyone else who worked those vats. But there was something else in those hands. Calluses in specific places that didn't come from the vats. Along the inside of the thumb and forefinger. The kind that came from rope work. Or from holding something long and balanced.

He was eating methodically. Without hurry. His eyes moved around the room as a man's eyes moved when he was used to being the only one of his kind in a place.

Declan looked at him with the same flat stare he gave everyone.

Alone. That was the first thing. A man alone was either dangerous or vulnerable, and this one didn't look dangerous. Didn't have the coiled readiness of a man expecting trouble. Just present. Contained.

Declan picked up his bowl and moved to the man's table.

The man looked up.

Dark eyes. Calm. Not startled. Not threatened. Just noting.

"Mind?" Declan said.

The man gestured to the bench across from him.

Declan sat.

They ate in silence for a while. The room moved around them. Irish voices. Tin cups. The fire smoking in the corner.

Declan watched the man's hands. The calluses. The particular way he held his spoon, not the grip of someone who'd grown up with cutlery, something older than that.

"You work the vats?" Declan said.

"Yes," the man said. His English was careful. Not uncertain, just considered. Like he chose each word deliberately.

"Hard work."

"Yes."

Declan ate. The man was not a mark. He could see that quickly enough. The coat was worn. The boots practical but not new. Whatever he earned at the salt works, he either spent carefully or sent it somewhere else. Nothing to take here.

He should have moved on.

But the hands held him.

"What else do you do?" Declan said.

The man looked at him. A flicker of something, not suspicion. Just assessment. The careful measurement of how much to give a stranger.

"Fish," he said.

"Where?"

A pause.

"Oneida Lake," he said. "I go tonight."

Declan had heard of Oneida Lake on the canal. Big water. East of Syracuse.

"What do you fish for?"

"Eels mostly. This time of year."

"How?"

The man studied him. The Irish boy with the flat gray eyes, asking questions about eels in an eating house in Geddes.

"Torch and spear," he said. "At night. When the water is dark."

Declan thought about the west. About the plains. About men on the canal talking about living off the land, off whatever the country provided. He didn't know how to do any of that. Had always taken what he needed from people. But people got scarce out on the plains, he'd been told. The land provided or nothing did.

He needed to know how the land provided.

"Show me," Declan said.

Not a question. Not quite a demand. Just direct. The way he said most things.

The man looked at him for a long moment. Reading him how men read each other when they were deciding something.

"John," he said. He extended his hand across the table.

Declan took it. "Shea."

John's grip was firm. Brief. The handshake of a man who meant what he said.

"You can come," John said. He went back to his stew. "If you don't talk too much."

Declan said nothing.

John glanced up. Something moved in his face. Not quite a smile. Just acknowledgment.

"Good," he said.

They finished their meal in silence.

Outside, the salt works steamed against the darkening sky. Onondaga Lake lay flat and gray to the west, its surface catching the last of the light.

John paused at the door and looked at the lake.

Not the way the salt workers looked at it, as a resource, a thing to be processed, water to be boiled until something useful was left. Something older than that. Something that had nothing to do with wages or the machinery ranged along its shores.

His face showed nothing.

But he looked for a long time.

Declan waited.

Then John turned east toward the road to Oneida Lake.

Declan fell in beside him.

Neither of them spoke.

The coal smoke drifted north across the water behind them.

The bare hills stood stripped and pale in the fading light.

And the lake lay still beneath it all, the same as it had always been and not the same at all.

* * *

They reached the south shore as the last light left the sky.

Declan had never seen water like it. Not the ocean, he knew the ocean, had crossed it in the dark hold of a ship. This was different. Inland water, still and flat and stretching out into darkness without end. No far shore visible. Just the lake going on into the night like it had no intention of stopping.

John moved without hesitation. He'd cached what he needed here. A bundle of cattails soaked in fat, tied tight, a spear of straight ash with a fire-hardened tip, a cord basket. He assembled these things in the dark with the ease of a man doing something he'd done a thousand times.

Declan watched.

"You are going to get your boots wet," John said as he shed his and stepped into the waters.

John lit the torch. The cattails caught bright and steady, a good, clean light that held without guttering in the still air. He waded into the shallows, the water coming up to his knees, the torch held low over the surface.

Declan took off his boots and left them on shore near John's and waded in.

The water was cold. Late summer had taken the worst of it, but cold enough to feel, the sandy bottom soft under his bare feet, patches of weed brushing his ankles.

John moved slowly. The torch close to the water, its light penetrating the shallows, turning the lake bottom gold and brown and shadow.

"Watch," John said.

Declan watched.

For a long time, he saw nothing but a sandy bottom moving slowly past. Weed. A small fish darting away from the light. The occasional glint of something.

Then John stopped.

Held the torch absolutely still.

Declan saw it.

An eel. Maybe two feet long, lying motionless on the bottom, boneless and still, not quite resting, not quite moving, just existing in that particular stillness they had. The torchlight had stopped it. Pinned it in place.

John's spear moved.

Fast. Certain. No hesitation between seeing and acting.

The eel came up on the end of the spear, twisting once and then going still.

John unthreaded it into the cord basket at his belt.

"You try," he said.

He handed Declan the spear.

Declan took it. Felt the balance of it. The weight distributed toward the tip the way a good tool weighted itself toward its purpose.

They moved on.

It took him four attempts before he got one. The first three times, he was too fast or too eager, the spear going where the eel had been rather than where it was. John said nothing after each miss. Just waited. Let Declan figure it out.

The fourth time, he made himself wait. Made himself watch until the eel was truly still, truly pinned. Made himself feel the spear as an extension of his arm rather than a separate thing he was throwing.

The eel came up twisting.

"Good," John said.

One word. But it meant something.

They worked the shallows for two hours. Moving slowly west along the shore, the torch burning low and steady, the basket filling. Declan got three more after the first. John got perhaps a dozen, each one taken with the same unhurried certainty.

When the torch burned low, they waded back to shore.

John built a small fire above the waterline. Cleaned the eels with a knife that moved through the work the way his spear had moved through the water, no wasted motion, no uncertainty. He showed Declan how to do it. The angle of the cut. How to peel the skin back. How to open the body without piercing the gut.

Declan watched once.

Then he did it himself.

John corrected him twice. The angle of the knife. The direction of the skin.

After that, he said nothing.

They cooked the eels over the fire on green sticks. The fat dripped and hissed in the flames. The smell was good. Rich and smoky and particular to this lake, this night, this fire.

They ate.

The lake was dark around them. Still. The moon had come up, and in its light, two long, low shapes were visible far out on the water. Islands, barely there, more suggestion than substance. Dark silhouettes against the silver surface, present but not quite real.

After a while, John spoke.

"Why do you go west?"

Declan looked at the fire. "Because there's nothing east."

John nodded. He understood that kind of reasoning.

"What will you do there?"

"Whatever pays," Declan said.

John was quiet for a moment.

"The buffalo," he said.

"I heard about them."

"My mother's people saw them. Far west. Said the ground shook when they ran." He paused. "They are going away. Like everything goes away."

Declan said nothing.

John looked at the fire. Then at the dark water. Then back at the fire.

"My name," he said. "My real name. Not John."

Declan waited.

"Gahsóhda'gę̨h," John said. He said it as if it were something that belonged to him completely. Not performing it. Not explaining it. Just saying it.

"What does it mean?" Declan said.

"Eel moving," John said. "Eel in the water." He looked out at the lake. At the dark islands on the moonlit water. "My clan."

Declan looked at the lake too.

"Gahsóhda'gę̨h," he said. He got it wrong.

John said it again. Slower.

Declan tried again. Closer.

John nodded once.

They sat with the fire burning down between them. The lake dark, still around them. Neither of them said anything else for a long time.

It was the most honest conversation Declan Shea had ever had with another person.

He didn't know that.

But it was.

He stayed two months.

Not because he planned to. He'd meant to move on after the first week. But the learning kept going, and the weeks accumulated without him marking them.

The woods along the south shore were dense hardwoods, mostly maple, oak, and beech, with alder thickets along the wet ground near the lake edge and open fields breaking the canopy here and there. Deer moved through it in the mornings and evenings. Rabbit ran the edges where the field met the wood. Squirrel worked the oak mast. And in the thick young growth where the trees crowded close and the undergrowth tangled, ruffed grouse held tight in the shadows until the last possible second.

John took him for deer first.

He taught Declan to move through the woods correctly. Not the method Declan used to move through city streets, direct, purposeful, arriving somewhere. The opposite of that. Slow. Low. Reading the wind before anything else. The bent grass. The disturbed leaf. The track that was an hour old versus the track that was a day old.

Declan was a poor student at first.

Too fast. Too direct. Too certain that the shortest line between two points was the right one. Every deer they approached heard or scented him before John had taken two steps.

John never expressed frustration. Just waited. Let the failure teach what words couldn't.

Slowly, something shifted.

Declan learned to be still in a new way. Not the flat waiting stillness of a predator watching a room, he'd always had that. Something different. The stillness of someone who had disappeared into the landscape. Who the deer didn't see because he'd stopped announcing himself.

The first deer he took himself, he shot at forty yards with John's rifle, a clean kill through the shoulder.

John nodded.

Then he showed Declan how to skin it.

This was the thing Declan took to fastest. Faster than the stalking. Faster than the eel spearing. The knife work. The particular knowledge of how an animal came apart, where the cuts went, how the hide peeled away from the muscle, how to work without piercing the gut, how to leave the hide intact and usable.

His hands understood it immediately.

John showed him once.

Declan did it himself the second time. Cleanly. Efficiently. Like something already in his hands waiting to be called out.

John looked at the hide laid out flat and smooth and said something in Onondaga.

"What?" Declan said.

"I said you have done this before," John said.

"I haven't."

John looked at him. "Your hands have."

Declan didn't answer. Cleaned the knife on the grass and didn't think about what his hands had done before.

The grouse came later.

John had a shotgun for birds. A different tool entirely, he explained, for a different kind of hunting. He loaned it to Declan without ceremony, showing him how to load and hold it.

They walked the thick young growth along the hardwood's edge, pushing through the tangle, John moving ahead, Declan behind.

The first grouse exploded from practically under Declan's feet.

There was no warning. One moment, the undergrowth was still, and the next it was a thunderclap of wings, the bird erupting straight up through the branches in a burst of sound that hit Declan in the chest before his mind had registered what was happening.

He flinched hard. The gun went nowhere near the bird.

John didn't laugh. Didn't say anything.

They walked on.

The second bird flushed ten minutes later from a tangle of brush. This time, Declan was ready for the noise, or thought he was. He mounted the gun. But he rushed it, swinging too fast, the shot going behind.

Still nothing from John.

The third bird held until they were almost on top of it, then came out low and fast from the tall grass and through a gap in the trees. This time, Declan made himself wait. Let the noise happen without flinching. Found the bird with the barrel. Swung through.

The grouse came down in a puff of feathers.

John picked it up. Handed it to Declan.

"Not too fast," he said.

"No," Declan said.

"Same as everything," John said. "Wait. Then move."

He turned and walked on into the thicket.

Declan stood holding the grouse.

Wait. Then move.

He'd been doing it wrong his whole life. Moving first. Acting before the moment was ready.

Or maybe not. Maybe it depended on what you were hunting.

He followed John into the trees.

John taught him to set snares, too. Simple constructions of bent sapling and cord that he could make from whatever the land provided. Where to set them. How to read the runs, the paths animals wore into the grass and soil by repetition. How to place the snare so it was part of the run rather than an interruption of it.

Declan set them wrong three times before he got it right.

When he got it right, John said nothing.

But the next morning, there was a rabbit in the snare.

They ate it that evening on the south shore, the water flat and dark in the October light, the trees along the shore going gold and red.

"You go soon," John said. Not a question.

"Yes," Declan said.

"West."

"Yes."

John looked at the lake. At the far darkness, where the islands were invisible now without the moon.

"The things I showed you," he said. "They come from this land. This lake. These hills." He paused. "The land out there is different. You will have to learn it again."

"I know," Declan said.

"The people out there," John said. "They know their land the way I know this one." He looked at Declan directly. "Remember that."

Declan looked at the lake.

"I'll remember," he said.

He meant it when he said it.

Whether he held onto it across the years and the miles and everything that happened after, that was a different question.

One the lake couldn't answer.

6

The Weighlock

The Weighlock Tavern sat on Clinton Square where the Erie and Oswego Canals met, a squat stone building that smelled of tallow candles and wet wool and the particular sourness of men who worked hard and didn't wash enough. A sign above the door showed a canal boat being weighed, though the paint had gone thin enough that it might have been anything.

Declan pushed through the door.

He was seventeen now, though he could have passed for older. The years since Clare had done their work on him. The docks, the slaughterhouse, the canal, filling out the frame his bones had laid down, layering muscle over it the way hard use does, dense and functional and without vanity. He stood an inch over six feet and moved like someone who'd learned early that size was only useful if you knew how to carry it. His face had lost whatever softness it might have had. The jaw had set hard. The eyes, gray, flat, with that quality of seeing everything and reacting to nothing, had stopped looking young somewhere on the Atlantic and hadn't looked young since.

* * *

Men noticed him when he walked into a room.

Most of them decided not to make anything of it.

The room was low-ceilinged and dark, a fire going in the hearth at the far end, tables filling the space between. Midday and already half full. Canal men mostly, boaters, lock tenders, mule drivers, with their particular smell of animal and road. A few men who looked like they moved salt for a living, their hands and faces stained white at the creases, the salt getting into every pore.

He found a table near the wall. Facing the door.

Always facing the door.

A girl came. Young. Tired around the eyes.

"Coffee," he said.

She brought it without a word.

He sat with it and looked at the room carefully, as he had learned to do. Not staring. Just taking inventory. Who had what. Who was watching what. Who was paying attention to anything beyond their own drink.

Most weren't.

Canal towns had a particular quality of inwardness. Men who spent their days moving things from one place to another developed a talent for not seeing anything that wasn't directly in front of them. The lock. The towpath. The next lock. Everything else was noise.

Good.

He found the man without looking for him.

Some men announced themselves. This one did it without trying. The coat first, good wool, the kind you ordered rather than bought off a peg. Then the boots, leather that had been tended to. Then the way he sat, taking up more space than he needed, one arm thrown over the back of his chair, legs spread, chin up. A man who moved through the world expecting it to accommodate him.

He was with another man. Canal trade by his look. Rough hands, practical clothes. But not an equal. The way he sat relative to the man in the good coat told you everything. Slightly turned toward him. Waiting for him to finish his sentences before starting his own.

The man in the good coat was talking. Loud enough that Declan could hear him from across the room without trying.

"— three boats by Friday or I pull the contract entirely. They want to do business with me, they deliver. Simple as that."

The canal man nodded. "Simple as that," he agreed.

The man in the good coat lifted his glass. A boy materialized and refilled it without being asked.

Declan watched.

* * *

The man had money on the table. Not careful about it, bills folded loose, sitting there like they didn't mean anything. A watch chain catching the firelight. The chain alone was worth more than a canal man earned in a month.

Declan drank his coffee.

Waited.

He was good at waiting. Had learned it young. Waiting was just watching, with patience attached.

The man's voice came again. Loud enough to carry.

"You there. Boy."

Declan looked up.

The man in the good coat was looking at him. Chin tilted. The particular expression of a man who'd spent his life having things fetched.

"Tell the girl I want the good bottle. Not what she's been pouring. The good one."

The room went on around them. Fire crackling. Men talking.

45

Nobody paying attention.

Declan looked at the man.

Just looked.

Flat and level and entirely without expression. He looked at him as a thing you'd already decided about.

The man's chin came down a fraction.

Something moved in his face. The sudden awareness that the calculation he'd made was wrong. That whatever this young man was, he wasn't the kind you sent for bottles.

He opened his mouth.

Closed it.

Declan stood.

He was aware, as he always was when he stood in a room full of men, of the effect of it. Conversations nearby faltered slightly. Eyes moved and then moved away. He hadn't asked for it, and he didn't perform it. It was just what happened when a man of his size moved with that particular quality of intention.

He walked across the room.

Stopped at the man's table.

The man looked up at him. The chin was fully down now. The arm had come off the back of the chair.

Declan reached out.

His eyes never left the man's eyes.

His hand found the bills on the table. Picked them up. Folded them once.

Put them in his pocket.

The man stared at him.

Declan waited.

One breath. Two.

* * *

Beside the man in the good coat, the canal man came up out of his chair fast with the reflex of someone who'd broken up enough trouble to think he knew how it went.

He didn't know how it went.

Declan hit him once. Short. The knuckles caught the man's throat just below the jaw. The kind of blow that didn't look like much and ended everything.

The canal man sat down hard, hitting the floor. Both hands at his neck. The sound he made wasn't a sound so much as the absence of one. Air trying to find a way through something that had closed.

The man in the good coat looked at his companion on the floor.

Looked at Declan.

Sat back down.

The room had gone to that different quality of quiet. The kind where everyone was suddenly very interested in what was directly in front of them.

Declan walked toward the door.

The barkeep was there. Broken nose badly set. The kind of face that had introduced itself to trouble so many times it had stopped being surprised. He stood with his arms at his sides and his eyes on Declan.

Declan stopped.

Looked at him.

The same look. Flat. Level. Patient. The look of a man who had nowhere else to be and nothing else to want and had already decided how this went.

The barkeep was big. Experienced. Had probably stopped a hundred men in a hundred rooms just like this one.

He looked at Declan's eyes.

Whatever he saw there made the decision for him.

He stepped aside.

Declan walked through the door.

* * *

Outside, Clinton Square was going about its business. Canal boats on the water. Mules on the towpath. Men moving salt and goods in both directions. The weighlock building squatting at the water's edge, boats lined up to be measured, taxed, and sent on their way.

The cold hit him.

He kept walking.

Behind him, through the door, he heard the man's voice rise. Outrage finding itself. Demanding.

Nobody did anything.

Nobody ever did.

That was the thing Declan had figured out somewhere between the Five Points and here. Most people, when it came to it, just wanted to be left alone. Wanted whatever was happening to happen to someone else and be over quickly.

He rounded the corner of Clinton Square and kept walking west.

The bills in his pocket.

The canal running beside him.

The cold smell of salt in the air.

And the west still out there somewhere, flat and endless and waiting.

* * *

He didn't go back to the boarding house.

Nothing there worth going back for. The bundle he'd arrived with, the knife, the spare shirt, the watch, he had on him. He always had it on him. The German woman could have the nail in the wall.

He walked west through the city.

Clinton Square fell away behind him. The canal basin. The weighlock building. The commercial buildings ringed the square, where men moved money and goods, and they didn't look up from their transactions long enough to see anything else.

He'd been in Syracuse, what? Three months, near enough. Longer than he'd planned. Longer than he'd stayed anywhere since Mulberry Street.

He didn't examine why.

The canal ran beside him, heading west. Boats moving. Mules on the towpath, their breath rising white in the cold morning air. The lock tenders going about their business. The same as it had been when he arrived, the same as it would be when he was gone, the machinery indifferent to any particular man passing through.

He passed a woman selling apples from a cart at the edge of the square. He took one without stopping, without looking at her, the motion so practiced and casual that she didn't register it until he was already past.

Old habit.

The city thinned. The buildings gave way to sheds and outbuildings and then to open ground. The road running west along the canal, the towpath beside it, the flat water between.

He stopped once.

Not for any particular reason. Just stopped.

To the south, the reservation lands of the Onondaga stretched away toward the hills. He couldn't see them from here. Didn't know exactly where they were. Just knew they were there, south of the city, reduced to seven thousand acres of what had been millions, the Nation confined to what the state had decided to leave them.

John was somewhere in that direction. Back from Oneida Lake. Back at the salt works, maybe, or resting before the next shift, or sitting somewhere quiet doing something Declan didn't have a word for.

Gahsóhda'gęh.

The name came to him without trying. He still couldn't say it right. Probably never would.

He stood there for a moment.

Then he turned and looked north. He dropped the apple core on the road, done with it.

* * *

Onondaga Lake lay flat and gray under the October sky. The salt works steamed along its southern shore, the coal smoke rising dark and heavy, drifting north across the water. The bare hills above it, stripped of every tree, the pale stumps marching up the slope in every direction, stood exposed to whatever weather came.

Declan turned west.

Picked up his pace.

The canal ran beside him. The towpath stretched ahead, flat and straight, without end. Somewhere out there, Ohio, Indiana, Illinois, the plains beyond, the west was waiting. Waiting as it had always been waiting. Indifferent. Vast. Full of whatever a man was willing to take from it.

The salt smell faded.

The city fell away.

Declan paid his fare and stepped onto the westbound packet, following the canal.

He didn't look back.

7

The Niagara

Buffalo sat at the edge of the continent.

That was how it felt standing at the waterfront for the first time, like the land had been building toward something and here it was, the last solid ground before everything opened up into water and then into whatever lay beyond the water. Lake Erie stretched north and west as far as he could see, gray and vast and moving with a chop that reminded him of the Atlantic without being the Atlantic. Bigger than Oneida Lake. Bigger than anything he'd seen since the crossing.

He stood at the waterfront for a while.

Not admiring it. Just taking its measure.

The city behind him was noise and commerce and the smell of the lake mixed with lumber and livestock and the particular energy of a place that existed entirely to move things from one place to another. Freight from the canal heading onto the lake boats. Goods from the lake heading onto the canal. Men going west. Men going east. Everyone passing through.

Buffalo was a city of passage.

Declan fit right in.

He'd arrived with enough money to eat and sleep for a week if he was careful. The bills from the Weighlock, the canal fare paid, still something left. Not much. Enough.

He found a room above a tavern near the waterfront. Cheap. The smell of the lake came through the window along with the noise of the docks. He didn't mind either.

He spent two days watching.

The waterfront taverns were full of men heading west. Emigrants mostly, families with everything they owned loaded onto wagons, heading for Ohio or Indiana or further. Men alone, like Declan, with less to carry and less to lose. Canal workers between jobs. Lake sailors between voyages. And mixed in among them, men coming back from the Mexican War. Soldiers mustered out, moving home or moving on, carrying whatever they'd brought back from the border and whatever they'd acquired along the route.

He heard it before he saw it.

A sound he had no name for. Not thunder, thunder came and went. Not the ocean, the ocean was restless, always shifting. This was steady. Constant. A low roar that seemed to come from the ground itself, from somewhere below sound, felt in the chest before it was heard by the ears.

Men at the canal basin had mentioned it. The falls. Worth seeing before you move on, they said. Everyone says that.

Declan followed the sound.

* * *

The road ran southwest from the city through scrub and open ground, the roar growing with every mile, becoming something physical, something that pressed against him as he walked. The air changed, too. Wetter, colder, a fine mist that appeared before he could see any water, settling on his coat and his face and the back of his hands.

Then the ground opened up, and he saw them.

He stopped.

He didn't mean to stop. His legs just stopped.

The falls were not what he'd expected. He hadn't known what he expected. Something large. Something impressive, a big building, a wide river, a lake stretching to the horizon. Something you could take the measure of and move on.

This was not that.

The water came over the edge in a curtain so vast it didn't look like water at first. It looked like the world was ending. Like the ground had simply stopped, and beyond it there was nothing but falling and the white chaos at the bottom where the falling became something else. A roiling, boiling violence of water on water that sent spray fifty feet into the air and created its own weather, its own wind, its own perpetual cloud that hung over the gorge like something alive.

The sound was everywhere. Not loud exactly, beyond loud. It had moved past the category of sound into something that occupied the body completely. He could feel it in his teeth. In his sternum. In the soles of his feet on the wet rock.

He stood there.

He didn't know how long.

Long enough that the mist had soaked through his coat, his hair was wet, and the cold had gotten into his hands.

He wasn't thinking about anything.

That was the strange part. Declan Shea, who was always thinking about something, the next move, the next town, the next mark, the next meal, was thinking about nothing at all. The falls had taken everything out of his head and replaced it with themselves.

He had no category for this.

No use for it. No way to take from it or exploit it or reduce it to something manageable. It just was. Enormous and indifferent and permanent in a way that made everything he'd done and everything he planned to do feel briefly, strangely small.

He thought about what the men on the canal had said.

The plains out there. Flat and endless, grass going to the horizon in every direction. Mountains that made the hills of Clare look like suggestions. Rivers so wide you couldn't see the far bank. And the buffalo. Millions of them, the ground shaking under their weight, the sky darkening with their dust.

He hadn't believed it. Not really. He'd filed it away as he filed things he couldn't verify. Possible, unconfirmed, adjust when evidence arrives.

But standing here.

Standing here with the falls filling his chest and the mist on his face and the world roaring at him from thirty feet away.

He believed it.

All of it.

The world was larger than he'd understood. Larger than Ireland. Larger than New York. Larger than anything the canal had shown him. And he was about to walk into the middle of it with a knife and the clothes on his back and whatever he could take along the road.

The falls roared on.

Indifferent.

Just as everything out there would be indifferent.

He didn't know that the Seneca, the Keepers of the Western Door, the westernmost nation of the Haudenosaunee, had named this place long ago. Onguiaahra. The strait. The neck of water between the lakes. A geographical fact, simply stated, by people who had no need to be overwhelmed by what they had always known was there.

He just stood in the mist and felt small.

Then he turned away from the edge.

* * *

His coat was soaked through. His hands were numb. The sound followed him as he walked back toward the city, fading slowly, never quite disappearing, still there in his chest long after he'd lost sight of the gorge.

He found the Lake House by its sound. Not the falls, the other sound, the human sound of men drinking and talking, and the particular quiet that settled over a card table when something was at stake.

He pushed through the door.

Five men around a table. An overhead lamp was casting yellow light across the cards, the faces, and the money in the center.

Declan bought in with two dollars and sat down.

He watched more than he played for the first hour.

That was the thing about cards. Most men thought it was about the cards. It wasn't about the cards. It was about the men holding them. How a man's jaw tightened when he had something good. The shift in another man's eyes when he was bluffing. The a third man reached for his drink every time he was uncertain.

Declan read them the way he read rooms.

By the second hour, he'd doubled his stake.

The soldier was still in the game. Broad through the shoulders. A face that had seen weather and violence in roughly equal measure. He had a tell. His thumb moved along the edge of his hand when he was uncertain, went still when he liked what he was holding.

And leaning against the wall beside his chair, a Mississippi Rifle. Model 1841. Stock intact. The percussion lock clean. A man who'd taken care of his weapon.

Declan had been watching it all evening.

The pot had been building for twenty minutes.

He'd been patient. Letting the smaller hands go. Waiting for the right moment.

When it came, he pushed most of what he had into the center of the table.

The other three men folded immediately.

The soldier looked at his cards. Looked at the pot. He had four to a straight and one card to draw. Good odds if the deck was feeling generous. His thumb moved along the edge of his hand.

He looked at his money.

Not enough.

Declan waited. Then, quiet and even —

"Can you call? Or do you fold?"

The soldier looked at him. Looked at his cards. Looked at the rifle leaning against the wall.

"How's about I cover with that?" he said. A gesture toward the rifle.

Declan looked at the pot. Let a beat pass, like he was calculating whether it was worth it.

Then he nodded.

The soldier drew one card.

He looked at it.

His thumb stopped moving.

"Show," Declan said.

The soldier laid down his cards. Four to the straight and a card that wasn't what he needed.

Declan laid down three nines.

The soldier stared at the table.

Declan's hands moved to the pot, gathering the bills.

"You pulled that third nine," the soldier said. Quiet. Almost to himself.

Declan's hands stopped.

He looked at the soldier.

Said nothing.

The table held its breath.

The soldier looked at the three nines. He looked at Declan's hands, still on the money. At the dealer who had found something very interesting to look at on the far wall.

He picked up the rifle.

Held it out.

Declan took it. Set it across his knees. Finished gathering the money from the pot with one hand, unhurried, while he ran his other hand along the barrel of the Mississippi.

The soldier put on his coat and left.

Nobody said anything.

Declan counted the money. Checked the action on the rifle. Sighted down the barrel at the far wall.

True.

He set it on the table and finished counting.

Eleven dollars and some change.

He picked up the rifle and walked out into the Buffalo night.

The falls were still in his chest.

He booked passage the next morning.

The lake opened up ahead of him, wide and gray and moving.

Beyond it, the West.

8

The Road to the Mississippi

The lake boat pushed off from Buffalo on a gray October morning, the water already showing its winter temper, short choppy waves, a wind out of the northwest that cut through wool like it wasn't there.

Declan found a place on the forward deck out of the worst of the wind and watched the city fall away behind them. Buffalo shrinking. The canal basin. The waterfront. The last solid eastern ground disappearing into the gray.

Ahead, the lake.

He'd thought Oneida Lake was big. He'd been wrong about that.

Lake Erie opened up around them as the boat pushed west, the shore to the south a thin, dark line, the northern shore entirely invisible. Just water in every direction, moving with a cold authority that reminded him of the Atlantic crossing, except the Atlantic hadn't pretended to be anything other than what it was. This was supposed to be a lake. It didn't behave like a lake.

* * *

There were maybe a dozen passengers. Emigrants mostly, heading for

Ohio. A family with three children who spent the first hour at the rail being sick. Two men in the fur trade by their looks. Weathered, quiet, watching the water with the ease of men who'd crossed it many times. A preacher heading west to save souls that hadn't asked to be saved.

And an older man near the bow, maybe sixty, wrapped in a blanket, smoking a pipe and watching the lake the way Declan watched rooms.

Dark hair going gray. The particular stillness Declan had come to recognize, not the stillness of a man waiting for something. The stillness of a man who had already decided about most things.

Declan watched him.

By midday, the wind had picked up, and most of the passengers had retreated below. Declan stayed on deck. So did the old man.

After a while, the old man spoke without looking at him.

"First crossing?"

"Yes," Declan said.

The old man nodded. Smoked.

"Big water," Declan said.

"Named for the people who lived here," the old man said. His English was careful and precise, each word chosen. "Erie. Cat Nation, some called them. Iroquoian people. Lived all along this southern shore."

Declan looked at the thin dark line of the Ohio shore in the distance.

"What happened to them?" he said.

The old man was quiet for a moment. The pipe smoke drifted south on the wind.

"My people happened to them," he said.

Declan looked at him.

"Seneca," the old man said simply. "Keepers of the Western Door." He gestured at the lake with the stem of his pipe. "Two hundred years ago. Beaver Wars. We fought over the fur trade, over access to the Europeans and their weapons. The Erie were in the way. We destroyed them. Absorbed some. Killed the rest." He drew on the pipe. "Within a few years, nothing left. Just the name on the water."

Declan looked at the southern shore.

A nation. Gone. Their name was all that remained.

"So your people did it to each other," he said. "Same as what's happening now."

The old man looked at him then. Really looked. The pipe held still in his hand.

"No," he said. Not angry. Just precise. "Not the same."

He looked back at the water.

"When the Haudenosaunee destroyed the Erie, we absorbed what remained. Their people became our people. Their children grew up Seneca. The land remembered them even if the nation was gone." He paused. "What is happening now is different. The white man do not want to absorb us. They do not want our children to become their children. They want the land without the people. They want us to disappear entirely." He drew on the pipe again. "That is a different thing."

Declan said nothing.

He wasn't interested in the distinction.

What he heard was simpler. The strong take from the weak. The Seneca took from the Erie. Now, white men were taking from the Seneca. The wheel turned. The strong became weak, and the weak became nothing, and the water kept the name of whoever it had belonged to last.

That was the nature of things.

Always had been.

The old man seemed to understand that Declan had stopped listening. He turned back to the lake and smoked in silence.

After a while, he spoke again. Not to Declan. Almost to himself.

"My grandfather fished this water," he said. "His grandfather fished it before him. Back further than that." He looked at the gray surface moving beneath them. "Now I ride a boat across it, owned by a man from New York who has never seen it before this year."

He said it without bitterness.

Just as a fact.

The kind of fact that had no remedy.

Declan looked at the water.

The wind pushed the boat west.

Neither of them spoke again.

By evening, they could see the Ohio shore.

* * *

The Ohio shore came up slowly in the gray October light, low and flat and nothing like what he'd been looking at his whole life.

No hills.

That was the first thing. Coming from Clare, where the land was always rolling toward something, always lifting or falling, always giving you a horizon that had shape to it, this was different. The land just went. Flat and wide and committed to it, the tree line at the edge of the cleared fields stretching in both directions without interruption, the sky sitting on top of it all like a lid.

He stepped off the boat at a small dock outside a settlement called Sandusky.

The ground felt different under his boots. Softer than New York. Darker soil, rich and black, where the recent rains had turned it. He crouched and pressed his hand to it as John had taught him to read ground.

Good land.

The best land he'd ever touched.

He stood and looked at the fields running back from the shore. Corn mostly, harvested now, the stalks cut and brown. A farmhouse, maybe a quarter mile back, was new enough that the wood hadn't weathered yet. Bright pale timber where it should have been gray if it had been standing any length of time.

A man was loading barrels onto a wagon near the dock.

"Is there a place to sleep in this settlement?" Declan said.

The man looked up. Took him in briefly. "Widow Hatch runs a boarding house. Half a mile up the road."

Declan nodded. Looked at the farmhouse again. The new wood. The young orchard beside it, the trees barely established, the stakes still in the ground.

"Everything here looks new," he said.

"Is new," the man said. "Most of it anyway. Land only opened up four or five years back."

Declan looked at the fields. Rich black soil. Flat and endless.

"They just give it away?" he asked.

The man shrugged. "File a claim. The government land office is in town. Dollar twenty-five an acre if you've got the money. Some of it's already gone, but there's plenty left."

He went back to his loading.

Declan looked at the land.

Four years ago, this had belonged to someone else. Now it was a dollar twenty-five an acre at the government land office.

He thought about what the Seneca man had said.

They want the land without the people.

He understood that.

He picked up his bundle and his rifle and walked toward the widow's boarding house.

* * *

The widow's boarding house was a two-story frame building at the edge of the settlement, clean and practical, run by a woman named Hatch who looked at Declan like she probably looked at every stranger who came through her door, measuring, cautious, deciding.

She gave him a room.

Supper was salt pork, boiled potatoes, and cornbread at a long table with four other men. A land speculator heading west, two brothers from Pennsylvania looking for farmland, and a quiet man who said nothing about where he was going or where he'd come from and ate quickly and left the table before anyone else.

Declan watched him go.

After supper, he sat by the fire in the common room. The widow moved through the house with the quiet efficiency of a woman who'd learned to manage everything herself. She didn't linger. Didn't invite conversation. But she watched. Every person in her house, every movement, every door.

He'd seen that kind of watchfulness before. In the Five Points. In people who were keeping something.

He didn't know what she was keeping.

Didn't care.

He was asleep before the fire burned low.

In the morning, he found a farmer heading southwest toward Columbus with an empty wagon. Offered to ride along and help unload at the other end.

The farmer looked at the Mississippi Rifle.

"You know how to use that?"

"Yes," Declan said.

The farmer nodded. "Climb up then."

Sandusky fell away behind them.

The road ran southwest through flat Ohio farmland, the harvested fields brown and wide on both sides, the sky enormous above it all. Every few miles, another farmhouse. Another new orchard. Another pale wood barn that hadn't had time to weather.

The land, opening up.

Getting flatter.

Getting bigger.

Declan sat on the wagon seat with the Mississippi across his knees and watched it all go past and said nothing.

The farmer talked enough for both of them.

9

Cincinnati

The city announced itself by smell.

Three miles out, the wind shifted and brought it; not woodsmoke, not the river, not the particular smell of a settlement finding its feet. Something else. Something that hit Declan in the chest and took him straight back to the slaughterhouse on the edge of the Five Points, where he'd worked his first months in America.

Blood and offal and the particular sweetness of rendering fat.

Pigs.

Thousands of them.

Cincinnati processed more pork than anywhere else in America, and the city wore the fact of it the way a working man wore his trade. Completely, without apology, in every surface and every breath of air.

He rode in on the farmer's wagon through streets that grew busier and louder with every block. German neighborhoods giving way to Irish neighborhoods giving way to the commercial center along the river. The Ohio River itself appeared between the buildings, wide and brown and moving with an authority that made the Erie Canal look like a drainage ditch.

He gave the farmer a nod of thanks at the edge of the commercial district and climbed down.

The farmer drove on without looking back.

* * *

Declan stood on a Cincinnati street corner and took stock.

He needed a coat. The one he had was wool and adequate for October, but the men around him, men who knew what was coming, were wearing heavier things. Buffalo hide. Oilskin. Layers built for serious cold. He'd be heading into his first plains winter, and he had no idea what that meant exactly, but the men on the canal and the lake boat had been specific about one thing.

You don't want to find out what it means without the right coat.

He found a trading post two blocks from the river. A long, low building stacked floor to ceiling with gear for men heading west. Blankets. Rope. Ammunition. Cooking equipment. Traps. And coats, heavy ones, the kind that had been thought about by men who'd spent winters where the wind came across a thousand miles of flat ground with nothing to stop it.

He spent some time going through them carefully.

The trader watched him with the patience of a man who'd seen every kind of westbound traveler and had learned that the ones who took their time choosing were the ones who came back.

Declan chose a heavy wool coat lined with rabbit fur, long enough to cover his thighs, with a collar he could turn up against the wind. Tried it on. Moved in it. Checked that his arms came free fast enough.

"Good choice," the trader said.

Declan looked at him.

The trader stopped talking.

He bought ammunition for the Mississippi. Two boxes of percussion caps. A good knife to replace the one from Clare that was getting thin from years of use. A wool blanket that could double as a bedroll.

He counted what he had left.

Not enough.

He needed more before he left Cincinnati.

* * *

He found it the same way he always found it.

The card game was in a tavern called the Boatman's Rest, two blocks from the river landing. The kind of place that existed in every river city. Rough, transient, full of men between one thing and the next. He sat down at nine in the evening with what he had and stood up at midnight with considerably more.

He didn't take everything.

That was something John had taught him without meaning to, about not stripping a place bare, about leaving enough that the thing you'd taken from could recover. John had meant it about the land. About not taking every eel, every deer, every rabbit from a place you might need to return to.

Declan applied it to card games.

Leave them something. They'll be back tomorrow. So will you.

He walked back to the boarding house through Cincinnati streets that smelled of the river, the slaughterhouses, and the cold coming down from the north.

The Ohio River ran dark and wide at the edge of the city.

On the far bank, Kentucky.

Slave territory.

He looked at it for a moment.

Then went inside.

* * *

He found a boarding house in a settlement called Peru, Indiana, two days west of the Ohio line.

The town sat on the Mississinewa River, the water running low and cold in the November light. The boarding house was run by a woman named Mrs. Keller. She was solid, efficient, the kind of woman who had built something in a place that didn't make building easy and wore the fact of it without comment. She fed her guests at a long table, whether they wanted to be fed or not, and charged extra if they didn't eat.

Declan ate.

There were six others at the table. A land surveyor. Two brothers, heading to Illinois to file claims. A Methodist preacher who said grace at such length that the food went cold. And a farmer and his wife who'd come into town to sell grain and buy supplies. The wife, small and sharp-eyed, with the particular alertness of a woman who had learned to pay attention to everything because nobody else would.

She'd come for cloth. She couldn't trust him to choose a pattern, the farmer had said when they sat down.

The farmer agreed.

It was the surveyor who brought it up.

"Passing through from the east, are you?" he said to the table generally. "Then you might not have heard. A woman died here in March. Frances Slocum. White woman, captured by Delaware Indians as a child, lived her whole life with the Miami. Refused to go back to her family when they found her." He shook his head. "Tragic story."

The farmer's wife set down her fork.

Just set it down. Quietly. The way a woman sets something down when she has decided to say a thing she has decided many times not to say.

"Tragic?" she said.

The surveyor shook his head. "Captured as a child. Never got home. Died among savages. Her family tried. Nobody could say they didn't try."

"She refused to go," the farmer's wife said.

"Well." The surveyor cut his meat. "After that long. Didn't know any better, probably."

"She knew perfectly well," the farmer's wife said. The edge in her voice, quiet but present now. "She spoke to her family when they found her. Knew who she was. Knew who they were. Chose to stay."

"Couldn't be helped," the surveyor said. "Too far gone by then."

The farmer's wife looked at him.

"She had a husband," she said. "Children. Grandchildren. A home. People who loved her and came to her for counsel. Her Miami family accepted her as their own from the day she arrived. Raised her as one of them. She was Miami. She knew it, and they knew it." She paused. "Can you say the same would have happened if a Miami child had been taken into a white family?"

Silence.

The preacher cleared his throat.

The surveyor studied his plate.

The two brothers became very interested in their food.

The farmer's hand moved to his wife's arm. Gentle. Brief. The pressure of a man who had learned that some opinions were better left unfinished in mixed company.

She stopped. She picked up her fork and continued to eat.

Mrs. Keller passed through the room just then, moving from the kitchen to the far end of the table with a fresh pitcher. She caught the farmer's wife's eye.

Nodded once.

Then went back to her business.

Declan ate.

He'd been eating the whole time. Hadn't looked up. Hadn't shifted in his seat.

But he'd heard every word.

He thought about the Seneca man on the lake.

They want the land without the people.

He thought about the Wyandot land at Sandusky. Four years gone.

He thought about Maconaquah, Little Bear, dying on the Mississinewa River eight months ago in the place she'd chosen over everything her birth had given her.

He didn't know what to make of any of it.

He just ate his food.

After supper, he went to his room.

Lay on the cot and stared at the ceiling.

Outside, the Mississinewa ran cold and dark toward the Wabash.

Miami water.

Still.

10

Illinois

He stopped in a town called Dixon, Illinois, two days west of the Indiana line.

Dixon sat on the Rock River, a rough commercial settlement that had grown up around a ford that men had been crossing for as long as men had been moving west. The main street had the usual collection of a frontier town finding its feet. General store, tavern, land office, blacksmith. And a barber shop, a narrow building with a striped pole outside that needed repainting.

Declan needed a shave.

He pushed through the door.

Two men ahead of him. He took a seat on the bench along the wall and picked up what was lying there. It was a pamphlet, worn soft at the edges from handling, the cover page reading:

LIFE OF BLACK HAWK Ma-ka-tai-me-she-kia-kiak Dictated by Himself

He looked at it for a moment.

Then opened it.

He wasn't a reader by habit. Had learned his letters in Clare well enough to get by, had read what he needed to read since, contracts, notices, the occasional newspaper when something caught his eye. He read just like he did most things. Functionally. Taking what was useful and moving on.

But something in the first pages held him.

The voice was direct. Unadorned. A man saying what he meant without apology or performance.

He read about the Rock River. About the Sauk village of Saukenuk that had stood at its mouth for generations, the corn fields, the lodges, the burial grounds of the ancestors. About the treaty of 1804 that the Americans said had ceded the land but that Black Hawk said had been signed by men who had no authority to sign it, who had been drunk, who had not understood what they were giving away.

He read about the slow pressure of white settlement moving in around Saukenuk. Farmers plowing up the corn fields. Moving into the lodges when the Sauk left for their winter hunts. Claiming the land while the people were gone.

He read about the return. Black Hawk coming back in the spring to find his village occupied. Going to the American authorities. Being told the land was no longer his. Being told to move west of the Mississippi.

He read about the war. The resistance. The defeat.

And then the surrender.

Black Hawk's words after the defeat at the Bad Axe River, where American soldiers had fired on women and children trying to cross the Mississippi to safety.

He read slowly here. Carefully, how you read something you want to make sure you've understood correctly.

I fought hard. But your guns were well aimed. The bullets flew like birds in the air, and whizzed by our ears like the wind through the trees in winter.

He turned the page.

I am now a prisoner to the white men. They will do with me as they wish.

But he can stand torture and is not afraid of death. He is no coward. Black Hawk is an Indian.

Declan sat with that.

The man ahead of him got out of the barber's chair. The barber looked at Declan.

Declan set the pamphlet down and took the chair.

"You know this river?" he said, while the barber worked the lather.

"Rock River?" The barber didn't look up from his work. "Been here since thirty-five. Before that it was Sauk country. Black Hawk's people. You read the pamphlet?"

"Some of it."

"Sad business," the barber said. "They fought hard. Couldn't win though. Too many of us."

He scraped the razor along Declan's jaw.

"What happened to him?" Declan said. "Black Hawk."

"Took him east. Showed him the cities. Washington. New York. Let him see how many white men there were. Then sent him back." The barber rinsed the razor. "Died a few years back. Out in Iowa somewhere. On a reservation."

He kept working.

"They say he never stopped calling the Rock River his home," the barber said. "Right up to the end."

Declan looked at the ceiling.

The razor moved.

He thought about the pamphlet. About the voice in it, direct, unadorned, without self-pity. A man describing what had been taken from him with the clarity of someone who had no reason left to soften anything.

That's what happens, Declan thought, *when you can't hold what's yours.*

He thought about the Rock River running outside.

Sauk water.

Like the Mississinewa had been Miami water.
Like Onondaga Lake had been Onondaga water.
Like the Hudson had been Mohawk water.
All the way west.
Always the same.
The barber finished. Declan paid. Picked up the pamphlet.
"Can I take this?"
The barber shrugged. "Been here two years. Nobody's claimed it."
Declan folded it and put it in his coat pocket.
He walked out into the Dixon street.
The Rock River ran west toward the Mississippi.
He followed it.

* * *

The land had been flattening for two days.

Illinois was nothing like Ohio, which had been nothing like Indiana, which had been nothing like New York. Each state west had taken something away: another hill, another tree line, another sense that the horizon had a shape to it. Now the horizon was just a line. Flat and absolute and stretching in every direction, like the earth had given up on variety entirely.

The sky was enormous.

He'd been told about the sky. Men on the canal, men on the lake boat, men in Cincinnati and Peru and Dixon, they'd all mentioned it eventually. The sky out west. How it sat on you differently when there was nothing between you and it. He'd nodded and filed it away under things that couldn't be understood until you were standing in them.

They'd been right.

He was on a freight wagon heading west, sharing the seat with a taciturn German hauler who had said exactly four words since

Dixon and showed no interest in adding to them. The Mississippi was wrapped in Declan's bedroll in the wagon bed behind him. The Black Hawk pamphlet was in his coat pocket. The knife was on his belt where it always was.

The road was rutted and muddy from recent rain, the fields on both sides harvested and brown, the occasional farmhouse set back from the road with that same pale new timber he'd been seeing since Sandusky.

Always new.

Always recently emptied of whoever had been there before.

He was maybe ten miles east of the river when he saw them.

At first, he thought they were hills. Natural rises in the otherwise flat land, the kind of thing you'd find anywhere. But they were wrong for hills. Too regular. Too deliberate in their shape. And too many of them, clustered together in a way that nature didn't cluster things.

"What are those?" Declan said.

The German hauler glanced over without slowing the horses.

"Mounds," he said. "Old ones."

That was all.

Declan looked at them as the wagon rolled past. The largest one rose maybe a hundred feet above the plain. Broad at the base, flattening toward the top. Grass covered now, brown in the November light. Around it, smaller mounds, dozens of them, arranged in patterns that suggested intention rather than geology.

Someone had built these.

A long time ago. Before anyone now living could remember. Before Illinois was Illinois. Before any of this road existed or any of these pale new farmhouses or any of the men who'd filed claims at the land offices in Sandusky and Peru and Dixon.

Someone had been here first.

He thought about the pamphlet in his pocket.

Then the mounds fell away behind the wagon.

He didn't look back.

* * *

He heard the Mississippi before he saw it.

The same way he'd heard Niagara. A presence before a sight, something felt in the chest before it registered in the eyes. Not a roar this time. Something lower than that. Deeper. The sound of an enormous weight moving with complete indifference to anything in its path.

The German hauler stopped the wagon on a low rise.

And there it was.

Wide.

Wider than he had words for.

The Ohio River had made the Erie Canal look like a drainage ditch. The Mississippi made the Ohio look like the Erie Canal. It was not a river the way he understood rivers. It was a moving landscape. Brown and vast and carrying everything, logs, debris, the remnants of things that had been somewhere upstream and were now somewhere else, with the same unhurried certainty that the falls at Niagara fell.

It didn't care.

That was the thing. Oneida Lake had been still and knowable. Niagara had been violent and overwhelming. The Mississippi was neither. It was simply present. Massive and indifferent and ancient in a way that made Niagara feel young.

He sat on the wagon seat and looked at it for a long time.

The German hauler said nothing.

On the far bank, the beginnings of St. Louis. Buildings. Smoke. The noise of commerce carried across the water.

He found a ferry crossing downstream.

Paid his fare.

Stood at the bow as the ferry pushed out into the current.

The Mississippi took them.

Powerful and brown and moving.

St. Louis came closer.

Behind him, Illinois fell away.

And somewhere ahead, past the city and the winter and everything that still had to happen, the west was waiting.

The way it had always been waiting.

Indifferent.

Vast.

His.

11

The Missouri

St. Louis hit him as the Five Points had hit him. The smell first, then the noise, then the particular density of a place where too many people were trying to do too many things in too small a space.

But bigger than the Five Points. Rawer. The Five Points had been old poverty, worn into the grain of the city over generations. St. Louis was new poverty, fresh and violent and still finding its shape. A city that had decided it was the gateway to everything and was making money off the decision as fast as it could before someone else made the same decision first.

He came off the ferry into a waterfront that made Cincinnati's look orderly.

The confluence of the Missouri and Mississippi was half a mile upstream, the two rivers meeting with the particular violence of things that had been moving separately for a long time and hadn't figured out how to do it together. The Missouri came in brown and fast and cold from the west, pushing against the slower Mississippi, the water between them a churning line of conflicting currents.

Declan stood at the waterfront and looked at it.

The Missouri.

That was the road west. Every man who'd been out there and come back had said it: follow the Missouri. It would take you where you needed to go if it didn't kill you first. Fast water. Unpredictable. Full of snags and sandbars and the particular malice of a river that didn't want to be navigated.

He looked at it for a while.

Then turned and walked into St. Louis.

He found a boarding house near the waterfront. Cheap. The smell of the rivers came through the window at night, along with the noise of the docks, the same combination he'd had in Buffalo, though the rivers smelled different from the lake. Older somehow. More complicated.

He had money. Not enough to last a winter without working.

He spent three days watching the city how he always watched a new place. The waterfront. The commercial district. The taverns. The particular geography of who had what, who wanted what, and where the two things met.

On the fourth day, he found the livery stable.

It sat two blocks off the waterfront, a large barn-like building that smelled of horses, hay, and manure, and the particular sweetness of animals kept in close quarters through cold weather. A man named Gruber ran it. He was a thick German with a permanently suspicious expression and hands that looked like they'd been made for a larger man.

Gruber looked at Declan as he looked at everything.

"You know horses?" he said.

"No," Declan said.

Gruber studied him. Most men lied. Said yes. Got found out in the first ten minutes and were useless.

"At least you're honest," he said. "I'll pay you three dollars a week. You muck the stalls, haul water, and feed. You do what I tell you and nothing else."

"Three dollars a week and you teach me to ride," Declan said. "By spring."

Gruber considered this.

"Two fifty," he said. "And I teach you enough not to kill yourself."

Declan nodded.

He started that afternoon.

The work was hard and physical and beneath almost everyone who came to St. Louis with ambitions. Declan did it without complaint. Mucking stalls. Hauling water in the cold. Brushing horses that didn't particularly want to be brushed. Learning the names of things, fetlock, withers, cannon bone, hock, not because he cared about the poetry of horses, but because knowing what something was called helped you understand what it did.

Gruber watched him work.

After two weeks, he said, "You pay attention."

Declan shrugged.

"Most men don't," Gruber said. "They think they already know."

He went back to his work.

That was the closest Gruber came to a compliment.

* * *

The riding started in the third week.

Gruber put him on a horse named Joker.

He didn't explain the name. He just brought the animal out of the stall, a big roan gelding, broad through the chest, with the particular expression of a horse that had opinions and intended to share them, and handed Declan the reins.

Declan got on.

Joker stood.

For maybe thirty seconds everything was fine.

Then Joker left the paddock track and walked to the far fence and put his head down and started eating the dead grass along the base of it.

Declan pulled the reins.

Joker ate.

Declan pulled harder.

Joker shifted slightly to reach a better patch of grass.

Gruber watched from the gate, arms folded, a slight upturn to the corners of his mouth.

Declan tried his heels. Tried the reins again. Tried both together. Joker was comprehensively unimpressed by all of it. He'd been doing this for years with men who outweighed Declan and knew more about horses than Declan ever would and he saw no particular reason to change his habits for a large Irishman with bad hands.

Declan sat for a moment.

Then he got off.

He came around to Joker's head. Took the halter in both hands, not rough, not gentle, just firm, and turned the horse's face toward him.

Joker tried to look away.

Declan didn't let him.

He held the horse's head steady and looked him in the eye. Whatever he said, if he said anything, Gruber couldn't hear it from the gate. He started to walk over. Joker had put three men on the ground in the last month alone, and a fourth in the hospital in October, and Gruber had been meaning to sell him and hadn't gotten around to it.

He was maybe ten feet away when he stopped.

Joker had gone still.

Not the stillness of a horse waiting for its chance. Something different. The ears forward. The eye on Declan with an expression Gruber had not seen on that particular animal in the two years he'd owned him.

Declan let go of the halter.

Got back on.

Joker walked the track.

Straight and steady and without any apparent interest in the grass along the fence.

Gruber stood in the middle of the paddock and watched.

He'd been working with horses for thirty years. He'd seen men who had a gift with them. Who spoke the language naturally, who the animals trusted without being asked to. Declan wasn't that. Whatever had happened at the fence wasn't gift, language, or trust.

It was something else.

Something the horse had understood and decided not to argue with.

Gruber went back to the gate.

He didn't ask what Declan had said.

* * *

The cards kept him alive through November and December.

St. Louis had no shortage of card games. The waterfront taverns ran them every night, rough affairs mostly, men with nothing to lose playing against men with everything to lose, the money moving around the table with the particular democracy of gambling, which didn't care where you came from or what you knew or what you'd done to get here.

Declan cared about none of those things either.

He played three or four nights a week. Never the same tavern twice in a row. Never taking everything. Leaving enough that the game would still be there next week and the week after. John's lesson applied with cold precision.

The livery work filled his days. The cards filled his evenings. The boarding house filled the hours between.

It was the most settled he'd been since Mulberry Street.

The westbound men were everywhere in St. Louis that winter. You couldn't sit in a tavern or eat at a boarding house table without finding one. Men who'd been out on the plains and come back, or men who were going out in spring and hadn't been yet. The ones who'd been out were easy to identify. Something in the way they sat. Something in the eyes. Not the flat predator stillness of Declan's own gaze but a different quality. The look of men who'd seen a lot of empty space and hadn't entirely come back from it.

Declan listened to them.

Not obviously. Not with questions or engagement or any of the social performances that invited reciprocal interest. Just present. Nearby. His ears open while his face showed nothing.

The fur trade was dying, they said. The beaver was nearly gone. Trapped out over thirty years of fashion in European drawing rooms that had never heard of the Missouri River. The mountain men were finished. The ones who hadn't died out there were drifting back east or adapting to whatever came next.

What came next, some of them said, was buffalo.

The hide trade was growing. Eastern factories wanted buffalo hides for robes and leather. The demand was there. The buffalo were still out there in numbers that strained belief. Millions of them, the old hands said, though the word millions didn't quite cover it. You had to see it. A man who hadn't seen it couldn't understand what millions of anything looked like moving across flat ground.

The work was simple. Find the herd. Get close enough for a clean shot. Drop as many as you could before they ran. Skin them where they fell. Stack the hides. Sell them.

Simple, the old hands said.

Not easy.

It was one of these men Declan found himself near on a January evening in a tavern called the Frontier House, two blocks from the Missouri River landing. An old trapper, really old, fifty at least, with a face like cured leather and hands that had done everything a man could do with his hands on the frontier, and they showed it. He'd been talking to another man who'd eventually wandered off, and now he was drinking alone with the comfortable solitude of someone who preferred his own company.

Declan moved to the adjacent seat.

The old trapper glanced at him.

Said nothing.

Declan set his coffee down on the bar. The old trapper sipped his whiskey.

"Buffalo," Declan said eventually.

The old trapper looked at him.

"You heading out?" he said.

"Spring."

The old trapper studied him how men who'd been on the plains studied young men who thought they were heading out in spring. Taking inventory. Assessing what would get him killed and what might keep him alive.

"You ride?" he said.

"Yes."

"You shoot?"

"Yes."

"You know the Crow?"

Declan looked at him. "No."

The old trapper nodded slowly. Like the answer was what he expected.

"The Powder River country," he said. "That's where the herds are thickest. Eastern Wyoming. Southeastern Montana. Crow territory." He drank. "The Crow have been there since before anyone can remember. They know that land same as you know your own hand. You go out there, you're in their country whether you think you are or not."

"Is that a problem?" Declan said.

The old trapper considered.

"Depends," he said. "On you. On them. On what you do and how you do it." He set down his glass. "The Crow are not the Sioux. They don't make war on white men like the Sioux do. But they're not welcoming either. They're watching. Always watching. And they understand exactly what the buffalo hunters are doing to their world, even if most buffalo hunters are too stupid to understand it themselves."

He picked up his glass again.

"Go careful," he said. "Learn what you can. Don't take more than you need."

Declan thought about John on the south shore of Oneida Lake.

Don't strip a place bare.

The old trapper finished his drink and left.

Declan sat with his coffee and thought about the Powder River.

He thought about the Crow.

He filed it all away.

* * *

February came and went.

March arrived cold, gray, and reluctant.

St. Louis sat on land that had belonged to the Osage Nation before the Americans arrived and decided it was too good a location to leave to people who weren't using it in the manner Americans thought land should be used. The Osage had been pushed west through a series of treaties that took everything and gave back less each time until there was nothing left to give back. Now their name survived on a river that ran into the Missouri upstream, the Osage River, carrying the name of the people who'd been removed from its banks as the Erie carried the name of the people the Haudenosaunee had destroyed.

Names on water.

It was the only monument most of them got.

April came.

The Missouri thawed completely. The waterfront came alive with the particular energy of men who'd been waiting out the winter and were done waiting. Wagons. Horses. Supplies being loaded onto flatboats heading upstream. The sound of the west opening up again after the cold.

Declan went to Gruber.

"I want to buy the horse," he said.

Gruber looked up from the harness he was mending.

"Joker," Declan said.

Something moved in Gruber's face. Not quite relief. The expression of a man whose problem is about to become someone else's problem.

He named a price.

Declan named a lower one.

Gruber accepted faster than he should have.

They both knew it.

Declan paid. Gruber took the money, counted it twice, and put it in his pocket.

"Don't let him near long grass," Gruber said. "You'll be there all day."

Declan fixed him with a look, turned, and walked out of the barn.

He saddled Joker in the early morning of the second week of April. The Mississippi Rifle wrapped in his bedroll and tied behind the saddle. The Black Hawk pamphlet was in his coat pocket. The knife on his belt. Enough money to get where he was going and enough sense to know that where he was going would provide what he needed after that.

He led Joker out of the stable.

Gruber watched from the door.

Neither of them said anything.

Declan mounted.

Joker stood.

He rode west through the St. Louis streets toward the Missouri River landing. The city fell away behind him block by block. The waterfront, the commercial district, the boarding houses, taverns, card games, and everything that had kept him through the winter.

At the landing, he found a flatboat captain willing to take a man and a horse upstream for a reasonable fare.

He paid.

Led Joker onto the flatboat.

The Missouri took them.

Fast and brown and cold and moving with a violence that made the Mississippi feel lazy.

St. Louis fell away.

The plains began.

$$12$$

The Powder River

The Missouri was nothing like the Mississippi.

The Mississippi had been vast and brown and moving with the indifferent authority of something that had been doing what it did since before anything else existed. The Missouri was different. Narrower. Faster. Angrier somehow, a river that hadn't made peace with its banks, that cut and shifted and changed its mind about where it wanted to go. The color of it was wrong too. Not brown exactly. Gray-brown. The color of the land it was pulling apart upstream and carrying east.

The flatboat pushed against it for three weeks.

Declan stood at the bow most of the time. Watching.

The land changed around them as they moved west and north. The trees thinned first. Then the hills flattened. Then the grass began, but not the grass he'd seen in Ohio and Indiana and Illinois, the managed grass of farms and cleared land, but something older and wilder and going in every direction without apology.

Prairie.

He'd heard the word, but it hadn't meant anything until now.

The wind came across it without interruption. That was the first thing he noticed. In every place he'd been, there was always something breaking the wind: a hill, a tree line, a building. Here, there was nothing. The wind just came. Steady and cold and smelling of grass and distance and something else. Something animal, maybe. Something that had been on that wind a long time.

The grass moved in long, slow waves, the whole plain shifting and resettling like water. The sky sat enormous above it. Not the enormous sky of Illinois, which had surprised him. This was different. Illinois had been flat, but it had still felt like land with sky above it. This felt like he was between two things of equal size, the grass ocean below and the sky ocean above, and the flatboat was moving through the seam between them.

He stood at the bow and watched it.

He'd grown up on an island. Crossed an actual ocean. Stood at Niagara and felt small. Stood at the Mississippi and understood the spine of the continent.

None of it had prepared him for this.

Not because it was violent or overwhelming.

Because it just went.

In every direction.

Forever.

He thought about what the old trapper had said in the Frontier House.

You have to see it. A man who hasn't seen it can't understand what millions of anything looks like moving across flat ground.

He wasn't there yet.

But he was getting there.

He left the flatboat at a trading post near the mouth of the Yellowstone River, where the two waters met in a wide, turbulent confluence that smelled of mud and distance. Fort Union sat on the north bank. A substantial trading post that had been doing business with the Crow, the Assiniboine, and the Blackfeet for twenty years, the kind of place that existed at the edge of the known world and had decided to make money off the fact.

He bought supplies. Dried meat. Ammunition. A second blanket. A small axe.

He asked about the buffalo.

The trader, a weathered French Canadian who'd been at Fort Union longer than most men survived anywhere, looked at him.

"South," he said. "And west. Follow the Yellowstone to the Powder River. That's where the herds are this time of year." He paused. "That's Crow country."

Declan just eyed the man.

The trader regarded him with the suspicion men reserve for boys who claim knowledge they don't have.

"You'll see them," he said. "Before you see the Crow."

Declan paid for his supplies and walked out.

Joker was where he'd left him, tied at the rail, pulling at a patch of grass at the base of the post.

Declan untied him.

South and west.

The Yellowstone ran beside him, cold and fast and moving in the right direction.

He followed it.

* * *

He smelled them before he saw them.

He'd been following the Powder River south for three days, the country opening up around him into something that had no equivalent in anything he'd seen. The grass ran to the horizon in every direction. The sky was enormous. The river cut through the plain in wide curves, the cottonwoods along its banks the only vertical things in a landscape that had given up on vertical entirely.

Joker had been nervous since morning.

Not spooked exactly. Just alert in a way he hadn't been. His ears moving. His nostrils working. Some information coming in on the wind that Declan couldn't read yet.

Then the wind shifted.

And Declan understood.

The smell hit him like a physical thing. Not bad exactly. Just enormous. The concentrated smell of animals in numbers he had no frame for. Hide and dung and the particular musk of something large living in vast quantity. It came from the south and west, filling the air complctcly, as the falls at Niagara had filled it with mist.

Joker stopped.

Declan let him.

They stood on a low rise above the river.

And then he heard it.

Low. Beneath sound almost. A vibration in the ground that came up through Joker's hooves and into Declan's legs and settled in his chest like a second heartbeat. Not thunder. Something more deliberate than thunder. Something with direction and weight and purpose.

He waited.

The sound grew.

Then they came over the rise to the south.

The first ones appeared at the crest and kept coming and kept coming and kept coming and didn't stop. Brown and massive, moving with a kind of unstoppable momentum that made the ground shake beneath them. Their heads swinging low. Their breath rising in clouds in the cold air. The sound of them was everywhere now, not just in his chest but in his teeth and in the soles of his feet and in the air around him.

He'd thought he understood what millions meant.

He hadn't.

You couldn't count them. Counting wasn't the right relationship to have with what he was looking at. They covered the plain from the river to the horizon. They covered the horizon itself. They were still coming over the rise to the south and there was no end to them visible and no suggestion that an end existed.

Joker trembled under him.

Not from fear exactly. Something older than fear. The particular response of a prey animal to a sight its instincts hadn't forgotten even if its life had given it no occasion to use that information.

Declan put his hand on Joker's neck.

Joker steadied.

Declan looked at the buffalo.

The old trapper had been right. A man who hadn't seen it couldn't understand what millions of anything looked like moving across flat ground.

He understood now.

He also understood something else. Something the old trapper hadn't said and probably couldn't have said in a way that would have meant anything before this moment.

There was enough here.

More than enough.

More than he could take in a lifetime.

He sat with it for a moment.

Then he moved.

He took Joker downwind and found a shallow draw fifty yards from the edge of the herd. Tied Joker to a root. Moved on foot through the grass, low and slow, repeating what John had taught him, reading the wind before each step.

The buffalo didn't see him.

They didn't look for what the wind didn't tell them was there.

He got within forty yards of the nearest one. A cow, heavy and slow, at the edge of the herd. He picked her not for size but for position. She was away from the main body, with enough space between her and the next animal that a shot wouldn't push the whole herd.

He waited.

Just like the grouse.

Wait. Then move.

He fired.

The cow dropped.

The herd shifted. A ripple of movement, a low rumble of unease. But they didn't run. He'd seen that too. If you dropped them cleanly, didn't wound one that ran and alarmed the others, the herd would often just move a few yards and settle again. They were too many and too dumb and too used to predators taking the edges to panic over one clean death.

He reloaded.

Slow. The Mississippi Rifle demanding its full attention. Powder, patch, ball, ram, prime. His hands working fast but not fast enough. By the time he was ready, the nearest animals had drifted fifty yards further.

He moved with them.

Dropped a second one.

Then the herd ran.

Something had shifted. A change in the wind, maybe, or just the accumulated unease of two deaths reaching whatever threshold the herd ran on. They went all at once, the ground shaking, the sound of them filling the plain, and within two minutes, there was nothing in front of him but churned earth and settling dust.

Two animals.

He stood in the middle of the torn plain and looked at what he had.

Two buffalo. More hide and meat than he could carry. More than he could process alone before the weather turned it.

He went to work.

The skinning took the rest of the day. The Mississippi Rifle was propped against the first carcass while he worked. It was useless now, a single-shot muzzleloader standing against a plain that had just swallowed sixty million animals and barely noticed.

He worked until dark.

Rolled in his blanket beside the stacked hides.

Lying on his back, he looked at the stars.

The plains sky at night was something else entirely. More stars than he'd seen anywhere, the darkness between them deeper, the whole thing pressing down close and cold and indifferent.

He thought about the two rifles he'd seen other hunters carrying.

Thought about the pairs of men he'd seen working the range. One shooting while the other reloaded. The mathematics of it simple and obvious now that he understood what he was dealing with.

Two rifles. Or two men.

One shooting. One reloading.

The herd barely noticing.

He looked at the stars.

He could do more than this.

Much more.

He closed his eyes.

Joker shifted in the dark nearby.

The plains were quiet.

Somewhere to the north, the herd was still moving.

* * *

He'd been at it six weeks.

Six weeks on the Powder River range, learning the work by doing it wrong until he did it right. He'd learned to read the wind before he moved. Learned to pick his position before the herd arrived rather than chasing it. Learned that a clean kill dropped the animal where it stood and didn't alarm the others, while a wounded animal that ran took the whole herd with it.

He was getting better.

Not good enough.

Three hides on a good day. Sometimes four. Once five, when everything went right, and the wind held, and the herd stood still long enough. He'd sold two loads at a trading post on the river. Rough money, enough to keep him in ammunition and supplies, but nowhere near what the range was capable of providing.

He could see that. Could see the gap between what he was taking and what was available to be taken.

The reloading was the problem. Always the reloading. The Mississippi Rifle demanding its full attention between every shot, powder, patch, ball, ram, prime, the whole ceremony taking two minutes on a good day, longer when his hands were cold or the wind was blowing. Two minutes was an eternity on a buffalo range. In two minutes the herd moved. In two minutes the angle changed. In two minutes the morning light shifted and the shot that had been there wasn't there anymore.

He was thinking about this on a Tuesday morning in October when he saw the other man.

Half a mile east, working the edge of a small herd that had broken off from the main body and was grazing along a creek bottom.

Declan stopped Joker.

Watched.

The man was already set up behind a low rise, a forked shooting stick planted in the ground, his rifle resting in it. He'd been there a while. Long enough to have read the wind and found his angle and settled into the particular stillness of a man who knew how to wait.

He fired.

Clean kill. The cow dropped where she stood. The herd shifted but didn't run.

The man reloaded. Slow and methodical. By the time he was ready the herd had moved forty yards.

He fired again.

Another clean kill.

Declan watched him work through the morning. Five animals. Patient. Accurate. Never rushed a shot. Never pushed the herd past its tolerance.

Good hunter.

When the herd finally moved off, the man stood and stretched.

He didn't look at Declan.

But the way he stood, not scanning the horizon and not checking his surroundings as a man does when he thinks he's alone, told Declan he'd known someone was sitting a horse half a mile east for the last two hours.

Declan rode over.

The man was already crouched over the nearest carcass, knife out, making his first cut.

He didn't look up.

"You going to watch or work?" he said.

Declan dismounted. Dropped Joker's reins. Joker stood, ground tied. He took out his knife.

Crouched over the second carcass.

They worked in silence. The flies already gathering in the October warmth. The smell of fresh blood and hide, and the particular rawness of an animal opened on open ground.

Declan worked as John had taught him. The angle of the first cut. How the hide peeled away from the muscle when you found the right plane between them. No wasted motion. No tearing. The hide coming off clean and intact.

After a while, the man glanced over.

Said nothing.

Went back to his work.

They finished the first two animals. Moved to the next. The sun climbed. The plains stretched away in every direction.

"Shea," Declan said.

The man worked his knife along the belly.

"Bill," he said.

That was all.

They worked through the remaining three animals without speaking. By the time they stacked the last hide the sun was still well short of noon. Declan straightened and looked at it. Then at the stacked hides. Then at the plain to the north where the herd had gone.

He looked at Bill.

Bill was looking at the sun too.

Doing the same arithmetic.

They'd skinned five animals in less than half a morning.

Two men working.

The day still ahead of them.

Declan picked up his rifle.

"Let's get my five," he said.

He rode north.

He didn't look back.

Behind him he heard Bill pull the shooting stick from the ground.

Heard him mount.

Heard Joker's hooves and then a second set of hooves falling in alongside.

They rode north together.

Neither of them said anything.

There was nothing to say.

That was the first day.

The second day, Declan was already at the creek bottom when Bill arrived in the gray pre-dawn, smelling of woodsmoke and whiskey and the accumulated roughness of a man who'd been sleeping out for years. He looked at Declan. Looked at the plain. Drank from his canteen. Picked up his rifle.

They worked the morning.

Eight animals in all.

The system arrived without discussion. Declan shot while Bill reloaded and handed the charged rifle back. Then Bill shot while Declan reloaded. One rifle always ready. The herd standing longer than it should have. The animals dropping one after another in the cold morning air.

It wasn't a new idea on the range. Other men had worked it out before them. But neither Declan nor Bill had been told, and neither had thought to ask. They'd arrived at it the same way they arrived at everything, alone, by necessity, later than they needed to.

By the end of the week, they were taking twelve animals on a good day.

Sometimes fifteen.

Bill drank in the afternoons. Declan ignored it. The man could shoot straight in the mornings. What he did in the afternoon was his own business.

They camped separately.

Ate separately mostly.

Spoke when something needed saying.

It wasn't friendship.

Neither of them would have known what to do with friendship.

It was something older and simpler.

Two men who recognized each other.

On the Powder River.

The plains going on in every direction.

The herd always somewhere to the north.

* * *

The trading post sat on the river as it had grown there, low and dark and smelling of hides and woodsmoke and the particular sourness of men who'd been out on the range too long and were making up for lost drinking time.

Declan was at the card table in the corner.

He'd been there two hours. Won some. Lost some on purpose. The particular economy of a man who knew how to manage a room full of people who might need managing later.

Bill was at the bar.

He'd been there longer.

Declan could hear him from across the room. The voice getting louder, the kind of loud that came after the bottle had been at a man long enough. Bill telling it as men told it after a good day on the range, the numbers growing slightly with each retelling, as numbers tended to do.

"Twenty," Bill said. "Got twenty today."

The room went on around him. Cards. Smoke. The fire.

Then a voice from down the bar.

"Twenty." Not a question. The particular tone of a man who'd decided something.

Declan didn't look up from his cards.

"Sour Bill got twenty." The man again. Louder now. Making sure the room heard. "Sour Bill, who can't hardly stand up, got twenty buffalo today."

A few laughs. The easy laughs of men who smelled something

coming and wanted to be on the right side of it.

Bill straightened.

Wobbly. But straight.

"I said what I said," he said.

The other man was big. Bigger than Declan even, and younger than Bill by twenty years and carrying the particular confidence of a man who'd picked his moment carefully. He pushed back from the bar.

Declan looked at his cards.

Looked at the man.

Looked at his cards again.

The man reached up to the wall.

A branding iron. Heavy. Hanging on the wall like some kind of decorative emblem. Why this shack needed atmosphere didn't matter. What mattered was how the man's hand closed around it. How his shoulders set.

Declan set his cards down.

He stood.

He crossed the room slowly. Not fast. Not with any urgency. He moved with the calm of a man who already knew how things would finish and saw no need to hurry toward it.

He stopped.

Maybe six feet from the man.

The man was still looking at Bill. Still smiling the smile of someone who hadn't registered the change in the room yet.

Then he registered it.

He turned.

Declan stood there. Gray eyes flat and level. The branding iron in the man's hand suddenly feeling heavier than it had a moment ago.

"What's yer plan for dat iron, mate."

Not a question. The voice quiet. The lilt of Clare in it, something that only came out at certain moments, in certain temperatures of feeling.

The man looked at him.

He was smiling still. The leftover smile of a moment ago, not yet caught up to what his eyes were seeing.

Then it caught up.

The smile faded from his face. Slow. Like a lamp turned down.

He looked at Declan's eyes.

What he saw there stopped him.

Not size, he was the bigger man. Not a threat exactly. Something colder than threat. The absolute stillness of a man who was not afraid of what came next. Who was, if anything, waiting for it. Who had looked at this moment and found it not daunting. Not even interesting, particularly. Just available.

The man was stuck.

He'd picked up the iron in front of the room. Put himself out there. Couldn't put it back down without becoming something he couldn't afford to become in a place like this.

But the eyes.

He looked around the room for something, support maybe, or permission, or just the confirmation that other men saw what he saw.

The other men were looking at their drinks.

The room had gone very quiet.

Declan took one step closer.

Just one.

And then he smiled.

It was the wrong kind of smile. The kind that had nothing to do with warmth or humor or any of the things smiles were supposed to mean. The kind that said, *go ahead.*

The man saw it.

And in the half-second between the smile and what came next, something moved in his face. The understanding of a man who has made a very specific kind of mistake.

Declan hit him.

Once.

The heel of his hand into the man's nose. Fast and economical, and without any of the windup that telegraphed a punch. The man's head snapped back. The branding iron hit the floor. The man hit the floor a half second after it, both hands at his face, the blood coming fast and dark between his fingers.

Declan looked down at him.

The man wasn't getting up.

Declan looked at the room.

The room looked at its drinks.

He picked up the branding iron. Set it back on the wall where it had been.

Walked back to the card table.

Sat down.

Picked up his cards.

Nobody said anything.

The fire crackled.

* * *

After a while, Bill picked up his bottle and walked over to the card table and sat down across from Declan. He didn't say anything either. Just sat there with his bottle and looked at Declan, as a man looks at something he's reassessing.

Declan looked at his cards.

"You in?" he said.

Bill looked at the cards on the table.

Looked at Declan.

"I don't play cards," he said.

"Then sit there and be quiet," Declan said.

Bill sat there.

He was quiet.

The man on the floor had stopped making noise.

Someone eventually helped him outside.

Nobody mentioned it again.

But something had shifted in the room. In how the men watched Declan when they believed he wasn't aware. In how they no longer watched Bill at all. And in how Bill remained at that table for the rest of the evening.

Not leaving.

Just there.

Present in a way he hadn't been before.

Like a man who has just discovered something about the ground he's standing on.

That it holds.

13

The Creek Bottom

He'd been hunting the same creek bottom for three days.

The herd moved through it in the mornings, grazing along the water before drifting south onto the open plain as the day warmed. He and Bill had taken twelve on the first day, nine on the second. The third morning, Bill didn't show, the whiskey having made its claim on him, and Declan worked alone.

Five animals.

He skinned them where they fell, rolled the hides, and stacked them. Left the meat. There was too much of it, no way to move it, and no market for it anyway. The hide buyers didn't want meat. Nobody wanted meat. The plains were full of meat, and the plains could have it back.

He rode back to camp.

The next morning, he returned to the creek bottom to find the herd's trail and follow it south.

She was at the second carcass.

He almost didn't see her. She was low to the ground, working with a knife, her movements small and economical in like someone who'd been doing this kind of work since she was old enough to hold a blade.

The grass around her was tall enough that she was almost part of it, with her dark hair, dark clothing, and the particular stillness of someone who had learned not to announce themselves.

Joker saw her first.

His ears came forward. He slowed without being asked.

Declan looked.

She was cutting meat from the carcass. Methodical. Working the spine, taking the backstraps, her hands moving with a practiced efficiency that reminded him of someone. She had already emptied the body cavity, heart, liver, and kidneys into her cache. She cut out the tenderloins with practiced accuracy, taking what she could carry.

He watched her for a moment.

She knew he was there.

Her head came up, like a doe when she hears a twig snap. Eyes hard on him, assessing the threat. She looked back down and kept working.

He rode closer.

Her head came up again, and she fixed him with those dark eyes.

The look took his breath.

Not the face exactly. Something in the bones of it. The jaw set hard. The eyes, direct and completely without fear, the kind of eyes that had decided something about the world and weren't interested in revisiting the decision. The concentration in them while she worked.

Maeve.

Not Maeve. But something that reached across ten years and the Atlantic Ocean and everything that had happened since and found the wound that hadn't closed.

He sat Joker.

She looked at him the way you looked at weather. Something that was happening. Something you worked around.

Then she went back to cutting meat.

He watched her hands. The angle of the knife. How she worked without waste, every cut deliberate, nothing taken that couldn't be used, nothing left that could be saved. The opposite of everything he did on this range.

He didn't say anything.

There was nothing to say. She was taking meat from an animal he'd killed and left. The meat was worthless to him. He had no claim on it worth asserting.

But he stayed.

After a while, she stood. She had a bundle wrapped in hide, maybe thirty pounds of meat, carefully folded and tied. She lifted it without difficulty. Looked at him once more.

The same look. Weather. Something happening.

Then she walked west into the grass.

He watched her go.

She didn't look back.

The plains went on around the carcass, the flies gathering in the morning warmth, the creek moving cold and indifferent over its stones.

Declan sat Joker for a long time after she'd disappeared into the grass.

He didn't know her name.

He didn't know anything about her.

He touched his heels to Joker.

Rode south after the herd.

Behind him, the carcass lay open in the morning sun.

Picked clean of everything she could carry.

The rest left for whatever the plains sent next.

*   *   *

He made camp at the cottonwoods above the creek bend.

A small fire. Coffee. Salt pork cut thin and fried in the pan. The kind of meal that required no thought and that he'd eaten so many times on the range, it had stopped tasting like anything.

He ate.

The plains darkened around him. The fire popped. Somewhere to the south, a coyote said something to the night, and the night didn't answer.

He wasn't thinking about the woman.

He wasn't thinking about anything.

He heard Bill before he saw him. The particular unsteadiness of a man navigating the dark on whiskey legs. The irregular footfall, the occasional stumble, the sound of someone working harder than he should have to just to stay upright.

Bill came into the firelight.

He looked as he did on the days the whiskey had been at him since morning. Eyes not quite focused. A looseness in his face that meant whatever he had been holding together through the day had let go.

He dropped down across the fire from Declan.

Didn't speak.

Reached into his coat for the bottle.

Declan watched him.

"Five today," Declan said.

Bill looked up.

"Should have been twelve," Declan said. "Could have been fifteen."

Bill said nothing. Set the bottle on his knee.

"Seven animals," Declan said. "Seven animals walked away today because you were in your blankets."

"I was sick," Bill said.

Declan looked at him.

The fire between them. The plains, dark beyond it.

"You were drunk," Declan said.

Bill's jaw tightened. He was a big man. Had been a dangerous man in his time and still was when the situation called for it. He wasn't accustomed to being spoken to this way. By anyone. And certainly not by a young Irishman who'd been on the range less than a season.

He looked at Declan.

Declan looked back.

The same eyes that had looked at the man in the trading post. The same eyes that had looked at the horse in Gruber's paddock. Flat, gray, and completely without doubt about how this went.

Bill held it for a moment.

Two moments.

Something shifted in his face. The same thing that eventually shifted in every face. The recognition that whatever was behind those eyes wasn't bluffing and wasn't performing and wasn't going to look away first.

"I need you functional in the mornings," Declan said. "What you do after noon is your business. What you do before noon is mine."

Bill looked at the bottle on his knee.

Looked at Declan.

"You understand what I'm saying, boyo?" Declan said.

It wasn't a question.

Bill put the bottle back in his coat.

"Yeah," he said.

Declan just nodded.

He went back to his salt pork.

Bill sat across the fire in silence. After a while, he pulled out his bedroll and lay down without another word.

The fire burned down.

The coyote called again to the south.

Still no answer.

Declan finished his coffee, poured the grounds into the dirt, lay back, and looked at the stars.

The plains sky at night. More stars than anywhere. The darkness between them absolute.

He wasn't thinking about the woman.

He wasn't thinking about anything.

He closed his eyes.

Tomorrow the herd would be south of the creek bend.

He'd find it before Bill was awake.

He always did.

14

The Willows

The post was already awake when Declan rode in the next morning. Smoke from the cookstove drifted low across the yard. A few hunters were sorting hides. Someone was hammering something metal inside. The usual noise of men and work.

He wasn't looking for her.

He saw her anyway.

She was at the trader's table under the awning, the bundle of meat laid out in neat, red folds. The trader, a thick-shouldered man with a French name nobody bothered to pronounce right, stood across from her with his arms crossed, already bracing himself.

She put a tin pot on the table. Hard. The sound carried.

Then she spoke. Crow. Fast. Sharp. The words came like stones skipping across water, quick, precise, each one landing where she meant it to.

The trader shook his head. "No, no," he said, waving a hand. "Not for that."

She ignored him. Took a small pouch of tobacco from his table and dropped it into the pot with a finality that made the trader's eyebrows go up.

He reached in, took the tobacco out, and set it back in its place on the table.

She put it back in the pot.

He took it out again, slower this time, watching her.

She stamped her foot. Not petulant, not childish. Just a line drawn in the dirt.

The trader barked a laugh. "Ahh, no. Not this time."

She said something sharp and clipped. A single word. Maybe two.

He shook his head again.

She gathered the meat in her arms, turned as if to leave.

The trader swore under his breath and called after her in Crow, a tone Declan didn't need translated. Half exasperation, half surrender.

She stopped. Turned. Walked back with the same unhurried certainty she'd had at the carcass.

She set the meat down. Picked up the pot. Took the tobacco. Tied the pouch to her belt without looking at the trader.

He chuckled, shaking his head. Said something in Crow that made the men nearby grin. The kind of line a man uses when he knows he's been beaten fair.

She didn't smile. Didn't acknowledge the victory. Just lifted the pot, adjusted the weight of it in her hand, and stepped away from the table.

She passed within ten feet of Declan.

Didn't look at him.

Didn't slow.

Didn't give any sign she recognized him from the creek bottom.

She walked out into the sunlight, the pot swinging lightly at her side, the tobacco pouch tapping against it with each step. The grass beyond the post swallowed her as it had yesterday, as if she belonged to it and it to her.

Declan sat his horse and watched her go.

He didn't know why.

He didn't know what it meant.

He only knew the same thing he'd known yesterday, that something in him had shifted, and he wasn't going to name it.

He turned Joker toward the sheds, toward the hides, toward the work that waited.

Behind him, the trader was still shaking his head, muttering in Crow, laughing at himself.

And she was already gone.

* * *

She left the trading post with the pot in one hand and the tobacco pouch tied at her belt, walking west toward the grass. The three Cheyenne men watched her go. They didn't bother to hide it. Men didn't hide much out here unless they were afraid of being seen.

Declan saw them watching.

Saw the way they leaned toward each other.

Saw the way their eyes followed her.

He turned away.

None of his business.

He took two steps toward Joker.

Stopped.

Maeve's face flickered across the woman's again. Not the features, but the jaw set against the world, the steady carriage, the choice not to look back.

He swore under his breath.

Turned Joker toward the river trail.

Followed.

The grass swallowed the sound of the Cheyenne men ahead. He kept his distance, letting the land carry the noise of their movement to him, the low murmur of voices, the rustle of bodies pushing through tall stems.

Then the voices sharpened.

A shout.

A woman's cry.

He nudged Joker forward.

They were in a shallow draw, half-hidden by willow scrub. The three men had her surrounded. One held her arms. Another was tying a rawhide cord around her wrists. Her cheek was reddened, the mark of a struggle, nothing more. She was breathing hard, eyes wide, but she wasn't pleading. She was furious.

She saw Declan first.

Her voice broke out in Crow, fast, high, urgent. Not words he knew, but the meaning hit him anyway. The same way it had in the trading post. The same way Maeve had once spoken to him when the world was coming apart, and she needed him to do something he didn't want to do.

Declan stopped Joker at the edge of the draw.

The Cheyenne men turned.

They weren't afraid.

Not at first.

Three young warriors, confident, sure of themselves, sure of the land beneath their feet. They looked at him as men look at a problem they haven't decided how to solve yet.

Then they looked at his face.

Something changed.

Declan stepped down from Joker.

Slow.

Deliberate.

The same way he crossed the room at the trading post, like the outcome was already decided, and the walking was just the space between.

He didn't reach for his gun.

He didn't need to.

He walked toward them with that cold, level stillness that had stopped bigger men than these. The kind of stillness that said he wasn't weighing options. He wasn't negotiating. He wasn't thinking at all.

He was already there.

The Cheyenne, holding her wrists, hesitated.

Just a flicker.

But it was enough.

The second man shifted his stance.

The third looked at Declan's eyes and stopped moving altogether.

Ashkáale was still speaking, the words tumbling out of her, sharp and bright with fear and fury. He didn't understand a single one, but he understood it all.

Declan kept walking.

The air tightened.

The men watched him come.

And in the space between one breath and the next, they understood what the man in the trading post had understood:

This was not a man you wanted to test.

Not here.

Not today.

Not ever.

* * *

The lead man moved first.

Not toward Declan. Sideways, a feint, the kind of movement designed to split attention, to make a man's eyes choose between two threats. Old tactic. Good tactic.

Declan didn't split.

He went straight at the one holding Ashkáale.

Fast.

The man had half a second to register that the white hunter wasn't stopping, wasn't slowing, and wasn't doing what men usually did when outnumbered, which was to hesitate. Then Declan's knife was in him. Low. Under the ribs. The particular angle John had never taught him, but that his hands had known since a cottage floor in Clare.

The man went down.

The second one was already moving, a short blade out, coming in from the left, quick and committed. A fighter. Declan took the cut across his forearm, barely felt it, got inside the man's reach, and hit him once in the throat with the heel of his hand.

The man went down.

Declan turned.

The boy was right there.

Maybe seventeen. The youngest of the three. He hadn't run. He'd stood and watched his two companions fall in the space of seconds, and the watching had held him in place, the mind not yet caught up to what the body needed to do.

Now his mind caught up.

But too late.

Declan was already moving toward him.

The boy backed up one step. Two.

His eyes found Declan's.

And stayed there.

Whatever he saw stopped him completely. Not the knife. Not the blood on Declan's forearm. The eyes. Flat and gray and absolutely without doubt. The eyes of something that had already decided and was just closing the distance between the decision and the conclusion.

No anger in them.

No hatred.

Nothing personal at all.

That was the worst of it.

The boy understood in that moment, not as a thought, as a certainty that arrived in his chest like a stone dropping into still water, that he was going to die. That the white man crossing the draw toward him wasn't going to stop. Wasn't going to negotiate. Wasn't going to give him the chance to run, fight, or speak.

He was already dead.

He could see it in the man's eyes.

Declan was three steps away.

Two.

A hand closed on his arm.

Hard.

The second man.

Not dead. On his knees in the grass behind Declan, one hand outstretched, fingers locked around Declan's forearm with the grip of a man using the last of what he had.

Declan spun.

Instinct. Pure and immediate.

The knife went in on the turn, the movement and the blade arriving together, no gap between them. The second man's grip loosened. His eyes went to something far away.

He fell.

Declan turned back.

The boy was thirty yards away.

Running.

Already into the willow scrub at the draw's edge, the stems closing behind him, the sound of his movement fading fast into the particular silence of grass that had swallowed a man whole.

Declan stood.

No rifle.

The Mississippi was back at camp. The knife was in his hand, and the boy was thirty yards into country he knew like his own hands, running with the controlled terror of someone who had looked into a demon's eyes and found himself still breathing.

Declan looked at the empty grass.

Looked at the knife.

Looked at the grass again.

Gone.

He stood with that for a moment.

The draw quiet around him.

The willows moving.

The two men still.

He hadn't wanted to let the boy go.

Hadn't chosen to.

It had just happened that way.

The dying man's hand on his arm had given the boy two seconds.

Two seconds was enough.

Declan wiped the knife on the grass.

Turned.

Ashkáale was on her feet. The rawhide cord, still around her wrists. She was looking at the two men on the ground. Then at Declan. Then at the grass where the boy had gone.

Her face was unreadable.

Not fear. Not gratitude. Something older and more careful than either.

Declan crossed to her.

She held her ground, didn't step back, didn't flinch when he reached for the cord. He cut it in one motion. The rawhide fell.

She rubbed her wrists.

He stepped back.

Looked west.

Pointed.

"Go."

She looked at him.

That look. The weather look. Something happening that she was accounting for and filing away.

Then she picked up the pot and the tobacco pouch from where they'd fallen.

Walked west.

Didn't look back.

He watched her go until the grass took her.

Then he looked at the two men on the ground.

Then at the grass where the boy had run.

He did the math.

One boy running meant the story reached the Cheyenne camp by nightfall. Meant warriors who valued their dead would be looking for the white hunter on the roan horse.

Not today.

But eventually.

He hadn't chosen that.

It had just happened.

He looked at the cut on his forearm. It would close on its own.

He mounted Joker.

He didn't know why he'd followed her.

Didn't know why he'd stepped down from Joker instead of riding on.

He knew what he'd done his whole life, kept his head down, done his work, stayed out of other people's trouble because other people's trouble was a cost with no return.

Today, he'd walked into it.

For reasons he couldn't figure.

The Cheyenne would come.
Not today.
But they'd come.
He filed it under problems to manage.
Touched his heels to Joker.
Rode back toward the creek bottom.
Behind him, the draw was quiet.
The willows moved in the wind.
The two men lay still in the grass.
The plains went on around them.
Indifferent.
Vast.
How the plains went on around everything.

15

Heávohe

Five years on the Powder River.

Five years of mornings that smelled of frost and grass and the particular richness of a land that hadn't been stripped yet, though the stripping was underway. Five years of following the herds north in spring and south in fall, of reading the wind before anything else, of skinning in the cold with hands that had stopped feeling the cold after the first winter.

Declan was twenty three now.

The plains had finished what the Five Points and the canal and the road west had started. He was lean and hard and brown from the weather, the boy from Clare so far beneath the surface of him that he sometimes forgot the boy had existed. His hands were scarred from the knife work. His eyes had gone even flatter than they'd been, if that was possible, the gray of them the particular gray of winter sky over the Powder River, the color of something that had decided about the world and wasn't revisiting the decision.

He was good at this work.

Better than most men on the range. He knew the herds the same way John had taught him to know the land, reading the grass, reading the wind, reading the particular behavior of animals that told you where they'd been and where they were going. He'd developed a patience on the stand that other hunters noticed and couldn't quite explain. Most men got eager. Pushed the herd too soon. Declan waited. Always waited. The stand lasting longer than it should have because he never moved until the moment was exactly right.

The Mississippi Rifle was worn from use, bright steel showing through the bluing.

He cleaned it every night. Kept it true. But five years of hard use on the range had taken something from it. The rifling inside the barrel smoother than it had been, the accuracy at distance less reliable. He'd been compensating for two seasons, getting closer than he needed to, adjusting for the drift he'd learned to expect.

The money was good.

Not as good as it could have been.

Bill was the reason.

Sour Bill had been declining for three years, how men declined when the bottle was winning, not dramatically, not all at once, but steadily, the way a river cuts a bank. More mornings lost. More afternoons that started early. The system they'd built, one shooting while the other reloaded, twelve animals on a good day, fifteen when everything went right, was working at maybe two-thirds of what it could have been. Seven or eight animals on a good day now. Sometimes less.

Declan had done the math a hundred times.

The partnership still made sense. Two men with muzzleloaders still outperformed one man with a muzzleloader, even with Bill's limitations factored in. The math held.

Barely.

And the Cheyenne hadn't made it easier.

The first time was the winter of 1849.

January. Declan alone at his camp on the Powder, Bill somewhere to the south sleeping off three days of whiskey. The fire burned low, and Declan was in his blankets when Joker moved.

Not spooked. Just alert. The particular quality of attention that meant something was there.

Declan lay still.

Listened.

Three of them. He could hear the difference between one man moving in the dark and two or three. The spacing of sounds, the slight variations in the way the grass moved. They were coming from the east, downwind, which meant they'd planned it.

He was already moving when they reached the edge of the firelight.

What happened next took maybe forty seconds.

When it was over, three men were on the ground, and Declan was standing in the dark with his knife and a cut across his left hand that he hadn't felt until after.

He looked at the three men.

Looked at the dark plains around him.

Joker stood nearby, ears forward, watching.

Declan wrapped his hand.

Put more wood on the fire.

Lay back down.

In the morning, he moved camp three miles north.

That was the first time.

The second time, Bill was there.

Spring of 1851. They'd sold a load of hides at the rough trading post on the Middle Fork and were riding back to the range, following the creek north through the cottonwoods. Late afternoon. The light going gold and long across the grass.

Declan felt it before he heard it.

That particular quality of stillness that wasn't natural stillness, the birds gone quiet, the insects stopped, the air holding itself.

"Bill," he said.

Bill had time to look up.

Then they came out of the cottonwoods.

Six of them. Young warriors, moving fast, the kind of fast that meant they'd been working themselves up to this for a while and didn't want to give themselves time to reconsider.

What followed was not a fight in any organized sense.

It was close and fast and brutal and over in less time than it took to describe. Declan took two of them before they reached him, a third as he came off Joker, a fourth with his back against a cottonwood trunk. The fifth pulled back when he saw what he was dealing with.

The sixth went for Bill.

Bill was not a fighting man. He was a hunter, capable with a rifle at distance, but close work with blades was a different thing entirely. He got his arm up in time, barely, and the warrior's knife caught him across the left cheek instead of the throat.

A deep cut. From the cheekbone to the jaw.

Bill went down.

Declan came off the cottonwood.

The warrior who'd cut Bill turned.

Looked at Declan's eyes.

Made a sound that wasn't quite a word.

Then he ran.

The fifth one was already gone.

Two got away.

Declan stood in the cottonwoods and looked at the four men on the ground. Then at Bill sitting against a tree with both hands pressed to his face, the blood coming fast and dark between his fingers.

"How bad?" Bill said.

"Bad enough," Declan said.

It was. The scar would be permanent, a thick diagonal line from cheekbone to jaw that never quite faded, that pulled slightly when Bill smiled, which wasn't often anyway.

Declan cleaned the wound with whiskey from Bill's bottle.

Bill didn't protest the use of it.

That night at the fire Bill looked at Declan across the flames for a long time without speaking.

Finally, he said, "You weren't scared."

Declan looked at the fire.

Declan just shrugged.

"Six of them," Bill said.

"I can count well enough," Declan responded.

Bill shook his head slowly, a small, uncertain motion from a man who couldn't quite place what he'd witnessed.

He drank from the bottle.

Didn't say anything else.

The third time was the summer of 1852.

Three warriors on the open plain, no cover, no surprise, just three men who'd decided today was the day and rode straight at Declan and Bill in the middle of the afternoon like the directness of it might accomplish what stealth hadn't.

It didn't.

Declan rode toward them.

Not away.

Toward.

Bill watched from fifty yards back, his hand on his rifle, as Declan went straight at three armed warriors on horseback with nothing but a knife and whatever it was that lived behind those flat gray eyes.

One of them pulled up.

Then the second.

The third kept coming. As Declan rode past, close, he left Joker and took the brave off his pony. By the time they both hit the ground, the brave was dead, Declan's hand covered in blood, and the steel of his knife glinting red in the sun. The other two were already turning and riding south, hard. Declan let them go, not because he wanted to, but because Joker couldn't catch two horses running flat out across open ground.

He mounted and rode back to Bill.

Bill was sitting his horse with an expression that had moved past surprise and past fear into something that didn't have a name. The expression of a man who has revised his understanding of what another man is capable of and isn't sure he likes the revision.

"One of these days," Bill said, "they're going to send enough of them."

Declan looked south where the two warriors had gone.

"Could be," he said.

He rode on.

Bill followed.

* * *

By 1853, the story had been traveling across the plains for four years. Declan didn't know exactly what shape it had taken in the telling; he had no way of knowing, no language for what the Crow and the Cheyenne said around their fires at night. But he'd seen the evidence of it.

At the trading post on the Middle Fork, the previous autumn.

He and Bill had ridden in to sell a load of hides. The post was busy. Half a dozen hunters, a few Crow men trading robes, the trader's usual chaos of commerce and argument, and the smell of hides and woodsmoke.

Declan was tying Joker to the rail when he felt it.

Being watched.

Not the casual attention of men noting a new arrival. Something more specific. More focused.

He looked up.

Three Crow warriors across the yard. Young men, well-mounted, the particular bearing of men who were somebody in their world. They were looking at him. Not pretending not to look. Just looking. Speaking to each other in low voices, their eyes on Declan.

Declan raised his head.

Looked back.

They stopped talking.

One of them looked away first. Then the second. The third held it a moment longer than the others, something in his face that wasn't quite fear and wasn't quite respect but lived in the territory between them, and then he turned and walked his horse around the side of the post and was gone.

Declan watched the space where they'd been.

Bill came up beside him.

"They know who you are," Bill said.

Declan looked at him.

"The Crow," Bill said. "The Cheyenne, too. Word travels out here same as anywhere." He pulled the stopper from his bottle. "Maybe faster." He drank. "They've been talking about you since that business in the willows. Story gets bigger every time it's told. The white hunter on the Powder River who kills like he's doing nothing more than swatting flies." He stoppered the bottle. "They think you're big medicine. Bad medicine." He looked at Declan with the scarred side of his face catching the afternoon light. "The kind of story they tell children to keep them close to camp at night."

He paused. Looked at his bottle. Looked at Declan.

"The Cheyenne call you Heávohe," he said.

Declan looked at him.

"Devil," Bill said.

Declan looked back at the corner where the Crow warriors had been.

Nodded once.

Filed it.

They sold their hides.

Rode back to the range.

16

Sour Bill

He heard the shots first.

Not the rapid crack of a man working close to the herd, the sound he was used to, one shot and then silence while the rifle was reloaded, the herd moving in those two minutes, the geometry of the stand changing and having to be reestablished. This was different. A shot. Then another. Then another. Evenly spaced. Not fast exactly, deliberate, each one considered, but continuous in a way that muzzleloader fire simply wasn't.

He turned Joker toward the sound.

The hunter was on a low rise, maybe a quarter mile east, prone behind a shooting stick, his body almost flat to the ground. A big rifle. Longer than the Mississippi. Heavier through the stock. Even at this distance, Declan could see the man work, the rifle coming back from his shoulder, his hands moving at the breech with a quick, practiced motion, the rifle going back up, settling, firing again.

The whole sequence taking maybe fifteen seconds.

Declan sat Joker and watched.

The herd was two hundred yards from the hunter. Maybe more. Further than Declan would have attempted a shot with the Mississippi.

At that distance, the ball lost too much velocity, the trajectory dropping unpredictably, clean kills becoming wounded animals that ran and took the herd with them.

But the hunter wasn't missing.

The animals were dropping where they stood. One. Then another thirty yards away. Then a third at the edge of the group. Clean kills, each one, the animal going down without the lurching stagger of a hit that wasn't quite right, just folding at the knees and settling into the grass with the particular finality of something that was done.

The herd shifted after each shot.

But didn't run.

Couldn't locate the threat. The hunter was too far away, the sound reaching them a half-second after the bullet, the direction of it confused by the wind and the distance. They milled. They turned. They pressed together and separated and pressed together again in how herds did when something was wrong, but they couldn't find what.

And in that milling, another animal dropped.

Then another.

Declan counted.

Seven animals in the time it would have taken him to reload the Mississippi twice.

He sat very still on Joker and watched the hunter work.

The man was unhurried. Methodical. He'd found his position and his range, and he was working the stand the way a man worked a card table when he had the measure of everyone at it, patient, precise, taking what was available without rushing and without waste.

Eight.

Nine.

The herd finally ran on the tenth shot, some threshold of unease reaching whatever the herd ran on, and the hunter lowered his rifle and watched them go with the expression of a man who'd gotten what he came for and was satisfied with the arithmetic.

Declan rode over.

The hunter was already on his feet, moving toward the nearest carcass. He looked up when he heard Joker.

A lean man. Older than Declan. Sun-darkened. The kind of face that had been out here long enough to stop looking like it came from anywhere else.

He looked at Declan as men looked at each other on the range, assessing, neutral, neither hostile nor welcoming.

Declan looked at the rifle.

"Sharps," the man said. Seeing where Declan's eyes had gone.

Declan nodded.

"You haven't seen one."

"No."

The man held it out.

Declan took it. Felt the weight of it. Heavier than the Mississippi by a third. The balance different, more weight toward the breech where the mechanism lived. He opened it. Looked at the falling block action, how the lever dropped the block, and exposed the chamber. Simple. Positive. No fouling from the muzzle, no loose patch, no ram.

He closed it.

Sighted down the barrel at the horizon.

True.

"How far?" Declan said.

"Clean kill?" The man considered. "Two hundred yards comfortable. Three hundred if you know your rifle and the wind is right." He paused. "Some men push it further."

Declan looked at the ten carcasses scattered across the grass.

Looked at the horizon where the herd had gone.

Looked at the rifle in his hands.

He handed it back.

"Where'd I get one?" he said.

"Fort Laramie," the man said. "Army post trader. He's got them." He took the rifle back and looked at it briefly, how you look at a thing you'd come to depend on. "Ride south. Two days, maybe three. Through the Cheyenne country."

He went back to his skinning.

Declan sat Joker for a moment.

Two days south.

Through Cheyenne country.

He thought about the willow draw. The two men in the grass. The boy running.

Filed it.

Touched his heels to Joker.

Rode back toward camp.

That evening, he told Bill.

"Fort Laramie," he said. "Two days south."

Bill looked up from his fire.

"Cheyenne country," Bill said.

"Yes," Declan said.

Bill looked at his bottle.

Looked at Declan.

"When?" he said.

"Tomorrow," Declan said.

Bill said nothing.

But in the morning, he was saddled and ready when Declan broke camp.

They rode south.

* * *

They came out of the north.

Declan heard them before he saw them, that particular sound that carried across flat ground, the drumming of hooves and the high, carrying call of men who'd worked themselves into something and weren't pulling back from it.

He turned Joker.

Seven of them. Maybe eight. Hard to count at the distance, the dust rising behind them, the ponies already at full gallop. Coming straight south. Coming straight at them.

"Ride," Bill said.

They rode.

The draw was maybe a mile south, a shallow cut in the plain where a creek ran in wet years, the banks low but enough. Declan had noted it that morning, the way he noted terrain. Old habit. Always know where the ground gives you something.

A mile.

He looked back.

The Cheyenne ponies were closing fast. Plains horses, light and quick, already at full speed when Declan and Bill had started moving. The gap between them shrinking with mathematics that didn't work in their favor.

They weren't going to make it.

He knew it before Bill said it.

"Not going to make it," Bill said.

Then Bill's horse went down.

Not a stumble. Not a fall. The animal dropped mid-stride, one moment running hard and the next simply gone, folding at the front legs, the impact throwing Bill forward and clear, rolling him twice through the grass before he came to rest face down.

Declan pulled Joker up hard.

Bill was already moving, pushing up, getting his bearings, looking at his horse lying still in the grass with a Cheyenne arrow in its neck.

They were shooting already.

Another arrow cut the air close enough that Declan heard it.

He dropped off Joker. Slapped him hard across the flank.

Joker ran.

Good.

"Behind the horse," Declan said.

They got behind the horse.

It wasn't much. The animal lay on its side, still twitching in the grass, and they pressed themselves against its back, and the cover it offered was real, even if it wasn't much better than open ground, better than nothing, the only thing the situation had given them, and they used it.

Declan raised the Mississippi.

The riders were two hundred yards out. Closing fast. He picked the lead rider, the one at the point of the V, the one whose death would require the others to make a decision.

Waited.

One fifty.

Fired.

The lead rider went down.

The oncoming line faltered, not stopped, not turned, but that fractional hesitation of men who'd expected no resistance yet and were now recalculating. In that hesitation, the V broke.

They split.

Two groups.

Four riding wide left. Three wide right.

Declan was already reloading. Powder. Ball. Ram. His hands worked the sequence without thought, the Mississippi's ceremony performed for the thousandth time.

Beside him, Bill fired.

A rider on the right went down.

"Good shot," Declan said.

Bill said nothing. Already reloading.

Both of them heads down behind the horse, hands working, the two groups of riders arcing wide around them now, looking for the angle, looking for the moment.

They found it.

The left group had swung wider than the right, coming around in a long curve that brought them in from the southeast, behind and to the left, where the dead horse offered less cover, where Declan and Bill had to turn to face them and expose their backs to the right group.

Declan heard them coming.

Both rifles empty.

Both men reloading.

The left group saw it.

Four riders at full gallop, the gap closing fast, the angle perfect, the moment exactly what they'd been riding to find.

They came in hard.

"Bill," Declan said.

"I see them," Bill said.

His hands working the ram. Not fast enough.

Not fast enough.

The first rider was fifty feet out.

Declan dropped the Mississippi.

Came up with the knife.

The first rider came over the horse.

Declan moved into him, not away, into. The knife finding the man as he came off the pony, the momentum of the horse carrying him past and down.

The second rider pulled his pony hard, trying to circle, find the angle again.

The third came straight.

Declan was moving toward him.

The fourth went for Bill.

He heard it, the sound of the impact, something wrong in it, the particular sound of a man taking something he can't absorb.

He couldn't turn.

The third rider was already on him.

What happened next happened fast and close and without any of the space that allowed for thought. Just the knife and the body and the ground and the knife again.

When it was over, Declan was on his feet, and two men were on the ground, and the second rider had pulled back and was circling at a distance, reassessing.

He turned.

Bill was down.

Not sitting up. Down. On his back behind the horse, one hand pressed to his side, the particular stillness of a man who's taken something serious and knows it.

The fourth rider was already twenty yards away and riding hard south.

Declan looked at the right group.

Still out there. Circling. Watching what had just happened to the left group and making their own calculations.

He went to Bill.

Bill's face was the color of old ash. The hand at his side, dark with blood.

"How bad?" Declan said.

Bill looked up at him.

Something moved in his face. Not fear. Something older than fear. The look of a man who has done the arithmetic and doesn't like the answer but accepts it.

"Bad enough," he said.

The same words Declan had used about the scar.

Declan looked at the right group still circling.

Three of them. Hanging back. Watching.

He looked at the Mississippi on the ground. Empty. He looked at his knife.

He looked at Bill.

Bill's breathing had changed. Shallow. The hand at his side losing its pressure.

"Go," Bill said.

Declan looked at him.

"Get the damn rifle," Bill said. "Go."

Declan picked up the Mississippi.

Began to reload.

The three riders watched him.

Declan said aloud to them, "If you're comin', come."

He raised the rifle.

They turned and rode north.

He watched them go.

Then he looked at Bill.

Bill was looking at the sky.

His chest was moving.

Barely.

Declan sat down beside him in the grass behind the dead horse.

The plains went on around them.

Flat and vast and indifferent.

How the plains went on around everything.

After a while, Bill's chest stopped moving.

Declan sat with that for a moment.

Then he stood.

Looked north where the three riders had gone.

Looked south toward Fort Laramie.

Looked at Bill.

He couldn't carry him. No horse. No way to move him across open ground.

He took Bill's rifle. His ammunition. His knife.

He looked at Bill's bottle, loose now by his side. Declan picked it up, took a swallow, and tucked the bottle under Bill's arm.

He started walking south, following Joker's tracks.

The sun was still high.

* * *

He found Joker two miles south.

Just over a low ridge, in a shallow swale where the grass grew tall and thick along a seep of water. Of course, that's where he was. Declan stood on the ridge and looked down at the horse grazing with the particular contentment of an animal that had found exactly what it wanted and saw no reason to look further.

He walked down.

Joker raised his head. Looked at Declan. Went back to the grass.

Declan took the reins.

"Had enough, have you?" he said.

Joker pulled at the grass.

Declan let him eat for another ten minutes. Then he mounted and rode south.

Fort Laramie took two days.

He rode through Cheyenne country. Nothing came at him. He occasionally caught a glimpse of Cheyenne braves on a ridge here, or watching him from a canyon rim as he rode on. Just watching. The plains stretched out around him, Bill's rifle across the saddle. He had Bill's knife in his saddlebags. The bottle, somewhere back in the grass beside a man the plains never really respected.

The fort sat on a rise above the confluence of the Laramie and the North Platte, the buildings pale adobe in the late afternoon light, the American flag moving in the wind above the parade ground. More substantial than anything he'd seen since St. Louis. Soldiers. Emigrants. Hunters. The commerce of a place that existed at the edge of everything and had decided to make the most of it.

He rode in.

Found the post trader's store without asking.

The man behind the counter was wide and efficient with the particular economy of movement of someone who'd been doing the same work in the same place for a long time and had stopped wasting effort on anything that didn't need it.

Declan looked at what was on the wall behind him.

The Sharps was there.

Two of them. One a carbine, shorter, designed for a man on horseback. The other a rifle, long barreled, heavy, the octagonal barrel catching the light. The sporting rifle. The one the hunter on the plain had been using.

"That one," Declan said.

The trader took it down.

Declan went through it carefully as he'd gone through the hunter's rifle on the plain. The falling block action. The weight and balance. The barrel sighted down at the far wall.

True.

"Ammunition," Declan said.

The trader named a price for the rifle and the ammunition together.

Declan paid it without negotiating.

He was turning to go when he saw it.

In the glass case on the counter. A Navy Colt. The 1851 model, he'd seen them on men coming through the range, the revolving cylinder, six shots without reloading. He'd always had the knife. Always been close enough for the knife. But the plains were changing, and the situations were changing, and a man who was going to be alone out there now, no Bill, no partnership, just himself and the Sharps and whatever came at him, a man in that situation might need something between the knife and the long rifle.

He looked at it.

Fingered his knife.

Looked at the Colt.

"That too," he said.

The trader lifted it out. Laid it on the counter.

Declan picked it up. Felt the weight of it. The balance was different from the knife, heavier in the hand, the grip filling his palm differently. He worked the action. Smooth.

"Ammunition."

He paid.

The trader reached under the counter.

"Holster," he said. He laid it beside the Colt. "Goes with it."

Then he reached to the wall behind him and lifted down a sheath, long and fitted for a rifle, the buckskin a light tan, fringed, and worked with a pattern that wasn't any white man's stitching. Geometric. Precise. The kind of work that took patience, knowledge, and a particular relationship to the material.

"Saddle sheath for the Sharps," the trader said. "Indian work. Cheyenne woman brought it in last month. Best leather work I get." He set it on the counter. "I'll throw it in."

Declan looked at it.

The pattern running along the length of it, diamonds and lines and symbols he had no way to read. The stitching was tight and even, and done by hands that knew what they were doing.

A Cheyenne woman's hands.

He picked it up.

Turned it over.

Said nothing.

He took the Sharps. The Colt. The holster. The sheath.

He walked out into the Fort Laramie afternoon and stood at Joker's side and fitted the sheath to the saddle and slid the Sharps into it. Settled the Colt at his hip.

Stood back.

Looked at it.

Then he mounted.

Rode north.

Back toward the Powder River.

Back toward the range.

Back toward whatever was left of the herd and whatever was left of the season and whatever came next in a life that had been moving in one direction since a cottage floor in Clare and showed no sign of stopping.

The Cheyenne sheath on his saddle.

The Cheyenne name on his back.

Heávohe.

Riding north.

17

Iichíilee

The camp announced itself before he could see it.

Not the usual sounds, the particular texture of a Crow camp in the afternoon, women working, children, horses at the picket line, the low, steady noise of people going about the business of living. This was different. Higher. More urgent.

Declan slowed Joker without thinking.

He came over the low rise above the camp and saw it spread out below him, lodges in their proper arrangement, but something wrong in the space between them. Riders gathered near the trader's post, talking in the urgent clipped way of men deciding something. Women in groups, as women gathered when something had happened, and the shape of it wasn't yet clear.

He read it as he read everything.

Raid. Recent. The horses were still unsettled at the picket line, moving with the particular nervousness of animals that had smelled something they didn't like and hadn't forgotten it yet. Two lodge covers with fresh damage. Not fire. Torn. Cut maybe. The ground between the lodges churned up more than it should have been.

Not his business.

He was calculating his route around the camp to the trading post when he saw her.

She was near the center of it, where the disruption was thickest. Talking to Whistling Crow, her gestures unguarded in a way he had never seen from her. Urgent, uncontrolled, the composure she wore like a second skin pulled thin. She was giving orders. She was doing what needed doing, but there was something in the set of her shoulders that stopped him cold.

She turned to speak to someone else, and he saw her face.

He dropped the mule's rope.

He'd seen women cry before. Had learned young what it cost them.

Joker was already moving.

He came down the rise at a gallop, the camp opening up around him, people stepping back, faces turning. He didn't see any of them. He had his eyes on her. She had her back to him. She was still talking, still giving orders, still holding whatever she was holding together.

Someone said something. She turned.

She saw him coming.

For a moment, she was absolutely still.

Not the stillness he knew from her, the controlled, deliberate stillness of a woman who had decided about most things and was at peace with her decisions. Something different. The stillness of a person who has been running on will alone for hours and has just seen the one thing that makes will unnecessary.

He pulled Joker up in front of her.

The horse was breathing hard. Declan wasn't.

He looked at her face.

One tear. Just one. She didn't lift her hand to stop it. She didn't look away. She just stood there, let it go, and looked at him with those direct, dark eyes, and in them he saw something he could not explain.

"How many," he said.

She took one breath.

"Two," she said. Her voice was completely steady. Like the tear hadn't happened.

"Which direction."

"Northeast." She pointed. "Before dawn. We didn't know until the morning."

"What did they take?"

She looked at him.

"Iichíilee," she said. "Declan, they took Iichíilee. She is ten years old."

It was the first time she had said his name. He didn't examine that.

He looked at Whistling Crow, who had come to stand beside her. "White men," the man said in careful English. "Two. On shod horses. The tracks are there. They were gone before the camp woke."

Declan looked northeast. Hours ahead of him. Two men on shod horses moving through country they didn't know with a child who didn't want to go.

He looked back at Ashkáale.

She was watching him. Not the weather look. Something else. Something he hadn't seen before.

He said nothing.

He touched his heels to Joker.

Behind him, he heard Whistling Crow say something in Crow, low and certain, to no one in particular.

Heávohe will find the girl.

* * *

He rode northeast and didn't look back.

Ashkáale watched him go.

Whistling Crow stood beside her. He said nothing more. He was old enough to know when words were the wrong answer to a thing.

She turned back to the camp. There was still work to do. There was always still work to do. She went back to it directly, without ceremony, her hands finding their purpose before her mind had fully caught up.

But her hands were not quite steady.

She noticed this and said nothing about it.

Around her, the camp moved with its urgent purpose: men out on the eastern trail, women settling the children, someone seeing to the damaged lodges. She moved through all of it and did what was needed and kept her eyes away from the northeast horizon.

She did not watch for him.

She told herself this.

He will come back or he won't, she thought. *That is the nature of things. You do not watch the horizon for what you cannot control.*

Her father found her at the damaged lodge cover, pulling the torn edge back into place, assessing what could be salvaged and what couldn't.

He stood beside her and looked at the damage without speaking for a moment.

"He went," her father said.

"Yes."

"You did not ask him?"

She pulled the torn hide taut. Examined the edge.

"No," she said. "Why would I ask him?"

Her father was quiet. Not the absence of thought but the presence of too much of it to put into words efficiently.

She kept working.

He kept standing.

"Ashkáale," he said.

"I know," she said.

He looked at the northeast horizon.

She did not.

* * *

He picked up their trail again a mile out of camp.

Shod hoofprints in the soft ground near the creek crossing, two horses, moving at a steady pace, not running. Men who thought they had time. Men who thought nobody was coming.

He followed it as John had taught him to follow things. Steady. Patient. Reading the ground for what it said, not for what he wanted it to say.

They'd made no effort to hide their trail. Why would they. Two white men in Crow territory in 1853 with a stolen child, they'd be thinking about distance, not pursuit. They'd be thinking about where they were going and what they'd get for her when they got there.

He didn't think about that.

He just followed the track.

The shod prints told him things. The horses were tired, their strides shortening as the hours passed, their prints deeper at the toe than at the heel, animals that had been pushed through the night and were feeling it. They'd stop soon. Make camp. Feel safe.

He rode steadily and didn't push Joker. He let the distance close.

He found them at midday.

A small camp in a hollow below a limestone outcrop. The kind of place men chose when they wanted to feel hidden without actually understanding the country well enough to be hidden. A fire, nearly out. Two horses picketed on a short line, heads down, exhausted.

And Iichíilee.

She was sitting against the limestone face, her wrists bound in front of her, her ankles tied. Her face was doing the thing faces did when a person had decided that crying was finished and what was left was something harder. She was ten years old. She had her aunt's jaw and her aunt's eyes. She saw Declan on the rise above the hollow, and her expression didn't change, but something in it shifted, the particular shift of a person who has been waiting for something and has just seen it arrive.

The two men were at the dead fire. One lying on his back, hat over his face. The other, sitting up, whittling, his back to the rise.

Declan came down quietly.

The sitting one heard him at the last moment and started to turn.

What happened next was brief and efficient and without drama, just how Declan did most things that needed doing. The sitting man went down first. The other sat up, stood, and did what men like him always do.

He ran.

Declan stood with his knife and watched him go. A soft man. A coward's run, stumbling through the brush, not looking back. He'd make it back to whatever town he'd come from, and he'd tell a story that didn't feature him the way he actually was in it, and that would be the end of him.

* * *

He walked to the girl.

Crouched in front of her.

She looked at him with those eyes. Ashkáale's eyes in a younger face.

"Iichíilee," he said. "Heávohe," she replied.

She lifted her bound wrists.

He cut the cord at her wrists, then at her ankles. She stood without help, rubbing her wrists, and looked at the man on the ground, and looked at Declan, and said something in Crow that he didn't fully catch.

Then she stepped forward and put her arms around him.

She was ten years old, taken in the night, sitting against that limestone for hours, and she held on with a fierceness that surprised him. He stood there with his hands at his sides, not knowing what to do with them, and the whole thing lasted maybe five seconds before she stepped back and looked up at him with her aunt's eyes as if it hadn't happened.

He put her on Joker.

The horse stood for it with the patience of an animal that had carried stranger things and expected to carry stranger things still.

Declan walked.

Four miles back to camp. He didn't mind the walk. It gave him time not to think, something he was good at, made good at through repetition and necessity, the same process that taught a man anything the world required of him often enough.

The girl rode above him in silence for a while.

He didn't speak. She didn't either. She was handling it as her aunt had, by not handling it loudly.

The camp appeared on the low rise ahead.

Joker walked on, unconcerned, and kept his opinions about the afternoon to himself.

She was at the camp's edge when they came in.

She had told herself she was not watching the horizon. That was true. She had been working. But she had known the moment he crested the rise, something in the camp shifted, a direction of attention, and she had known.

She walked out to meet them.

She did not run.

She looked at Iichíilee on the horse. Read the girl's face completely, in an instant. Unharmed. The fear finished, the fury beginning.

She put her hands up, and the girl came down into them.

She held her.

One moment. Her face in the girl's hair. Her eyes closed. Everything she had been carrying since before dawn, finding somewhere to go, just briefly, just long enough.

Then she stepped back.

Checked the girl over with her hands, wrists, arms, face, and the cord marks. Said something low and direct. The girl answered. Ashkáale nodded once.

That was that.

She looked up at Declan.

He was standing at Joker's head. The flat gray eyes gave nothing back, the same as always, except that he was here and he had gone without being asked, and they both knew what that meant, and neither of them was going to say it.

"Your mule," she said. "Whistling Crow's son has him at the rise."

Something moved in his face.

"Thank you," he said.

She stepped forward then. Just briefly. Her hand on his arm for one moment. Not a grip, just a touch, the particular touch of a person acknowledging something they have no word for. Then she stepped back.

His jaw tightened.

She held his gaze for one moment longer.

Then she turned back to Iichíilee, took the girl's hand, and walked back into the camp.

She heard Joker's hooves behind her. Moving toward the rise. Moving away.

She did not watch him go.

Iichíilee did.

The girl stood at her aunt's side and watched the man ride away until the rise took him, and when he was gone, she looked up at Ashkáale with those careful eyes.

"Baáhpitche," she said. "You should have seen their faces when they saw it was Heávohe."

Ashkáale looked at her niece.

She said nothing.

But something moved in her face, just briefly, just for a moment, before she put it away.

"Come," she said. "There is work."

There was always work.

She took the girl's hand, and they went back to it.

18

Ashkáale

The herds were thinner now.

Not gone, not yet. Changed. The great black rivers of animals that had once rolled across the plains in a sound like a storm had become scattered bands, broken shapes moving across a country that no longer belonged to them as it once had.

Declan saw it before he heard it.

A carcass. Then another. Then a third. Dozens. All within a quarter mile of each other. Hide gone. Meat left. Bones already picked clean by wolves and birds. The grass around them trampled flat, the earth torn up by hooves that had milled and turned and milled again before running on.

He sat Joker and looked at the waste.

Not with outrage. Not with sorrow. Just the cold assessment of a man who understood the arithmetic of the plains and knew when the numbers were changing.

He rode on.

Another carcass.

Another.

A whole line of them stretching toward the horizon like some kind of ledger written in meat.

He dismounted. Squatted beside one. The hide had been taken clean. A sharp knife, quick hands. White hunters. The kind who worked in crews now, not alone. The kind who used wagons and teams and left the meat to rot because the hides were worth more than the time it took to cut the rest.

He touched the head with one hand. The meat was still warm.

He stood.

Joker flicked an ear. Looked north.

Declan looked too.

A small group of riders on a ridge. Crow. Five of them. Watching him, as men watched a fire on the horizon, not afraid of it, but aware of what it meant.

He didn't move.

They didn't either.

One of them lifted a hand. Not a greeting. Not a warning. Just a gesture that acknowledged what was in front of them. The carcasses, the waste, the thinning herds, the world shifting under their horses' hooves.

Declan lifted his chin once.

The riders came down the ridge.

Slow.

Unhurried.

How men moved when they had already decided there was no danger in the moment.

They stopped ten yards from him.

The lead rider was older, hair bound in two long braids, a hawk feather tied at the back, looked at the carcasses. Then at Declan. Then at the Sharps in the saddle sheath.

He said something in Crow. Declan caught pieces of it. Buffalo, white men, waste. Words he'd learned over the years without meaning to. Words that had become part of the landscape, the same way the wind and the grass had.

Declan said nothing.

Another rider, younger, sharp-eyed, pointed at the sheath on Declan's saddle. Said a word Declan knew well enough.

Heávohe.

Declan didn't react.

The older man said something sharp to the younger one. A reprimand. The younger man lowered his eyes.

The older rider looked at Declan again. Said something in Crow, slower this time, the cadence deliberate, as if he were speaking to a man who understood more than he let on.

"The Cheyenne watch for you," the man said.

"They speak your name in their camps. They have not forgotten the willows."

Declan said nothing.

The older man nodded once, as if that silence was the answer he expected.

The rider's eyes went to the sheath on Declan's saddle.

Then back to him.

"The girl told her story," he said.

"Our people remember."

Declan didn't answer.

He pointed east, a long, sweeping gesture toward the horizon where the land dipped and rose again in low folds.

Soldiers.

Declan saw them now. A patrol moving along the ridge, blue coats catching the sun, Crow scouts riding with them. Easy in the saddle. Talking. Laughing. Not captives. Not subordinates. Allies.

The older Crow rider said something else. A single word Declan didn't know, but the tone of it was unmistakable.

Change.
The riders turned their horses.
Moved off.
Declan watched them go.
Watched the soldiers on the ridge.
Watched the thinning herds.
He didn't feel anything about it.
He just filed it.
As he filed everything.
He mounted Joker.
Rode out, looking for the herd.
The plains went on around him.
Quieter.

* * *

The camp was on the Bighorn, in the shadow of the mountains.

Forty lodges, maybe more, the tipis arranged in a particular order that wasn't random. Clan groupings, family groupings, the social geography of a people who knew exactly where everyone stood in relation to everyone else. The smoke rising straight in the still afternoon air. The smell of meat drying. Of horses. Of fires that had been burning in this place for three days and would burn for three more before the camp moved on.

Búahisshish and Iilaxpáake rode in from the south.

Nobody ran to meet them. Nobody made a show of their arrival. But the camp noticed. The camp always noticed, the slight shift of attention, the women who paused in their work without appearing to pause, the children who moved toward the riders with the casual drift of children who happened to be going that direction anyway.

Búahisshish dismounted at his lodge.

153

His wife took his horse without being asked.

Iilaxpáake was already talking.

He was that kind of young man.

* * *

At the fire outside Daxpitcheehísshish's lodge, three men sat.

The chief himself, sixty years old now, the years visible in his face but not in his bearing. He sat as he always sat, with the particular stillness of a man who had learned that the world came to him if he waited.

Búahisshish sat across from him.

Iilaxpáake stood.

Young men stood. They hadn't yet learned the patience of sitting.

"We saw him," Búahisshish said.

Daxpitcheehísshish looked at the fire.

"On the plain south of the Tongue," Búahisshish said. "Working the herd. Alone now." He paused. "The other one is gone."

The chief nodded once. He'd heard. Word traveled.

"He is good with that rifle," Iilaxpáake said. He couldn't help himself. "It is said he can drop ten animals in the time it takes a man to reload twice."

Búahisshish looked at him.

Iilaxpáake lowered his eyes slightly.

"He saw us," Búahisshish said. "He didn't move. Didn't reach for the rifle."

"No," Daxpitcheehísshish said. "He wouldn't."

The fire moved between them.

"The Cheyenne have not forgotten the willows," Búahisshish said.

"No," the chief said again.

"They say Heávohe now when they speak of him." Búahisshish

looked at his hands. "The story has grown. Three more dead since the willows. Each time they sent men. Each time—" He stopped.

"Each time he walks away," Iilaxpáake said.

Nobody reprimanded him for it this time. It was simply true.

Daxpitcheehísshish looked at the mountains to the west. The Bighorns catching the last of the afternoon light, the peaks still holding snow in the high places.

"Our people remember the willows differently than the Cheyenne do," he said.

Búahisshish nodded.

"He saved her," Iilaxpáake said. The young man's voice had changed. Something in it that wasn't quite reverence but lived near it.

"He killed two Cheyenne," Daxpitchcchísshish said. "What hc saved or didn't save, that is a question only he could answer. And he is not a man who answers questions."

He picked up a stick and turned it in the fire.

"She said he looked at her and pointed west," he said. "One word. Go."

"Just go," Iilaxpáake said.

The old chief nodded his head.

"Just go," the chief said.

* * *

Across the camp, near the edge where the horses were picketed, Ashkáale was working a hide.

She had it staked flat on the ground, a buffalo cow, taken three days ago by her brother's hunting party. She worked the fleshing tool across it in long, even strokes, her movements the particular rhythm of a woman who had been doing this work since she was old enough to hold the tool.

155

Iichíilee sat nearby, watching.

The girl was eleven now. Old enough to start learning. Young enough that everything still looked like something she couldn't wait to know.

"Like this?" the girl said. She had a small piece of hide in her lap, working it with her own tool.

Ashkáale glanced over.

"Flatter," she said. "You're scraping, not cutting. The tool goes flat against the hide, not into it."

Iichíilee adjusted her angle.

"Better," Ashkáale said.

They worked in silence for a while. The sounds of the camp around them, children, horses, the low talk of women at the next lodge, someone singing somewhere to the north of the camp.

"Búahisshish is back," Iichíilee said.

"I know," Ashkáale said.

"He rode south this morning."

"I know."

Iichíilee worked her piece of hide. Looked up.

"Did they see him?"

Ashkáale's tool moved across the hide.

"See who?" she said.

The girl was quiet for a moment.

"Are you afraid of him?" she said.

"Afraid of who?" she said.

Ashkáale looked up from the hide.

Looked at her niece.

"No," she said. "I am not afraid."

"The other girls say—"

"I know what the other girls say," Ashkáale said. "Work your hide."

Iichíilee worked her hide.

But she watched her aunt from the corner of her eye, as girls watched the women they were trying to understand.

***

At the edge of the camp, near the water, Ashkáale's father found her before the sun went down.

She was still working. The hide, almost done.

He stood beside her for a moment without speaking. An old man's habit, the pause before the words, the gathering of what needed to be said.

"Búahisshish saw him today," he said.

"Yes, it is that talk of the camp," she said.

"On the plain, south of the Tongue."

"Yes."

He watched her work.

"You are thirty years old," he said.

"I know how old I am."

"A woman of thirty—"

"Father."

He stopped.

She kept working.

He tried again.

"There are men who have asked," he said. "Good men. Men with horses. Men who would—"

"Men who want a woman who smiles more," she said.

He was quiet.

"You told me that," she said. "Last winter. And the winter before."

"I tell you because it's true," he said. "A smile does not hurt," he said as he grinned foolishly at her. "See?" He was not being unkind. Just a father, who had been having this conversation for ten years, and hadn't found the right words yet. He suspected the right words didn't exist.

"The world is changing," he said. "Faster than we can see it changing. A woman alone—"

"A woman alone does what she has always done," Ashkáale said. "She works. She provides. She teaches." She nodded toward Iichíilee, who had gone back to the lodge. "She remembers."

Daxpitcheehísshish looked at the hide staked flat on the ground.

"From whose hunt is this?" he said.

"Your nephew's."

"He has a wife to work his hides."

"His wife is nursing," Ashkáale said. "She has enough."

He looked at the mountains.

"The soldiers came again," he said. His voice had changed. The father conversation over. The chief conversation beginning.

Ashkáale's hands slowed.

"When?" she said.

"Three days ago. While you were south." He paused. "They want scouts again. Young men to ride with them against the Lakota."

Ashkáale set the fleshing tool down.

Looked at her father.

"And?" she said.

He was quiet for a moment.

"Iilaxpáake has volunteered," he said.

She looked at the mountains.

The Bighorns catching the last light. The peaks going gold then gray.

"He's a fool," she said.

"He's young," her father said.

"The same thing."

Daxpitcheehísshish looked at his daughter. The scar that wasn't there anymore but that he still saw sometimes, the mark the rawhide had left on her wrists before the white man had cut it. Before the word. Go.

"The soldiers are the only thing between the Lakota and us," he said. "Between the Cheyenne and us. You know this."

"I know it," she said. "I don't have to like it."

"No," he said. "You don't."

He stood beside her for another moment.

Then he walked back toward the lodge.

She picked up the fleshing tool.

Kept working.

The hide almost done.

The mountains going dark.

The camp settling into evening around her, the fires brightening as the light faded, the children called in, the particular quality of quiet that fell over a Crow camp when the day's work was done and the night's rest was beginning.

Iichíilee came back.

Sat beside her aunt without being asked.

Picked up her own piece of hide.

They worked together in the firelight.

Shadow and Little Bird.

The mountains behind them.

The plains ahead.

The world was changing around them, just like her father said it would.

Faster than they could see it changing.

19

Ho'néheevàhtóohe

He'd been hunting since dawn.

The mule trailed behind him, hides lashed tight across its packs, the animal plodding with the particular resignation of something that had long ago accepted its place in the world. Joker moved easy beneath him, the afternoon light flattening the land into long folds of grass and shadow.

He heard the whoops before he saw anything.

Sharp. Rising. The kind of sound men made when they were already committed to the thing they'd come to do.

Joker lifted his head.

Declan touched his heels to him and rode up the low rise.

From the top he saw it.

A small Crow hunting party, five men, running hard across the plain, their ponies stretched out, the dust rising behind them in a long torn ribbon. And behind them, closing fast, a Cheyenne war party. Ten. Maybe twelve. Hard to count at that distance, the speed of them, the dust, the movement.

The Cheyenne were already in the run.

Declan sat Joker.

Held the mule's lead rope in one hand.

Watched.

The Crow riders angled toward a shallow cut in the land, a dry creekbed that might have offered something if they'd had another hundred yards. They didn't. The Cheyenne ponies were too fast, the gap closing with the particular inevitability of men who had chosen their moment well.

One Crow rider went down first.

Not from a shot. From a lance. The Cheyenne rider came alongside him at full gallop, the strike clean and practiced, the Crow man falling sideways off his pony and hitting the ground in a roll that didn't end in anything but stillness.

The others didn't look back.

They rode harder.

Declan watched the second one fall. An arrow this time. The man reaching back as if to pull it free, then slumping forward over the neck of his pony before sliding off entirely.

The Cheyenne whooped again.

A sound of triumph. Of momentum.

The Crow reached the dry creekbed.

Three of them.

They turned their ponies. Tried to make a stand.

It wasn't enough.

The Cheyenne hit them like weather.

Fast. Loud. A blur of horses and bodies and weapons. Dust rising in a thick cloud that swallowed the center of the fight, leaving only the edges visible, a pony rearing, a man falling, the flash of a lance, the arc of a club.

Declan watched it as he watched everything.

Cold.

Still.

Measuring the angles. The distances. The choices.

One Crow rider broke free of the dust. Young. Quick. Bow in hand. He loosed an arrow at a Cheyenne rider and turned his pony hard, trying to reach open ground.

He recognized one of the Crow riders when he broke from the dust.

The young one.

The one with the quick hands and the sharper eyes.

He'd seen him once near the Bighorn camp.

Iilaxpáake rode hard, bow in hand, turning in the saddle to loose an arrow that went wide. He tried to angle toward open ground, but the Cheyenne were already on him. Two riders cutting him off with the practiced ease of men who had done this before.

One came alongside him.

Close.

A short thrust with a lance.

Precise.

Iilaxpáake arched once and fell.

The Cheyenne didn't slow.

The dust settled.

The fight was over.

Five Crow dead on the plain and in the creekbed.

The Cheyenne moved among the bodies with quick, efficient hands, taking weapons, taking quivers, taking the Crow ponies. They left their own dead pony where it had fallen. No one looked at it twice.

They mounted again.

Turned south.

Rode off in a long line of dust and noise that faded into the distance.

He watched them go.

Declan sat Joker and looked at the bodies for a long moment.

He squinted and looked at the one he recognized.

He'd seen him before.

Once. At the trading post on the Middle Fork. The young one who'd pointed at the sheath and said the word. The one the older rider had checked.

That was all he knew of him.

It didn't change anything.

He didn't move.

Didn't feel anything about it.

He just filed it.

How he filed everything.

Then he turned Joker and rode on, the mule following, the plains settling back into their quiet as if nothing had happened at all.

** * **

They painted their faces black before they rode in.

It was the custom. You had killed, and you wore it, and the camp would see it from a distance and know before the advance riders came through. Ho'néheevàhtóhe did his own face, working by feel, as he had since he was young, the grease and pigment going on smooth and even. Around him, the others did the same. No one spoke. They had been riding for three hours, and the talk had been used up on the plain.

Five Crow ponies strung on a line behind Táhpeno, who had taken them. Good horses. The Crow knew horses, and these were no exception, deep-chested and clean-legged, and Táhpeno had strung them himself and checked the lead twice on the ride back. You did not lose what you had taken.

Ho'néheevàhtóohe looked at the sky. Two hours of light left. Good. They would come in with the sun still on them.

He chose four men to go ahead, Táhpeno and three others, and told them what to do with their eyes, not with words. Táhpeno grinned and kicked his horse forward and the four of them went out at a run, whooping, the scalp poles raised. Ho'néheevȧhtóohe watched them go. Then he reformed the rest into two lines and they rode side by side at a walk, the black faces forward, the Crow ponies trailing behind.

The sound reached them before the camp was visible. Women's voices carrying across the flat ground, the high keening of the victory songs, and then children's voices underneath that, and then the whole camp moving toward them like water running downhill. He could hear the excitement in it and it settled something in him that had been drawn tight since the plain.

The women came out singing, their arms raised, and the children ran alongside the horses, and the old men stood at the edge of the camp and watched with the particular stillness of men who had done this themselves and were now done with it. One of them caught Ho'néheevȧhtóohe's eye and nodded once, and Ho'néheevȧhtóohe returned it.

They rode through the camp in their two lines. The scalp poles passed from hand to hand and the women sang over them. The Crow ponies were examined and admired and Táhpeno stood next to them receiving what was due him without false modesty, because false modesty was its own kind of lie. A man did what he did or he did not. Táhpeno had taken five horses from under the Crow and deserved to stand straight.

Ho'néheevȧhtóohe dismounted and handed his horse to his youngest brother and went to find something to eat.

Later, when the camp had settled and the fire was low, he sat with five of the men from the party. Not all of them. The young ones were elsewhere, doing what young men did after a successful raid, and Ho'néheevȧhtóohe had no quarrel with that. He had been young once and remembered it clearly enough.

The five with him now were the ones worth talking to.

Táhpeno. Ho'néoxháaestse, who was not young and had not been for some time. Two brothers named for their father's horse and a man called Ésevone whose left hand was missing two fingers from an old fight with the Pawnee. A fire. Enough meat. The darkness coming down over the plain like a hand lowered slowly.

They talked about the raid. It was work they had done well, not boasting, because there was no one here to perform for, but accounting. What had gone as planned, and what had not. The Crow had gotten into the creekbed faster than expected. The two who went down early changed the shape of the thing. Táhpeno had ridden wide, and that was right. The young one who tried to break for open ground, they all remembered him. Fast. Almost.

Then Ésevone said it.

"The white man was watching from the ridge."

No one spoke for a moment.

"I saw him," Táhpeno said.

"We all saw him," said Ho'néheeváhtóohe.

He had seen the man the moment he appeared on the rise, sitting his horse without moving, the mule behind him with hides lashed across its back. A hunter. Alone. Just watching, the way a man watches something he has already assessed and filed and does not intend to act on.

Ho'néheeváhtóohe had made his decision in the space of a breath. Leave him. You did not interrupt your work to address a man watching from a ridge, not when the work was going well, and the watcher was alone. And there was the other thing, which he had not said yet.

"Bad medicine," said one of the brothers. "A white man watching the dead."

"He did not watch the dead," Táhpeno said. "He watched us work. He was already gone when we stripped the ponies."

"It doesn't matter when he left."

Ho'néheeváhtóohe fed a stick into the fire. "You know who he was."

The brother looked at him.

"The one the Cheyenne call Heávohe." Ho'néheevàhtóohe said it flat, without ceremony. It was a name, not an invocation. "The white hunter on the Powder River. The one who has been here since before some of you had wives."

Ésevone turned the meat on the fire with his three-fingered hand. "I have heard this name."

"Most people have."

"And you think this is the same man."

"I know it is the same man. I have seen him before at the trading post on the Middle Fork. You remember him when you see him." Ho'néheevàhtóohe paused. "He is not a man who looks like other men."

The fire shifted and settled. Outside the circle of light the camp moved with its ordinary sounds, dogs and children and the low talk of people winding toward sleep.

"So," said the brother. "Bad medicine."

"Or," said Táhpeno, "he saw what we did and he will carry it. The Cheyenne took five Crow horses in their own country. Heávohe watched it and did nothing. He sat his horse and he watched and he rode away." He looked around the fire. "There is no bad medicine in that. There is only the truth of what happened."

"Heávohe does not frighten easily," Ho'néheevàhtóohe said. "This is known. If he sat his horse and watched and rode away, it means he made a judgment. He judged that what we were doing was not his business."

"Or he judged that ten of us was too many."

"He has faced worse numbers than ten." Ho'néheevàhtóohe said it without heat. It was simply true, and all of them knew it was true, and there was no use pretending otherwise. "He sat his horse because he chose to. Not because he was afraid."

The brother was quiet.

"Then what does it mean," Ésevone said.

"It means he saw us. It means he knows we are in this country and what we are capable of." Ho'néheeváhtóohe looked at the fire. "That is not the worst thing."

Ho'néoxháaestse had said nothing since the man on the ridge was mentioned. He sat with his forearms on his knees and looked into the fire and the others had left him to it, because this was his way and they all knew his way. He spoke when he had finished thinking and not before, and when he spoke it was usually worth the wait.

Now he spoke.

"The young one," he said. "The one who tried to reach open ground."

He did not say anything else for a moment.

"I fought against him. Two winters back, on the eastern fork. A Crow hunting party, six of them. We were four." A pause. "He was the one who almost cost us Ésevone's horse." He looked at Ésevone. "You remember."

Ésevone nodded slowly.

"He was fast," Ho'néoxháaestse said. "And he did not panic. Even when it was going wrong for them, he did not panic." He looked back into the fire. "He was going to be a good warrior."

No one answered this. There was nothing to answer. It was not a challenge, and it was not grief exactly; it was something that did not have a clean name, the acknowledgment that the man you had just killed was worth killing, that he had made the ground mean something. It sat with all of them for a while.

Ho'néheeváhtóohe looked out past the edge of the firelight, past the camp, out to where the plain ran dark and flat toward the horizon. He could not see them now, but he had seen them that morning, riding in the thin pale lines of smoke rising in the south and east, too many and too far spread to be cook fires. The hunters' fires. Running their camps in lines across the plain, as a man runs a net across a river, working the herds from every direction at once.

Not just one white man watching from a ridge with a mule and hides.

The other thing.

He thought about the herds they had ridden through two days south. Thinner than last year. Thinner than the year before. He had noticed and said nothing because there was nothing useful to say and the raid was the thing in front of them, but he had filed it, as you filed everything that might matter later.

One of the brothers yawned and said something to the other about sleep and they went. Ésevone followed. Táhpeno sat a little longer, looking at the fire, and then he too rose and went without a word.

Ho'néoxháaestse remained.

The two of them sat in silence for a while.

"The young Crow," Ho'néoxháaestse said finally. Not asking. Just settling it.

"Yes," Ho'néheevàhtóohe said.

"He chose well. At the end. He chose open ground instead of the creekbed. It was the right choice. It only did not work."

"It almost worked."

"Yes." Ho'néoxháaestse looked at the fire. "Almost."

They sat a while longer. The camp quieted around them. The dogs settled. The smoke from the hunters' fires was invisible now in the dark, but Ho'néheevàhtóohe knew the direction, and he looked that way without meaning to, as you look toward a sound you cannot quite identify.

Then he banked the fire and went to sleep.

20

Bíawacheeitchish

The man's name was Whistling Crow, and he made things that held together.

Declan first saw his work at the trading post on the Middle Fork. A pair of moccasins on a trapper who'd worn them through two winters, and they still looked right. He asked about them. The trapper told him. It took Declan three months to find the camp.

Now he stood in front of Whistling Crow's lodge and said what he wanted. A coat first. Buffalo hide, heavy, wool side in, long enough to cover his thighs. He'd had three coats in eight years, and none of them were right. Too short, too stiff, seams that let the wind in. He drew what he wanted in the dirt with a stick. Whistling Crow looked at the drawing and said nothing.

Then moccasins. He pulled off his right boot and held it up. Whistling Crow took it, turned it, pressed his thumb along the sole. Set it down. Said something to his wife, who came and looked without touching. Whistling Crow held up four fingers.

"Four what?" Declan said.

Whistling Crow pointed at the Sharps rifle on Declan's back.

"Not the rifle."

Whistling Crow held up four fingers again.

Declan pulled two pieces of silver from his coat and held them out flat on his palm. Whistling Crow looked at them as a man looks at something he's already decided about.

It was somewhere in the middle of this that Declan looked up.

He was aware of the camp around him, as he was always aware of his surroundings, the position of the horses, the number of men he could see, the dogs, the sight lines. He filed it as he went. If you stopped filing, you got dead. But this was different. His eyes went to a place at the edge of the camp, drawn by movement, and then they stopped.

She was sitting with a girl working something in her hands, a length of hide stretched across her knee. She was talking, and the girl was listening with the particular quality of attention children have when the story is the right kind of story. Ashkáale's hands kept moving while she talked. She didn't look up.

He had seen her before. He had seen her at the trading post on the Middle Fork, at the edge of the camp when the older riders came down from the ridge, and, of course, he had seen her in the willows that time. He had seen her from a distance more than once over the years without meaning to. He had filed her each time. Shadow, that was her name.

But he had not seen her here, in her own world, in the plain light of a morning when nothing was at stake. She looked different. She looked like what she was.

He looked back at Whistling Crow.

"Two silver," he said. "And I'll bring you a robe besides. A good one. Taken clean."

Whistling Crow considered this.

She was telling it the way her mother had told it to her, which was the way her mother's mother had told it before that. Not with the careful shape of a lesson but with the ease of something simply true.

"Bíawacheeitchish," she said. "You know this name."

Iichíilee nodded, though her nod had the quality of a name half-known, heard but not held.

"She was Crow," Ashkáale said. "Born Gros Ventre, but Crow from the time she was ten. A raiding party took her, and a warrior of our people raised her as his own." She smoothed the hide with the heel of her hand. "From the time she was a girl, she wanted what the boys wanted. To ride, to hunt, to know how to fight. Her father let her. He was a wise man."

"Did she fight?"

"She fought. When the Blackfoot came raiding, she stood at the walls of the fort. She did not run." Ashkáale looked at the girl. "She killed two men that day. Two. And then she went after their horses."

Iichíilee's eyes were wide.

"She led war parties after that. She came home with horses and scalps, and the council of chiefs gave her a seat among them. Third place among all the leaders of her band." Ashkáale's hands kept moving, pulling the sinew through the hide with the small bone needle, even and steady. "She married four women who ran her lodge while she was at war. She had her own guns, her own horses, her own medicines. The devices on her robe were her own brave acts, each one."

"What did she look like?"

Ashkáale thought about this. "I did not see her myself. I was too young when she died. But my mother knew women who knew her. They said she looked neither savage nor warlike. That when she was at rest, you would not have known her from any other woman." She paused. "It was only when she moved toward something that you understood what she was."

Iichíilee sat with this.

"Three years ago," Ashkáale said. "She went north to make peace with the Gros Ventre, her birth people. To bring them and our people together." She pulled the sinew tight. "They killed her."

The girl was quiet.

"There was another," Ashkáale said, before the silence could settle wrong. "Biliíche Héeleelash. Among The Willows. She is alive now, not far from here. A war leader, a pipe carrier." She glanced at Iichíilee. "Do you know what she wears when she rides to war?"

The girl shook her head.

"Her finest clothes. Her best dress, her best moccasins, her finest beadwork. Everything that says she is a woman." Ashkáale let that sit for a moment. "She does not dress like a man to be taken seriously. She dresses like herself. She rides into the fight, and she is taken seriously, or she is not. Either way, she keeps riding."

Iichíilee looked down at her hands.

"I am telling you these names," Ashkáale said, "because no one will write them down. You understand? The ones who write things down do not know our stories, or they know them wrong. So you will remember. Bíawacheeitchish. Biliíche Héeleelash." She looked at the girl steadily. "Say them."

"Bíawacheeitchish," Iichíilee said. "Biliíche Héeleelash."

"Again."

She said them again.

"When you have daughters," Ashkáale said, "you will tell them. And they will tell their daughters. That is how it stays alive." She went back to her work. "Now. Help me with this edge."

Declan did not hear any of it. He was too far across the camp, and the words were not his. But he looked up twice more while the bargaining went on, and both times she was there, hands moving, talking to the girl, unhurried. The second time, she did not notice. The third time, she did.

She didn't look away. She looked at him as she looked at most things, directly and without performance. He was the one who looked back at Whistling Crow.

Three silver, in the end. And the robe. Whistling Crow spat in his palm, and Declan did the same. They pressed their hands together. The coat would take three weeks. He could come back or send someone. He said he'd come back.

He was walking toward Joker when he heard it.

Not words first. A sound, the particular register of men coming fast with intent, the quality of it different from any other kind of fast. His body knew it before his mind did. He had his hand on the Sharps before he'd taken another step.

* * *

The Lakota came in from the north, riding low and hard and straight for the horse herd at the edge of camp. Not a war party in force—a raid, fast and targeted, the kind that was in and out before a camp could organize. They were good. They knew what they were doing.

The Crow camp came up fast. Men reaching for weapons, women pulling children into lodges, the particular controlled chaos of people who had done this before and knew their parts. Two Crow warriors went straight at the raiders without hesitation, cutting off the angle to the horses. An older man was shouting something that organized the response the way a rock in a stream organizes water.

Declan went for Joker.

The horse was tied at the near edge of camp, thirty yards ahead of him. He was moving fast, Sharps in hand, reading the raid as he went. Nine riders, the main body driving toward the herd, two peeling wide to cut off any defenders who tried to flank. Standard. He'd seen the shape of it in the first three seconds.

Then he saw the three who had broken south.

Not toward the horses. Away from them. Toward the edge of camp, where the lodges thinned, and the grass began. Toward where Ashkáale and Iichíilee had been sitting.

He didn't decide anything.

He just turned.

Joker was behind him now. He didn't think about that.

The three riders had found them between the lodges. Ashkáale was on her feet, her back against the lodge wall, the skinning knife out and low, her body between the raider and the girl. Iichíilee was behind her, pressed flat against the hide wall, silent, understanding the situation completely.

One of the raiders had already dismounted. A young man, quick-eyed, moving toward Ashkáale with the particular focus of someone who had done this before and expected it to go a certain way. He was watching the knife. Calculating the moment.

The other two were still mounted, watching the lodge entrance, watching the main fight, watching everything at once, as men watched when they were working fast and didn't want to be surprised from behind.

Ashkáale saw Declan before they did.

Nothing changed in her face. She didn't look relieved. She didn't look away from the man moving toward her. She just noted it. Filed it, kept her eyes on the threat in front of her.

The dismounted raider was four feet from her when Declan hit him from the side.

Not a tackle. Not a collision. Something more deliberate. Declan came in at the angle that took the man's feet first, dropping him sideways, the knife going in before they reached the ground. Fast.

He was up before the man stopped moving.

The two mounted raiders had turned at the sound.

They saw the man on the ground. They saw Declan between them and the woman, the knife still in his hand, the flat gray eyes moving from one to the other with the calm assessment of a man deciding the order of things.

The nearer one came off his horse hard and fast, a tomahawk already moving, committed before he'd finished his decision. Declan stepped into it, inside the arc, where the weapon was useless, got a hand on the man's wrist. Turned the momentum against him. The ground took him. Declan's knee found the back of his neck once, sharp. The man went still. And that was two.

He straightened.

The third man hadn't moved.

He was still mounted, his pony shifted sideways beneath him, the animal reading what the man's eyes were reading. He looked at his two companions on the ground. He looked at Declan. He looked at the knife.

He looked at Declan's eyes.

Something decided itself in his face.

He reined his pony hard and rode back into the main fight, which was already collapsing. Two more Lakota down, the rest pulling out, the Crow warriors driving them off the horses with the organized fury of men defending what was theirs. They were good fighters. Fierce, fast, operating on their own ground with the total commitment of men who understood exactly what was at stake.

The last raiders cleared the camp at a run.

Then it was over.

The particular silence that followed violence, not quiet exactly, but the absence of a specific kind of noise, the camp refilling itself with voices and children and the restless movement of horses that had been frightened and weren't finished being frightened yet.

Declan wiped the knife on the grass.

Looked at the two men.

Looked at Ashkáale.

She had not moved from the lodge wall. Iichíilee was still behind her, one hand gripping the back of her aunt's dress, her face visible at Ashkáale's side. Wide-eyed. Breathing hard. But steady. The girl had held.

Ashkáale looked at Declan the way she'd looked at him in the willows eight years ago. Not gratitude. Not fear. The weather look. Something happening that she was accounting for, measuring, filing it.

Her eyes went to the two men on the ground.

Then back to him.

He looked away first.

He turned and walked to Joker, checked him over with both hands, neck to flank, lifted each hoof. The horse stood for it with his ears back, aggrieved at the noise and the smell and the general disruption of his afternoon. Declan said something to him that Whistling Crow's wife, watching from ten feet away, could not hear. Joker's ears came forward slightly. Declan dropped the last hoof and straightened.

The young warrior came up on his left. One of the men who'd fought well in the initial response, maybe twenty, looking at Declan with something that was not quite admiration and not quite unease, but lived in the territory between them.

He said something in Crow. Then, in broken trade language: "You fight for the woman again. Like the willows. She sees you."

Declan looked at him.

The warrior didn't step back, but he wanted to. Something had changed in the air between them.

"I fought for the horse," Declan said. His voice was flat and cold and had nothing in it. "Say that again, and I'll lay you in the grass."

The warrior said nothing. Declan held his gaze for three seconds, which was two seconds longer than necessary, then turned, untied Joker, and walked him out of the camp without looking back.

Behind him, Ashkáale had gone to where the dead Crow were being gathered. Two men from the band. She knew them both. She sat with one of them for a moment. A quiet man who had been kind to Iichíilee when she was small. She sat with him and did nothing. Just sat.

She heard the exchange with the young warrior. She heard Declan's voice without knowing the words, the particular flat cold of it, and she saw the warrior's face change. She saw Declan walk Joker out without looking back.

Iichíilee came and stood beside her.

"Who is that?" the girl said.

Ashkáale watched the edge of the camp where he had gone.

"Heávohe," she said.

"He is a good man."

Ashkáale thought about this. A man who walked into a willow draw for a stranger. A man who had a clear path to his horse and did not take it.

"I don't know what he is," she said.

She picked up the hide she had dropped when the raiders came. Found her needle. Went back to work.

But her eyes went once more to the edge of the camp where the grass lay flat and the plain opened out, already empty. Just once. Then she looked back at her work and did not look up again.

21

The Bozeman

The winters came and went, and each one left something behind that hadn't been there before.

The Lakota pressure had been steady since before anyone in the camp could remember. Raids, skirmishes, the slow grinding contest over hunting ground that went back further than the oldest elder could say with certainty. But from 1858 onward, its quality changed. Not more violent exactly. More deliberate. The Oglala and the Hunkpapa were moving west with a purpose that felt less like raiding and more like occupation, pushing into territory the Fort Laramie Treaty had guaranteed to the Crow, grazing their ponies on Crow grass, running Crow buffalo, camping on Crow water as if the treaty were a thing that had happened to other people.

Daxpitcheehísshish watched it from the ridges and said little.

He was a man who had learned that the first response to a thing was rarely the right one. You watched. You measured. You let the shape of it declare itself before you committed to an answer.

What he saw over those years declared itself plainly enough.

The Lakota were not raiding.

They were moving in.

* * *

Declan came back for the coat in October, three weeks after the bargain with Whistling Crow, as he'd said he would.

Ashkáale knew he was coming because Iichíilee told her, and she knew Iichíilee told her because the girl had been watching for him, which meant the girl had been watching Ashkáale watch for him, which meant nothing in this camp was private from a twelve-year-old girl with sharp eyes and too much time to think.

She went to her brother's lodge and helped his wife with the curing work and did not come out until the sound of Joker's hooves had been gone from the camp for an hour.

Iichíilee found her there.

Sat down beside her without being asked.

Picked up a piece of hide and started working it.

Said nothing for a long time.

Then: "He asked Whistling Crow about you."

Ashkáale's hands did not stop moving.

"What did Whistling Crow say?"

"That you were working at your brother's lodge." A pause. "He looked that direction for a moment."

"Then he left," Ashkáale said. Not a question.

"Then he left."

Ashkáale worked the hide.

Outside, the camp went about its business. Horses. Children. Smoke from the cooking fires drifting south on the cold air.

"Work your piece," Ashkáale said.

Iichíilee worked her piece.

* * *

Two years passed.

The soldiers came more regularly after that. Not in force, not yet, but patrols moving through the Yellowstone country with Crow scouts riding ahead of them, the scouts easy in their saddles, talking with the soldiers in the manner of men who had found a working arrangement with each other. Daxpitcheehísshish met with the patrol commanders. Listened. Spoke carefully. Translated nothing he didn't intend to translate.

At the fire outside his lodge one evening, he told Ashkáale what they wanted.

"Scouts," he said. "Eyes on the Lakota movements. Information about the trails."

She was working a length of sinew, pulling it through her fingers to soften it. She kept working.

"And in return," she said.

"Protection. Their rifles between the Lakota and us."

"Their rifles." She said it the way you repeat something to hear how it sounded.

"Yes."

She pulled the sinew through her fingers.

"And what do they want for themselves?" she said. "The soldiers. What are they here for?"

Her father looked at the fire.

"The land is opening," he said. "Men coming west for gold. The strikes are north of here, past the Yellowstone. They want a road through our country to reach them."

She looked at him then.

"Through our country," she said.

"Yes."

She went back to the sinew.

The fire moved between them.

"So," she said. "White men on our land so that more white men can come onto our land."

"The Lakota are already on our land," her father said. "The Cheyenne. They have been taking it for thirty years. The soldiers push them back." He paused. "We could fight the soldiers, too. We could fight everyone at once." He looked at her steadily. "How does that end?"

She said nothing.

She knew how it ended. She had thought it through every way she knew how to think through a thing, and it always ended the same way. You could not fight in every direction at once. You chose your enemies by choosing your allies, and there were no clean choices left, if there had ever been any.

"I understand it," she said finally.

"But," her father said.

"But I don't have to like it."

He almost smiled.

"No," he said. "You don't."

* * *

Iichíilee was fourteen now. Old enough to see what was happening. Old enough to ask.

"Why don't we fight?" she said one evening. Not to the camp, not to anyone in particular. Just to her aunt, as young people put their hardest questions to the person they most trusted to answer them honestly.

Ashkáale's hands kept moving on the hide.

"We fight," she said. "We have been fighting."

"Then why are they still coming?"

Ashkáale set the fleshing tool down.

She looked at the mountains. The Bighorns were catching the last of the afternoon light, the peaks going gold and then gray as they always did, indifferent to what happened in the valleys below.

"Because there are more of them," she said. "And because the Cheyenne fight with them. And because the buffalo—" She stopped.

"Because of the hunters," Iichíilee said.

"Yes."

The girl sat with this.

"Someone said we should make peace with the Lakota," Iichíilee said. "Fight the whites together."

Ashkáale looked at her.

"Who said this?"

"Some of the young men. After the last raid."

Ashkáale picked up the fleshing tool. Went back to work.

"The Lakota have been killing our people since before your grandfather was born," she said. "They killed ten of our warriors the year you were three years old. They killed Iilaxpáake." She pulled the tool across the hide in one long, even stroke. "You do not make peace with a people by forgetting what they have done. You make peace with them when they stop doing it. The Lakota have not stopped."

"But the whites—"

"I know," Ashkáale said.

She said it with a flatness that ended the conversation. Not because she didn't have more to say. Because what she had to say was not something she was ready to say out loud.

The whites are taking the buffalo. The buffalo are the life. Without the buffalo, there is nothing left to fight for and nothing left to fight with. And Declan Shea has been on the Powder River for seven years taking buffalo, and he is one man. There are a thousand more behind him.

She worked her hide.

Said nothing.

* * *

Over the next three years, the Bozeman Trail cut through everything.

John Bozeman had pushed north from the Oregon Trail in 1863, threading through the Powder River country east of the Bighorns. Through Crow land, though Bozeman did not stop to ask, to reach the Montana gold fields faster than any other route. Within a season, it was carrying hundreds of wagons. Within two seasons, thousands. Men with families. Men alone. Men with nothing but a mule and the idea of gold and no particular concern for whose ground they were crossing.

The Crow watched them from the ridges.

Ashkáale watched them from the ridges.

She watched the wagons move through the valley below in long, slow lines, the white canvas catching the sun, the dust rising behind them in columns that hung in the still air for an hour after the last wagon had passed. She watched the grass they trampled and the wood they cut and the game they frightened and the creeks they fouled, and she watched all of this with the flat, careful gaze she brought to everything she wasn't ready to name.

The Lakota were furious. The trail ran through what they now considered their hunting ground, ground they had taken from the Crow and did not intend to share with anyone. They raided the wagon trains, and when the Army sent soldiers to protect them, they raided the soldiers too. The forts went up along the trail. Fort Reno, Fort Phil Kearny, Fort C.F. Smith, each one sitting on the plain like a declaration.

Fort C.F. Smith sat in the Bighorn Valley.

In Crow country.

Daxpitcheehísshish looked at it for a long time, the first time he saw it.

He said nothing.

Neither did Ashkáale, standing beside him.

But she felt the particular cold of a thing that cannot be undone. The fort was there. It would stay there. Whatever came next, the ground under it was no longer simply Crow ground. It was something more complicated than that, something that didn't have a clean name, which was how most of the changes came, without clean names, without the courtesy of announcing themselves as the permanent things they were.

* * *

Declan came back to the camp in the spring of 1865.

Not for anything he needed. He had the coat, the moccasins. He came with hides to trade, which was reason enough, which was the reason he gave himself.

He rode in on Joker with the mule behind him and the Sharps in the Cheyenne sheath and the Colt at his hip and the flat gray eyes moving across the camp how they always moved across everything, reading, filing, registering threat and non-threat and the geometry of the space and the people in it.

He tied Joker at the trader's post.

He found Whistling Crow.

He didn't find Ashkáale.

She was there. He knew she was there the same way he knew where every person in a room was without looking directly at them. Some peripheral awareness that he had stopped trying to explain to himself. She was near the horse pickets, working, her back to him.

Don't, he thought.

He traded his hides.

He resupplied.

He checked the mule's packs and prepared to leave.

She came past him on her way somewhere else entirely. She didn't slow. She didn't look at him. She came within ten feet of him and kept walking and said, without turning her head, without breaking stride:

"Your hides are getting smaller. The animals are smaller now."

Then she was past him and gone around the edge of a lodge and out of sight.

He stood there.

She's right, he thought. *They are smaller.*

He mounted Joker.

Rode out.

* * *

Iichíilee was shelling dried corn at the edge of the lodge when Ashkáale came back.

She sat down. Picked up a cob. Started working on it without speaking.

Iichíilee shelled her corn.

After a while, she said, without looking up: "He watched you go."

Ashkáale's hands did not stop.

"He watches everything," she said.

"Not the way he watched you."

Ashkáale set the cob down. Picked up another one.

The mountains stood behind them, the same as they had always stood. The plain stretched ahead. The smoke from the Army fort in the valley drifted north in a thin pale line.

He is one of them, she thought. *He is exactly one of them. Every hide he takes is one less reason for us to be here. Every season he hunts is a season closer to the end of everything this place has ever been.*

I know what he is.

"Work your corn," she said.

Iichíilee worked her corn.

* * *

That winter, Daxpitcheehísshish sent four young men to ride with the soldiers.

Scouts. Information on the Lakota movements. Eyes on the trails.

He stood outside his lodge and watched them ride out in the cold morning air, their breath rising white, the soldiers moving alongside them easy and unhurried. Four young men who had been boys in this camp not long ago, who had learned to ride and shoot and read the land as their fathers had taught them, riding now in a direction that felt different from the directions men had ridden before.

Ashkáale stood beside her father.

She said nothing.

He said nothing.

The scouts moved south along the Bighorn, and the mountains rose behind them white and permanent against the winter sky, and the camp watched them go in the particular silence of people who understood that some departures were different from others and didn't yet know exactly how.

"It is the right decision," Daxpitcheehísshish said quietly.

Ashkáale looked at the empty ground where the riders had been.

"I know," she said.

She went back inside.

22

The Hundred Slain

The Lakota called it the Battle of the Hundred Slain before the whites had finished burying their dead.

The story reached the Bighorn camp in pieces, as stories traveled on the winter plains, rider to rider, fire to fire, each telling adding what the last one left out until the shape of it was clear. December 1866. Fort Phil Kearny. A captain named Fetterman had ridden out with eighty men and a certainty about himself that the Lakota had been waiting all autumn to answer. Crazy Horse and ten warriors showed themselves on the ridge, taunting, retreating, showing their backs like decoys, and Fetterman had followed them over Lodge Trail Ridge and into two thousand warriors waiting in the cold.

It was over in twenty minutes.

Eighty-one men dead. Not one left to tell it from the Army's side.

The prophecy had said one hundred soldiers would be dead at the hands of the warriors. The morning of December 21st, the medicine man Crazy Mule rode out from the camp to read the signs. He rode out and came back. Rode out again. Three times, the vision was not yet complete. On the fourth ride, he came back with his arms spread wide, miming the weight of a hundred dead soldiers lifted from the ground. The day was right.

Daxpitcheehísshish heard the story and sat with it.

He was thinking about Jim Bridger.

The old scout had been at Fort C.F. Smith that autumn. Crow riders had told him, had told him plainly, directly, in the language of men reporting fact, that they had ridden through the Lakota encampment on the Tongue River and it had taken half a day. Half a day to ride through one camp. Red Cloud was building something that had no precedent on these plains. The warriors numbered in the thousands, and they were organized, and they intended to close the Bozeman Trail and kill everyone on it.

Bridger had reported this to the Army.

The Army had said that Bridger exaggerated about Indians.

Daxpitcheehísshish looked at the fire.

His people had done their part. His people had put their eyes on the ground and reported what those eyes had seen. The Army had decided they knew better.

Eighty-one men dead in twenty minutes.

* * *

Ashkáale heard the story from her father that night.

She sat across the fire from him and listened to the whole of it. The warning, the dismissal, the decoy, the ridge, the twenty minutes. When he was done, she sat with it.

"They didn't listen," she said.

"No."

"The Crow told them, and they didn't listen."

"No."

She looked at the fire.

They will never listen, she thought. *Not to us. Not to anyone who looks like us, speaks like us, or knows what we know. They will ride over the ridge every time because they cannot imagine that we might understand something they don't.*

She didn't say it. It wasn't a new thought. It was just sharper now.

"What does this mean for us?" she said.

Her father picked up a stick and turned it slowly in the fire.

"It means Red Cloud is stronger than the Army thought," he said. "And it means the Army will send more soldiers." He looked at the burning end of the stick. "More soldiers means more forts. More forts means more of this." He gestured, a small motion that took in the camp, the mountains, the plain beyond. All of it. The whole of what was left.

Ashkáale worked her sinew.

Outside, the winter camp settled into the night. Dogs. Low voices. The cold coming down off the mountains with its particular authority.

"And our scouts," she said. "The men who ride with the Army. Are they safe?"

"For now," her father said.

"For now," she said.

* * *

The next two years ground on, slow and relentless, each season leaving less than the last.

Red Cloud pressed the Army hard along the trail. The forts were under constant siege, the wood-cutting parties attacked, and the supply trains were picked apart on the open ground between the posts. The Crow scouts at Fort C.F. Smith moved in and out of danger as men moved in and out of dangerous work, carefully, with the knowledge that careful was not the same as safe.

Ashkáale knew two of the men riding with the soldiers by name.

She had known them since they were boys. She didn't ask about them when the riders came back. She watched their faces when they came in, counted heads, and went back to her work.

Both came back.

Not everyone did.

* * *

Declan was on the Powder River range when the Fetterman news reached him.

He heard it at a rough trading post two days south of the Tongue. Hunters talking, the story already garbled by distance and retelling, the number of dead varying wildly depending on who was telling it. He filed what was confirmed. Eighty men. All dead. Army taking it badly.

He drank his coffee.

Looked at the plain through the trading post's single window.

The herd had been thin this season. He'd ridden further than the previous year to find it, taken less when he did, and come back with a load that would have embarrassed him in 1855. The range was changing. Not gone, not yet, but different. Quieter. The ground that had shaken under sixty million animals now shook under fewer each year, and the silence between the herds was growing.

He filed this, too.

The Army trouble was north of his range. The Lakota raids were mostly north. The Bozeman Trail ran east of where he worked. None of it was his business, and he had no stake in any of it. He made it a point not to acquire stakes in things that weren't his business.

But the range is getting smaller, he thought, *and it is getting smaller in the direction of the trouble.*

He paid for his coffee.

Rode out.

* * *

The treaty came in the spring of 1868.

It came after Red Cloud had won. Thoroughly, undeniably, in a way the Army couldn't paper over. The Bozeman Trail forts were abandoned. The soldiers walked out, and the Lakota burned them before the smoke from the chimneys had cleared. Red Cloud signed the treaty only after the forts were gone, not before, which was the first time in anyone's memory that a Plains nation had fought the United States to a standstill and made them close their forts as the price of peace.

But the treaty that made peace with the Lakota also made a reservation for the Crow.

The commissioners came to Fort Laramie in May. Daxpitchee-hísshish rode to meet them with seven other chiefs and headmen of the Mountain Crow, the River Crow, the Kicked in the Bellies. He rode in his finest clothing, the shirt with the quillwork, the leggings his wife had made, the hawk feather at the back of his head. He rode as what he was. As what he had always been.

What he signed away was thirty million acres.

Thirty million acres of the territory that the 1851 treaty had guaranteed to the Crow. The Powder River country. The Tongue River country. The eastern range where the buffalo had run in numbers that were already becoming memory. All of it ceded to the United States government, which would, in turn, recognize it as hunting ground for the Lakota, the very people who had been taking it from the Crow by force for twenty years. The government was now making official what the Lakota had taken by conquest, and the Crow were signing the paper.

What he kept was a reservation in the heart of the old territory. South of the Yellowstone. The Bighorn country. The mountains. And this was the thing he had held out for, the thing the commissioners had finally agreed to after two days of negotiation, the right to hunt on the ceded lands as long as those lands remained unoccupied by settlement.

It wasn't nothing.

It wasn't enough.

He made his mark on the paper.

* * *

Ashkáale stood at the edge of the camp when he came back.

She had not gone to Fort Laramie. Women did not ride to treaty negotiations. She had stayed with the camp, worked her hides, and helped Iichíilee with the curing, and said nothing about where her father had gone or what he had gone to do.

She had known what he had gone to do.

She watched him ride in. His face told her what the paper said. Not in its particulars, she would learn those later, but in its shape. The face of a man who has done the necessary thing and is carrying the weight of it.

He dismounted.

She didn't go to him. He would eat first, rest, and then they would talk. That was the way of it.

Iichíilee came and stood beside her, a grown woman now.

"What did he give them?" the girl said.

Ashkáale watched her father walk toward his lodge.

"The Powder River," she said. "The Tongue. Everything east of here." She paused. "He kept the mountains. He kept the hunting rights on the land he gave away, as long as no white men settle it."

Iichíilee was quiet.

"Will white men settle it?" she said.

Ashkáale watched her father disappear through the lodge flap.

"Yes," she said.

* * *

Later, at the fire, Daxpitcheehísshish told her what he had kept.

She listened. She asked her questions carefully, as she asked all her questions, not to challenge, but to understand completely.

"The hunting rights," she said. "You got that in writing."

"I got it in writing," he said.

"And you trust their writing."

He looked at the fire.

"I trust it as much as I trust the writing from 1851," he said. "Which guaranteed us the Powder River." He let that sit. "But it is in writing. And it is more than we would have without it."

She worked her sinew.

"You did what you could," she said.

"Yes."

"It won't be enough."

"No," he said. "Probably not."

The fire moved between them.

Thirty million acres, she thought. *The Powder River. The Tongue. The ground where the buffalo still run, where the grass is still thick, where our people have hunted since before any name we have for time. Gone. Signed away to the United States government so they can give it to the Lakota who took it from us by force. And we have kept the mountains and a promise about hunting rights that will last exactly as long as the Americans find it convenient.*

And somewhere on that ground right now, Declan Shea is hunting what is left of the buffalo that used to belong to this world.

She said none of this.

She went back to work.

* * *

Three weeks after her father returned from Fort Laramie, Declan rode into the camp.

Hides to trade. Same as always. The Sharps in its Cheyenne sheath, the Colt at his hip, Joker moving under him with the long-suffering resignation of a horse that had accepted its situation.

Ashkáale saw him come in from where she was working near the picket line. She turned her back before he reached Whistling Crow's lodge.

She worked.

She was aware of him in the camp, as she always was. Some peripheral register, she had stopped trying to explain or argue with. She knew when he moved, where he was, when he stopped. She knew when he finished his trading and walked toward Joker.

She did not look up.

She heard him mount. Heard Joker's hooves as he turned toward the camp's edge.

Then the hooves stopped.

She did not look up.

After a moment, the hooves started again, moving away, and she listened to them fade into the distance, and the plain swallowed the sound the way it swallowed everything.

Iichíilee was beside her.

She hadn't heard the girl come.

"He stopped," Iichíilee said. "Before he rode out. He stopped his horse and looked this direction for a moment."

Ashkáale's tool moved across the hide.

"Then he left," she said.

"Then he left."

Ashkáale worked.

The mountains stood behind her. The plain stretched ahead. The reservation boundary was somewhere out there now, drawn on a paper she hadn't signed, marking the edge of what was left.

She worked the hide.

She did not look up again.

23

Closer

The buffalo were moving west.

Not all at once. Not in the dramatic way the old men described the great migrations of their youth, the ground shaking for two days, the sky darkening with dust. Just west. Season by season, the herds pulling toward the mountains the way water pulled toward low ground, following something Declan couldn't name but could read in the grass and the tracks and the particular silence of ranges that had been full the previous year and weren't full now.

He followed them.

Which meant he followed them into Crow country.

The trading post sat at the base of the Bighorn foothills, a low building of rough timber and mud mortar that smelled of hides and tobacco and the particular sourness of men who'd been out too long. It had been there perhaps five years, long enough to have worn grooves in the ground where the horses tied, long enough for the trader to know which men were worth extending credit to and which weren't. Declan was neither. He paid cash and asked for nothing extra, and the trader left him alone, which was the arrangement Declan preferred with most people.

The Crow camp was a quarter mile east, pitched in the bend of a creek where the grass was good and the water ran clear. They came here in the trading seasons, the camp and the post existing in the proximity of people who needed each other, didn't entirely trust each other, and had worked out an arrangement that served both without requiring either to pretend otherwise.

Declan came to the post.

Ashkáale was in the camp.

Four times a year, more or less. That was how it worked out.

In the spring of 1869, she stayed.

She had told herself she would go to her brother's lodge when she heard Joker's hooves on the hardpan. She didn't go. She stayed where she was near the creek bank, working a length of rawhide, and when the sound of him in the trading post reached her, the low exchange with the trader, the particular way Joker moved when he was tied and unhappy about it. She kept working, said nothing, and didn't look up.

He came out of the post and walked toward Joker, and stopped.

She felt it without looking. The stopping. The particular quality of stillness that meant he was aware of her just as she was aware of him.

She looked up.

He was looking at her.

Not the weather look. Not the filing look. Something she didn't have a clean name for. Something that lasted three seconds, then he looked away, untied Joker, mounted, and rode out without looking back.

She looked back down at her rawhide.

Iichíilee was sitting ten feet away, working her own piece, and had seen all of it.

Neither of them said anything.

* * *

In the autumn of 1869, Iichíilee spoke to him.

Ashkáale heard it from inside the lodge where she was helping her father eat. Daxpitcheehísshish had been moving slowly since the summer, the old injuries in his hip making themselves known as old injuries do. Not dramatically, just steadily, the body presenting its accounting. He ate less than he used to. He sat longer at the fire.

She heard her niece's voice outside, in trade language, asking something she couldn't quite make out. Then Declan's voice, low and flat, answering.

She kept her attention on her father.

He was watching her face.

"Go," he said.

"I'm eating with you."

"You've finished eating." He looked at his own bowl. "Go listen to what she's asking him."

She went out.

Iichíilee was standing near the post's hitching rail, looking up at Declan on Joker with the particular directness she'd had since she was a girl. She had asked him about the Sharps rifle, how far it shot, and how long to reload. Practical questions. Hunter's questions. The kind a young woman asked when she had grown up watching men work the range and had decided she wanted to understand it.

Declan was answering. Briefly. Without performance. The rifle shot clean to three hundred yards in good conditions. Reloading took fifteen seconds if your hands were cold, less if they weren't.

Iichíilee nodded. Asked something else.

Ashkáale stood at the edge of the camp and listened.

She didn't join them. But she didn't go back inside either.

When Declan finally looked up and saw her standing there his face did the thing it did, the filing, the registering, and then he looked back at Iichíilee and finished answering her question and touched his heels to Joker and rode out.

Ashkáale watched him go.

Iichíilee came and stood beside her.

"He knows a great deal about rifles," she said.

"Go help your uncle's wife," Ashkáale said.

Iichíilee went.

* * *

The summer of 1871, and it started with a horse.

The Crow camp had been pitched at the post for two weeks, trading furs and dried meat for ammunition and cloth, and the particular items the camp needed going into the summer hunt. Declan had come in from the range three days prior and was camped a short ride south, coming to the post each morning to resupply and sell his hides.

The white hunter's name didn't matter. He'd been out six weeks, and he was tired, and his horse had strayed or been stolen four days back, and he'd been nursing a grudge about it ever since. He came into the post on foot, which did nothing for his mood. He came out of the post and saw a Crow man leading a pony toward the camp. The pony had a mark on its face, and the hunter's eyes went straight to that mark. His mouth went ahead of his judgment.

"That's my horse," he said.

The Crow man stopped. He was young, twenty, twenty-two, with the particular bearing of a man who had earned his standing and wasn't accustomed to having it challenged in front of his people.

"It is not your horse," he said. His English was careful and flat.

"The hell it isn't. Look at that mark on its face."

"This is my horse," the Crow man said. "I have had this horse three years."

The hunter took a step toward him. "I want a closer look at that animal."

The Crow man's hand moved. Not to a weapon. Just moved. The involuntary adjustment of a man whose body had decided something before his mind had finished the thought.

Declan was sitting on the post's step with his coffee. He had been watching since the hunter came out of the door. He watched as he watched everything, reading it, filing it, deciding.

He didn't move. This was none of his business.

Ashkáale came out of the camp.

She walked straight to the two men, put herself between them, and looked at the pony's face. She turned back to the hunter.

"Your horse," she said in trade language. "What mark did it have?"

The hunter barely glanced at her. "Star. Right here." He touched his own forehead. "Full star. And that's a star on that animal's face, and that animal is mine."

"This is a crescent," Ashkáale said. "Small. Off-center. Not a star."

"Lady, I know my own horse."

He took another step toward the Crow man. The Crow man held his ground. His jaw was set, and his eyes had gone to that particular flat place that meant the next step was going to cost somebody something.

"I said I want a closer look—"

Declan stood up.

That was all. He rose from the step with his coffee still in his hand, unhurried, and he was simply standing now where he had been sitting, and both men felt the change in the air before they turned to look at him. When they did look, the hunter saw the flat gray eyes moving from him to the Crow man and back again, with the calm assessment of a man who had already decided how this would go and was waiting to see if anyone wanted to find out.

The hunter's next step didn't happen.

He stood very still.

The post trader had come to the door. A few Crow men from the camp had drifted over. The geometry of the moment had shifted entirely, and the hunter could feel every part of it.

He looked at the pony's marking. He looked at it how a man looked at something when he needed a reason to do what he'd already decided to do.

The crescent was obvious now.

"Could be a mistake," he said. To nobody in particular.

"Could be," the trader said from the doorway.

The hunter walked away. Not fast. Not slow. The walk of a man preserving what dignity the situation had left him.

The Crow man watched him go. Then he looked at Declan, a long, level look that said he had seen what Declan had done and understood it. Then he led his pony back toward the camp.

Ashkáale turned.

She saw Declan standing at the step. She thought she had handled it. She had pointed out the marking, and the hunter had looked and backed down, and that was the end of it.

She almost said something to him.

She didn't.

She walked back toward the camp.

Declan watched her go. Then he set his coffee down on the step and took up Joker's reins and swung up into the saddle and sat there a moment looking at nothing in particular.

Then he rode out.

* * *

Late summer of 1872.

Daxpitcheehísshish did not ride to the trading post that season. His hip had become something more than an inconvenience, something that kept him at the fire in the mornings longer than it used to, that made Ashkáale watch him when he stood with an attention she tried not to make obvious. He was not dying. Not yet. But the plains had a way of taking things incrementally, and she had started to understand that her father was one of the things the plains were taking.

She came to the post herself for the trading. Three pack horses with furs. A list of what the camp needed in her head: ammunition, cloth, two good knives, and salt.

Declan was there.

She had known he would be there. The range brought him here the same way it brought her. Neither of them had arranged it. It had just become the geography of their lives.

She traded her furs. Got what the camp needed. Tied the packs onto the horses and led them toward the camp.

He fell into step beside her.

Not beside her exactly. A few feet to her right, leading Joker, moving in the same direction at the same pace. Neither of them had decided this. It had just happened.

They walked in silence for a while.

Then he said, in trade language, halting, the words chosen carefully. Words chosen in a language when a man didn't have enough of them: "Your father. He is well."

Not a question. The careful phrasing of a man who suspected the answer and was giving her a way to answer it or not.

She looked ahead at the camp.

"He is older," she said.

He nodded.

They walked.

"The herd," she said after a while. "You find it still."

"Further than before," he said. "Smaller than before."

She looked at the mountains.

"Yes," she said.

That was all. Four exchanges in trade language, none of them saying what either of them meant, all of them meaning something neither of them was ready to say. The camp was fifty yards ahead. She would turn toward it, and he would turn toward his own camp to the south, and that would be the end of it.

She stopped at the camp's edge.

He stopped too. Joker shifted, ears forward, looking at something in the middle distance.

She looked at him then. Directly. Not the weather look. Not the filing look. The look of a woman who has been watching a man for fifteen years and has run out of reasons to pretend she hasn't.

He looked back.

Three seconds. Four.

"Heávohe," she said. Just his name. The Cheyenne word for what he was. She had never said it directly to him before.

Something moved in his face. Just slightly. Something that didn't have a name in any language either of them spoke.

He mounted and touched his heels to Joker.

Rode south.

She watched him go.

Iichíilee was at the camp's edge behind her. She had watched all of it, the walk from the post, the four exchanges, the stopping, the look, the name. She had watched her aunt's face and Declan's face and the thing that had passed between them that neither of them would acknowledge.

She was smiling.

Not broadly. Just at the corners. The smile of a young woman who has been watching something for a long time and has finally seen it become what she knew it was going to be.

Ashkáale turned and saw it.

"Work your hides," she said.
Iichíilee's smile didn't go anywhere.
She went to work her hides.

24

Gold From The Grass Roots

The survey column came through in the summer of 1873, and it was not a thing you could miss.

Declan saw it from the range, a dark line moving along the north side of the Yellowstone, visible from three miles out, the dust rising in a column that hung in the still summer air for hours after the thing itself had passed. He sat Joker on a low rise and watched it move. Counted what he could count from that distance. Wagons. Soldiers. More wagons. Civilians in numbers that didn't belong out here. Men with equipment he couldn't identify from this distance, men who moved differently from soldiers and hunters, men who stopped and looked at the ground and made notes and moved on.

Surveyors.

He knew what surveyors did. He'd seen them in Ohio, in Illinois, moving ahead of the settlers, as scouts moved ahead of an army. They measured the ground. They drew the lines. They decided what the ground was worth, to whom, and what could be done with it.

He watched the column for a while.

He touched his heels to Joker, and the horse moved off the rise at his own pace, which was slower than it used to be. Declan noted it the way he noted everything. Filed it. Rode back to the range and went to work.

Change coming, he thought. *Adjust when it arrives.*

* * *

Ashkáale and her father watched it from the ridge above the Bighorn.

Daxpitcheehísshish sat his horse with the careful stillness of a man managing pain, the hip that had been taking things from him incrementally for three years now, the mornings that started slow, the rides that ended earlier than they used to. He had come to the ridge because he needed to see it himself. He would not send others to look at a thing this important and take their word for it.

He looked at the column for a long time.

Two hundred and seventy-five wagons. More soldiers than the Crow camp had people. Civilians moving through a former Crow hunting ground, the way water moved through a channel, as if the channel had always been there and had always been theirs.

Ashkáale sat her horse beside him and said nothing.

The column moved west along the Yellowstone. Slow and enormous and indifferent to what it was moving through. The surveyors stopped periodically, clustered around their instruments, made their measurements, and moved on. The soldiers flanked them with the bored efficiency of men doing a job they'd done before.

"They are measuring the ground," Daxpitcheehísshish said.

"Yes," Ashkáale said.

"When men measure ground," he said, "they have already decided it belongs to them."

He turned his horse and rode back toward camp.

She stayed a moment longer.

The column moved on until the dust was all that was left of it, hanging pale and still in the afternoon air above the Yellowstone. Then the air cleared, and the river ran on, and the ground was the same ground it had been before the column came through it.

But it wasn't.

She knew it wasn't.

She rode back to camp.

* * *

The Panic came in the autumn of 1873.

Declan heard about it at the trading post. Something had gone wrong in the eastern financial markets, banks failing, the railroad money drying up, men in New York losing fortunes in an afternoon. He listened to the hunters and traders talk about it with the attention he brought to things that might affect his work.

The railroad construction stopped.

He filed this as: *the surveyors will be back. The railroad will be back. The money runs out, and then it comes back, and when it comes back, it brings more men than before.*

He went back to work.

The range was smaller than it had been the previous year. He rode further for less. He filed this, too.

* * *

The news about the Black Hills came in the autumn of 1874.

It reached the trading post as all news reached the trading post, in pieces, from different directions, each piece slightly different from the last, the shape of the thing emerging gradually from the accumulation of accounts. A cavalry column had gone into the hills that summer. A lieutenant colonel named Custer. A thousand soldiers, journalists, a brass band on white horses. They had gone in looking for a place to build a fort and came out talking about gold.

Gold from the grass roots, Custer had written to the newspapers.

Gold from the grass roots.

Declan sat at the trading post's rough table with his coffee and listened to the men talk about it. He watched their faces, reading them, filing what he read. The way the eyes went when the word gold was spoken. The particular quality of attention that settled over a room when men heard something that made them forget whatever they'd been thinking about a moment before.

He knew that look.

He had seen it his whole life, wearing different clothes.

It was the look of men who had decided they wanted something and were calculating how to get it. The look of men who had found a reason, gold, destiny, progress, God's plan, whatever word made the wanting sound like something other than wanting, and were getting ready to move.

He had seen what came after that look.

In the Five Points, when men decided what was in a room was worth taking. On the ship crossing the Atlantic, a man looked at Maeve too long. In the trading posts and saloons and card games across twenty years of moving west, the look was always the same, and what came after it was always the same.

Someone would lose something.

Someone always lost something when men looked like that.

He thought about Maeve's brush. The bone handle. How she had carried it across an ocean in her hand, not tucked away, not put somewhere safe, just in her hand, like letting go of it meant letting go of the last of what their mother had been. Whoever had taken it from her hadn't needed it. They had just wanted it and had taken it because they could.

That was all this was.

Men who wanted what was in those hills and had found the word that made the wanting sound like destiny.

He finished his coffee.

Set the cup down.

Rode out.

* * *

The news reached the Crow camp through a scout who had ridden with the Army that summer. A young man named Plenty Strikes who had been east and come back with the particular quietness of someone who had seen something he was still working out how to say.

He told it at the fire.

The hills were Lakota land by treaty. The soldiers had gone in anyway. They had found gold, or said they had found gold, or the newspapers had said they had found gold, the scout was not entirely certain of the difference. What he was certain of was the newspapers. He had seen them in the fort. Seen the men reading them. Seen the look on the faces of the men reading them.

He described the look.

Ashkáale was working near the edge of the fire's light, not sitting in the council, not invited to sit in the council. She worked her rawhide and listened.

Iichíilee was beside her.

The scout finished his account. The men talked. Her father sat at its center, the stillness of a man who has already understood the thing being discussed and is waiting for the others to catch up.

Ashkáale worked.

The Lakota will fight, she thought. *They have no choice. And when the Lakota fight, the Army will come in force, and when the Army comes in*

force, everything changes again. Everything always changes again.
  And the buffalo.
  She didn't finish the thought.
  She worked her rawhide.
  Iichíilee watched her face. Said nothing.

* * *

The prospectors started coming through in the spring.
  Not the Army. Not surveyors. Just men. Ones and twos and small groups, moving east through the Bighorn country on their way toward the hills, riding with the particular urgency of men who had heard something and were afraid someone else would get there first.
  They moved through the Crow hunting ground without stopping. Without asking. Without appearing to register that the ground they were crossing belonged to anyone.
  Ashkáale watched them from the camp's edge one morning.
  A group of six, moving fast, their pack animals loaded heavily. They didn't look toward the camp. They didn't look at anything except the direction they were going.
  She watched them until they were gone.
  Iichíilee came and stood beside her.
  The plain stretched out ahead, the Bighorns rising behind them, the sky enormous above it all. The same as it had always been. The same ground her father's father had hunted. The same ground that the treaties said was theirs.
  "How many will come?" Iichíilee said.
  Ashkáale watched the empty ground where the six men had been.
  "All of them," she said.
  She went back to work.

* * *

That evening, Declan came to the trading post.

He had been on the range for two weeks and came in with a load of hides that was smaller than the load from two weeks before, which had been smaller than the load from the week before that. He sold them without comment, resupplied, and sat with his coffee.

The trader mentioned the prospectors moving through.

"Saw some," Declan said.

"More every week," the trader said. "Government says stay out, but they're not staying out."

Declan drank his coffee.

"Bad for business," the trader said. "Men moving through aren't men stopping to trade."

Declan set his cup down.

He was thinking about the range. About the herd moving further west, further north, pushed by the pressure of men moving through from every direction now. Hunters, soldiers, surveyors, prospectors, all of them taking something or disturbing something or simply passing through in numbers that the land hadn't been asked to absorb before.

The silence between the herds was growing.

Rode back to his camp.

The plain was quiet around him. The stars came out over the Bighorns, and the night was cold and clean and still. Joker moved beneath him, steady enough, though the night cold had gotten into the old horse's joints, and Declan could feel it in how he carried himself. Something careful in it, something that hadn't been there ten years ago. Twenty-five years was a long time for a horse. A long time for anything out here.

Adjust when it arrives, he had told himself a year ago, watching the survey column move along the Yellowstone.

It had arrived.

He wasn't sure yet what the adjustment was.

25

What Goes Unsaid

The northern herd was dying.

Not quickly. Not all at once. But the mathematics of it were past arguing with now, and Declan had stopped arguing with them. He rode further each season and found less and came back with loads that would have shamed him ten years ago. The southern herd was already gone, finished, stripped, the plains south of the Arkansas as quiet as a room after everyone has left it. The hunters had moved north, and the northern herd was absorbing the pressure as a man absorbed blows, standing through the first ones, the second ones, beginning to buckle somewhere around the third or fourth.

He'd been counting.

This was the fourth year of the northern herd taking what the southern herd had already taken, and the count was wrong in a way that wasn't going to get better.

He rode into the Crow camp in October of 1875 with Joker moving slowly beneath him and a load of hides that wasn't worth the weeks it had taken to accumulate them. He had come to the trading post first. Sold the hides. Resupplied. Then he'd looked at Joker in the thin autumn light and made a decision he hadn't planned to make.

The horse needed rest. Real rest. Not the overnight kind, but the kind that took days, good grass, water, and the particular relief of not being asked to do anything for a while.

The camp's creek was good. The grass along it was the best within three days' ride.

He rode into the camp, tied Joker at the picket line, unsaddled him, stood back, and looked at the horse for a moment.

Twenty-six years old. The broad chest was still there, the opinions still there, but something in the way he stood had changed. Something careful. Something that hadn't been there when he'd looked into Declan's eyes in Gruber's paddock and decided not to argue.

Declan put his hand on the horse's neck.

Joker's ear flicked back. Then forward.

Declan took his hand away and went to find somewhere to sit.

* * *

Ashkáale saw him come in.

She was at the fire outside her father's lodge, working a piece of elk hide, when she heard Joker's particular footfall on the hardpan. She kept working. She heard him unsaddle. Heard the particular silence that meant he was looking at the horse as she sometimes looked at her father, taking inventory of what time was doing.

She kept working.

After a while, she heard him settle somewhere across the camp, and the camp went back to its ordinary sounds.

She worked the hide.

She was aware of him; she was always aware of him, some peripheral register she had stopped trying to argue with years ago. She knew where he was in the camp without looking. She knew when he moved, when he was still, when he was watching her, and when he was watching something else.

He was watching her.

She kept working.

* * *

Daxpitcheehísshish came out of the lodge in the late afternoon.

He moved slowly now. The hip had taken the summer badly, and the autumn wasn't giving it back. He walked to the picket line with the careful deliberateness of a man who had made a negotiation with pain and was keeping his end of it. He stopped at the picket line and looked at the horses there, and his eyes found Joker.

He stood in front of the horse for a moment.

Joker looked at him.

The old chief reached into his coat and produced an apple. Wizened, small, the last of the autumn stores, and held it out on his palm. Joker looked at it. Looked at the man. Took the apple with the careful delicacy of a horse who had strong opinions about most things and had decided this was not one of them.

Daxpitcheehísshish began to talk.

Not loudly. Just the low, even murmur of a man saying something that needed to be said to someone who would listen without judgment. What he said, Declan couldn't hear from across the camp and wouldn't have understood fully if he could. The old man's hand moved to the horse's neck, and Joker stood for it. He stood still, ears forward, with the expression of a horse that had found something he recognized.

Declan watched this from where he sat.

He didn't move. Didn't speak. Just watched the old chief and the old horse in the late afternoon light and filed what he saw in a place he didn't have a label for yet.

* * *

Ashkáale brought him food that evening.

Not brought, set down near him, without ceremony, without looking at him directly, on her way to somewhere else. A piece of roasted meat and some dried berries in a small bowl. She set it down and kept moving.

He looked at it.

Looked at her back as she walked away.

He ate.

Later, she came back and sat near the fire, not far from where he was. Not beside him. Near him. The distance was still there, but smaller than it had been. She had her work with her, a length of sinew she was pulling through her fingers to soften it, and she worked without looking at him, and he sat without looking at her, and the fire moved between them.

After a while, he said, in Crow: "The herd. Where did you find it last?"

His Crow was not perfect. It had the particular roughness of a language learned without a teacher, learned from years of listening and necessity, and the slow accumulation of words that mattered. But it was real. It said what he meant.

She looked at him. Something crossed her face, not surprise exactly. More like the acknowledgment of something she had suspected.

"North of the Tongue," she said. In English. Clear and flat and deliberate. "Two weeks ago. A small band. Maybe three hundred animals."

He nodded.

"I found four hundred south of here in September," he said. "Further west than I've ever had to go."

"Yes," she said. "They are going west. Into the mountains." She paused. "There is nowhere further to go after the mountains."

They sat with that.

The fire popped. Somewhere in the camp, a child was being put to sleep, a woman's voice low and rhythmic in the dark.

"The southern herd," she said. "It is gone."

"Yes."

"Completely."

"Yes."

She pulled the sinew through her fingers.

"How long for the northern herd?" she said. It wasn't quite a question.

He looked at the fire.

"Five years," he said. "Maybe less."

She nodded once. The nod of a woman receiving information she had already calculated and was having confirmed.

"And then what will you do?" she said.

He was quiet for a moment.

"Find something else," he said.

She looked at him then. Directly. The way she had looked at him the previous summer at the camp's edge when she had said his name for the first time.

"There is not always something else," she said.

He held her gaze.

"No," he said. "Not always."

* * *

Iichíilee came and sat with them after a while, quiet and unobtrusive, taking up her own work near the fire. She had learned years ago how to be present without disrupting, and she deployed this skill now with the practiced ease of someone who had been perfecting it since childhood.

They talked.

Not about the buffalo anymore. About other things, the camp, the coming winter, the Army patrol that had come through two weeks prior. Declan's Crow filled in where his English didn't reach, and Ashkáale's English filled in where her Crow didn't say quite what she meant, and Iichíilee stepped into the gaps occasionally, a word here, a phrase there, with the lightness of someone performing a task so natural it barely registered as effort.

At some point, Declan said: "Iichíilee. She is a grown woman now."

Ashkáale glanced at her niece.

"Yes," she said.

"She should have a man," Declan said. "Someone to help take care of her. Every woman deserves that."

Iichíilee went very still beside her aunt.

She was looking at her work. Not at Ashkáale. Not at Declan. Just at her work.

Ashkáale said nothing.

The sinew moved through her fingers. The fire moved. The night sounds of the camp moved around them. Everything moved except Ashkáale's answer to what Declan had said.

Declan looked at her.

She did not look up.

He looked across the camp to where Joker stood at the picket line in the dark, the old horse a pale shape in the firelight, and Daxpitcheehísshish was no longer there, but the apple was gone, and Joker was standing easy in a way he hadn't stood in a long time.

After a while, Declan said he would sleep and stood and went to his bedroll.

Ashkáale worked her sinew.

Iichíilee worked beside her.

* * *

He left in the morning.

He saddled Joker slowly, checking everything twice as he had started doing, not from doubt but from the particular care that had crept into how he handled the horse over the last year. Joker stood for it with his ears back, but not pinned. Resigned rather than resistant.

Ashkáale was at the creek with the morning's water when he rode out.

He looked back once.

She was looking at him.

Neither of them did anything with that. He turned and rode south, and the camp sounds faded behind him, and the plain opened up, and Joker moved beneath him at the careful pace that was his pace now.

* * *

Iichíilee found her aunt at the fire an hour later.

She sat down. Picked up her work. Said nothing for a while, as she had learned from watching Ashkáale, letting the silence do what it needed to do before the words came.

Then: "Why didn't you tell him?"

Ashkáale kept working.

"Tell him what?" she said.

"That you don't need a man to take care of you." Iichíilee watched her aunt's hands move over the hide. "You have never needed that. You would have said so. To anyone else, you would have said so."

The fire moved between them.

Ashkáale pulled the sinew through her fingers.

"Why didn't you?" Iichíilee said.

Ashkáale was quiet for a long moment. The camp moved around

them. The mountains stood behind them. The plain stretched ahead toward where Declan had gone, already invisible, already swallowed by the distance.

"Because he is right," she said.

Iichíilee looked at her aunt.

Ashkáale went back to work.

Iichíilee said nothing.

She picked up her own piece and worked beside her aunt in the quiet of the morning, and the fire burned down between them, and neither of them spoke again for a long time.

26

1872

The stand lasted four hours.

Declan had found the herd the evening before, a group of maybe three hundred animals, a small group by the standards of what the range had been when he first rode out in 1849, a reasonable group by the standards of what it was becoming. He'd made his camp downwind, a mile back, and waited for the morning light.

He was in position before dawn.

The Sharps was loaded. The rest of the ammunition laid out in the order he'd use it, not because he needed the reminder, he'd done this enough times that his hands knew the sequence without instruction, but because order was how you kept the stand from becoming chaos. Order was how you kept the animals from running before you were done with them.

The herd was in a shallow bowl below the rise where he lay. The wind was right. The light was coming up slow and gray from the east.

He picked the lead cow.

Always the lead cow. John had taught him that, without knowing he was teaching it, as you watched a thing and let it tell you where the decision was. In a herd the lead cow was the decision. Drop her, and the herd stood confused, milling, looking for direction that wasn't coming. Move to the next animal before the first one has finished falling. Keep moving. Don't let them run.

He settled the Sharps.

Breathed out.

The lead cow dropped.

He was already moving to the next animal.

He worked methodically, how he worked everything. No hurry. No drama. The Sharps spoke, and an animal went down, and he moved to the next one, and the Sharps spoke again. The herd milled. Stepped around the fallen. Lowed with a low sound that carried across the bowl and meant nothing to them yet, not danger, not flight, just confusion. Just the herd waiting for someone to tell it which way to go.

Nobody told it which way to go.

He took thirty-seven animals before the herd finally broke and ran.

He lay on the rise and watched them go. The thunder of them diminishing. The dust rising. The bowl going quiet except for the ravens that were already gathering, appearing from nowhere as ravens did, as if they had been waiting just beyond the visible world for exactly this.

Thirty-seven animals.

Four hours.

He stood. Began the walk down into the bowl.

Behind him, to the north, east, and south, the plains went on. And on every part of those plains that he could not see, in every direction, other men were lying on other rises with other rifles, working other herds with the same methodical patience, the same order, the same arithmetic.

He knew this.

He went to work on the hides.

Whistling Crow sat his horse on the ridge above the Powder River and looked at what the morning had become.

He had ridden out before dawn. Not for any purpose; he was past the purposes that once lifted him from his robes before the light. Just to look. Just to be on the ridge as he had been all his life, reading the country in the manner the country demanded.

What the country was telling him this morning, he did not want to hear.

He counted the smoke columns.

One to the north, maybe four miles. One northeast, further. Two to the east, close enough together that they might have been one camp or might have been two. One due south, low and gray against the pale sky, the particular smoke of a fire that had been burning since before dawn and had settled into itself.

Five camps.

All of them hunters.

He sat his horse and looked at the smoke and thought about what five camps meant in terms of men and rifles and hides and the particular mathematics of what a good hunter with a Sharps could do in a morning.

He had watched them come in since the treaty. The year after, a few. Then more. Then more than that. Each season, the camps on the horizon multiplied, the fires visible at night in directions where there had been no fires before. Each season, the herd came through smaller than the last, moving faster, the animals thinner, as if they too were reading the country and understanding something about it that the men doing the killing had not yet understood.

He thought about his father.

His father had stood on this same ridge. Not this exact ridge, the Powder River country had been Lakota ground in his father's time, and a Crow man on this ridge then would have been a dead man. A ridge like it, in the country to the west that was still Crow country, still Crow in the way that meant something. His father had stood on a ridge and watched the buffalo come through for three days. Three days of animals moving south, the ground shaking, the dust rising into the sky like weather, the sound of them something you felt in your chest before you heard it with your ears.

Three days.

His father had said, *You cannot count them. You can only stand with them and understand that you are small and they are not.*

Whistling Crow looked at the smoke columns on the horizon.

He thought about the sound his father had described.

He listened.

The plains were not quiet. The wind moved through the grass. A hawk called somewhere to the south. Somewhere, far off, the direction of the nearest smoke, the flat report of a large rifle carried across the distance.

Then again.

Then again.

He sat his horse for a long time.

Then he turned and rode back toward the camp.

He did not look at the smoke columns as he went.

There was nothing useful to be gained from looking at them.

Granger kept his ledger as he kept everything, precisely, without sentiment, with the understanding that numbers were the only honest language and that everything else was conversation.

He had been at the trading post on the Powder River for six years. He had come out from St. Louis with a contract from the hide company and a head for figures and no particular feelings about the plains one way or another. The plains were where the hides were. The hides were what the eastern factories needed. The factories made leather belts, boots, machine straps for the mills that were running day and night back east, the industrial appetite for leather apparently without limit. Granger's job was to sit at the post and buy what the hunters brought in and ship it east on the wagons that came through every three weeks.

He was good at his job.

He opened the ledger to the current page. September, 1872. The season was at its peak. The hunters, who'd been out since April, were coming in now with their final loads before the weather turned, the wagons running east as fast as Granger could fill them.

He ran his finger down the column.

Harmon. 340 hides. $1.25 each. $425.

Burke and his crew. 1,240 hides. $1.10 for the bull hides, $.90 for the cows. $1,240 roughly, he'd do the precise figure later.

Three men whose names he hadn't caught, just passing through from further north. 280 hides between them. Rough work, the hides not properly fleshed, he'd docked them accordingly.

The Irishman. Shea. 312 hides, good clean work, full price. $390.

He added the column.

The number was large. It had been large all season. It had been larger than the season before, which had been larger than the season before that. Each year, Granger sent more hides east, and each year the company sent word that demand was still growing, keep buying, the factories couldn't get enough.

He closed the ledger.

Outside the trading post, a wagon was being loaded. Two of his men, stacking hides in the bed, working fast, the bales dense and heavy, the smell of them something you stopped noticing after the first week and never noticed again. The wagon would go east tomorrow. Join the other wagons on the trail east. Join the railroad at the nearest point and ride the cars to the processing facilities in St. Louis, Detroit, and Philadelphia, where other men with other ledgers would receive them and add their own columns.

He thought sometimes about the end of it.

Not the moral end. He wasn't a man given to moral thinking about his work, the same way a millwright didn't think about the moral implications of grinding grain. He thought about the practical end. The supply end. There were a finite number of animals on the plains and an apparently infinite appetite for their hides, and at some point those two things were going to meet each other, and that was going to be a problem for the company and for his livelihood and for the hunters who depended on the trade.

He didn't know when that would be.

He looked at the column of numbers in his ledger.

He supposed it would be a while yet.

He went back to work.

The plain did not know what was happening to it.

That was the thing. The grass grew as it always had. The creek ran the same as it had always run, cold and clear over its stones, indifferent to the season and the decade and the century and everything that had happened on its banks since the first thing happened on its banks. The sky came up every morning the same as it had always come up, moving through its colors in the same order, indifferent to what moved beneath it.

The ravens knew.

They had been following the hunters since the hunters arrived. Moving with them across the range, as they had once moved with the wolves, opportunists, readers of the country, students of the gap between a thing living and a thing not living. They went where the dying was. There had always been dying on the plains. There had never been dying like this.

They now moved in flocks, where they had moved in pairs before.

They had learned that the sound of the Sharps meant food. They gathered at the sound of it before the animal had finished falling, appearing from the empty sky the way ravens appeared, as if the killing itself had summoned them.

The wolves knew too.

They had been following the herds since before anything on the plains could remember. Moving at the edges. Taking the old, the weak, the ones that wouldn't have made it through the winter anyway. The wolves were part of the arithmetic of the plains, as old as the grass, as certain as the creek, as permanent as the sky.

They were moving differently now.

Not at the edges of the herds. At the edges of the hunters' camps. At the carcasses left in the hunters' wakes. The skinned bodies lying open in the sun, the meat going to waste in quantities the wolves couldn't process, more food than they had evolved to understand. They ate until they couldn't eat, and the carcasses kept coming, and there was no framework in the wolf's understanding of the world for what was happening to the world.

The grass grew.

The creek ran.

The sky came up every morning.

And across the plains in every direction, from the Powder River to the Yellowstone to the Republican and the Arkansas, the rifles spoke their flat certain language all day long, and the ravens moved toward the sound, and the hides went east on wagons and then on railcars, and the numbers in Granger's ledger grew, and Whistling Crow sat on his ridge and counted smoke columns, and Declan Shea walked through the bowl below his stand and began the work of adding thirty-seven hides to the season's total.

And underneath all of it, underneath the rifles and the ravens and the wagons and the ledgers and the smoke on the horizon, something was happening to the plains that the plains had no word for.

Something that had never needed a word before.

Because it had never happened before.

27

The Greasy Grass

Declan heard it before he understood what he was hearing.

He was three miles north of the Little Bighorn River, working a shallow draw where the grass was still good, and the herd had been two days ago. The sound came from the south and east, not thunder, the sky was clear, something lower than thunder and more sustained, the particular quality of a sound that meant men in numbers doing what men in numbers did.

He stopped working.

Joker's ears went forward.

Declan sat on a low rise and looked south and saw nothing but grass and sky and the particular shimmer of a June afternoon on the Montana plain. The sound went on for a while. Then it stopped. Then it started again differently, more scattered, less organized, the sound of something concluding rather than something beginning.

Then it stopped entirely.

He sat for a long time after it stopped.

Something large, he thought. *Something that doesn't turn around.*

He didn't ride toward it. That had never been his way. You didn't ride toward large sounds unless you had a reason, and his reason for being in this country was the herd, and the herd was north of him, not south.

He rode back to his camp.

* * *

The ravens told him part of it.

By the following morning, they were visible from three miles. The particular circling pattern of birds that had found something significant, dozens of them, the kind of number that meant the ground below had more on it than any single animal could account for. He watched them from his camp without moving toward them.

He was breaking camp when the scouts came through.

Four of them. Crow. Riding hard from the south with the particular urgency of men who had been somewhere and needed to be somewhere else as fast as the horses under them could manage. They came up the draw at a run, and Declan stepped back from Joker and let them pass and watched their faces as they went.

He knew one of them. Had seen him at the trading post on the Bighorn. A young man, Goes Ahead, who had the quiet competence of someone who had been doing difficult work since he was old enough to be trusted with it. Goes Ahead had ridden with the Army. Had ridden with Custer.

He looked at Goes Ahead's face as he passed.

He had seen men's faces after bad fights. Had seen what bad fights left in a man's eyes when the fight was over, and the accounting began. Goes Ahead's face had that in it, the particular flatness that came after something that couldn't be unfiled, that sat in a man permanently from the moment it happened forward.

The four riders went north without stopping.

Declan watched them go.

He stood in the quiet of the morning, with the ravens circling to the south, the grass moving in the wind, and the particular silence of a plain that had just absorbed something large and was settling back around it.

Everything changes now, he thought.

He didn't know exactly what had happened. He would learn the specifics later, at the trading post, in pieces, how he always learned things. Two hundred and sixty-eight soldiers were dead. Custer and five companies of the Seventh Cavalry were wiped out to a man in less than an hour. The largest gathering of plains warriors anyone had ever seen, waiting in the valley of the Greasy Grass, where the Lakota and the Cheyenne and the Arapaho had come together under Sitting Bull and Crazy Horse and done what the Army had spent ten years insisting couldn't be done.

What he knew now, watching the ravens, watching the dust of the four riders settle north, was enough.

The Army would come back from this harder than it had come back from anything.

And the range would get smaller faster than he'd planned for.

He mounted Joker.

Rode north.

* * *

The news reached the Crow camp three days later.

Not from the scouts. Goes Ahead and the others had gone directly to the Army post, their report belonging first to the men who had sent them. It reached the camp how everything reached the camp, rider to rider, fire to fire, each telling adding what the last had left out.

Ashkáale heard it from Iichíilee, who had heard it from a young man who had ridden in from the east with his face doing something faces did when they were carrying something too large for them.

She set down her work.

She sat with it as her father had taught her to sit with difficult things. Not immediately, not performing composure, but actually sitting with it, letting the shape of it declare itself before she tried to understand what it meant.

Two hundred and sixty-eight soldiers are dead.

Custer dead.

The six Crow scouts who had ridden with him, alive, most of them, having been sent back before the final charge, having watched what they could not stop from a ridge a mile and a half away. They had warned him. She knew this without being told because it was the pattern, the same pattern that went back to Bridger at Fort C.F. Smith, back to Fetterman, back through every warning the Crow had ever given the Army that the Army had decided it knew better than to heed.

They had warned him.

He had not listened.

And now two hundred and sixty-eight men were dead on Crow land. Her people's reservation, the ground the 1868 treaty had kept for them, the valley of the Little Bighorn where the Lakota had come without consent and the Cheyenne had come without consent, and the battle had been fought without anyone asking the Crow what they thought about any of it.

She picked her work back up.

Her hands were steady.

* * *

Her father received the news at the fire outside his lodge.

He was very old now. The hip had taken the summer and the summer before, and each winter returned him slightly less than it had found him. He sat at the fire in the mornings and the evenings and moved between them carefully, with the particular economy of a man who had made his peace with what his body could still do and had stopped arguing with what it couldn't.

He listened to the account without interrupting.

When it was done, he sat for a long time looking at the fire.

The men who had brought the news waited. They were young, and they were frightened in the particular way of young men who had seen the shape of something large and couldn't yet see all of its edges. They waited for the old chief to tell them what it meant.

He looked at the fire.

"The Lakota won the battle," he said finally. "The Americans will win the war."

He said nothing else.

After a while, he went inside.

****

Ashkáale found him there later, sitting in the dim of the lodge with his hands in his lap, looking at nothing in particular.

She sat beside him.

She didn't speak immediately. Neither did he. Outside the camp moved with its ordinary sounds, children, horses, women at their work, the sounds of a people going on with the business of living regardless of what the world was doing around them. It was what you did. You went on.

"The scouts," she said. "They came back."

"Yes," he said.

"They warned him."

"Yes."

She looked at her hands.

"He didn't listen," she said.

"No."

The fire between them was small, just enough for the evening chill. The lodge was warm and close and smelled of the hides, and the smoke, and the particular smell of a life lived in one place long enough for the place to take on the smell of the life.

"What happens now?" she said.

Her father was quiet for a moment.

"The Army comes back with everything it has," he said. "It has been embarrassed, and it does not forgive embarrassment." He shifted slightly, the hip making its presence known. "The Lakota and the Cheyenne will be pushed onto reservations. All of them. Whatever is left of the buffalo will go with them." He paused. "And we will still be here."

"Because we chose correctly," she said. Not proudly. Just stating it.

"Because we chose to survive," he said. "Whether we chose correctly —" He stopped. "I do not know how to answer that question. I am not sure it has an answer."

She sat with that.

Outside, a child was laughing at something. The particular uncomplicated laughter of a child who didn't know yet what the adults around her were carrying.

"The scouts," Ashkáale said. "Goes Ahead. The others. They put on their warrior clothes before it started."

Her father looked at her.

"They were told to leave," she said. "But they put on their warrior clothes first. They took off the Army uniforms and put on their own clothes." She paused. "They wanted to die as Crow if they died."

Her father was quiet for a moment.

"Yes," he said. "I heard this."

"They didn't die."

"No."

She looked at the small fire.

"I think about that," she said. "What it means to put on your own clothes when you think you are going to die. To say, whatever happens, I am this. Not what they made me wear. This."

Her father looked at her for a long moment.

"Yes," he said quietly. "I think about that too."

* * *

Iichíilee found her aunt at the creek that evening, washing the day's work from her hands in the cold water.

She sat on the bank beside her and said nothing for a while.

Then: "Plenty Strikes came back today. He was with the column on the Rosebud, not the Little Bighorn. He is not hurt."

Ashkáale looked at the water moving over her hands.

"Good," she said.

"He said the soldiers are angry," Iichíilee said. "Not sad. Angry. He said there is a difference in how they carry it."

"There is," Ashkáale said.

"He said more soldiers are coming. Many more."

"Yes."

Iichíilee looked at the mountains going dark against the evening sky.

"Heávohe," she said. "Have you heard from him?"

Ashkáale took her hands from the water. Dried them on her dress.

"He was north of here," she said. "Working the range."

"He would have heard it."

"Yes."

"Is he all right?"

Ashkáale looked at the creek running cold and clear over its stones, the same as it had always run, indifferent to what the world was doing on its banks.

"Declan Shea," she said, "has been all right through things that would have finished most men." She stood. "He will be all right through this."

She walked back toward the camp.

Iichíilee sat on the bank a moment longer, looking at the water.

Then she followed her aunt.

* * *

Three weeks later, Declan came to the trading post.

He sold what he had. Resupplied. Sat with his coffee and listened to the men talk about what had happened and what was coming. The Army was already moving. Sheridan had been given everything he asked for. The Lakota and the Cheyenne would be pushed onto reservations before winter. The hunting grounds, the unceded territory, the Powder River country, all of it, would be opened.

He listened.

He thought about Goes Ahead's face in the draw that morning. The thing that had been in it that Declan didn't have a category for. He had one now. He had seen it before and hadn't recognized it at the time, but he recognized it now.

It was the face of a man who had done everything right and watched it go wrong anyway. Who had read the ground correctly and reported what he saw and been ignored and then been sent back to watch from a ridge while the thing he had tried to prevent happened below him.

He knew that feeling.

Not from war. From the range. From the seasons of reading the herd correctly and watching it diminish anyway. From the years of understanding exactly what was happening and having no means of stopping it.

He drank his coffee.

Outside, a group of prospectors was moving east. Then two soldiers riding west. Then a wagon he didn't recognize carrying equipment he couldn't identify.

Traffic. More of it every season. The plains filling up with the particular noise of people who had decided the land was available.

He set his cup down.

Rode north toward the Crow camp.

He didn't examine why.

* * *

Ashkáale was at the fire when he rode in.

She looked up when she heard Joker. The old horse moving at his careful pace, Declan sitting him as he had always sat him, easy, upright, the flat gray eyes already reading the camp.

He dismounted.

He walked to the fire and sat across from her without being invited and without apologizing for not being invited, which was the way he had always done things.

She looked at him.

His face had the thing in it she had seen in the returning scouts' faces. Not the same, nothing in Declan's face was ever quite what you expected, but related to it. The thing that came after watching something you couldn't stop.

She didn't say anything.

He didn't either.

The fire moved between them.

After a while, he said, in Crow: "Your father."

She looked at the fire.

"He is the same," she said. "Older every morning."

He nodded.

They sat.

The camp sounds moved around them. The evening coming down off the mountains with its cold. The horses at the picket line, shifting and settling.

"The scouts," he said. "Goes Ahead. The others. They came back."

"Yes," she said.

"I saw their faces."

She looked at him then.

He was looking at the fire. His jaw set as it did when he was carrying something he hadn't decided what to do with yet.

"They put on their own clothes," she said. "Before it started. They took off the Army uniforms."

He looked at her.

"They wanted to die as themselves," she said. "If they died."

Something moved in his face. Just slightly. The thing that moved when she said something that found a place in him, he didn't know was there.

"They didn't die," he said.

"No," she said. "They didn't."

The fire between them burned down slowly in the cooling evening air and neither of them moved to add wood and neither of them left and the dark came down over the camp and the mountains and the plain and all of it went on as it always went on, indifferent and permanent and entirely unconcerned with the people sitting beside the fire trying to find the words for what they were living through.

28

The Silence Between The Ridges

The Army finished its work in the winter of 1876-77.

Not quietly. Not cleanly. But finished. The Lakota and the Cheyenne pushed onto reservations, their camps burned, their horses taken, the leaders who had held out the longest were brought in cold and hungry and without options. Crazy Horse surrendered in May of 1877 and was dead by September, killed at Fort Robinson under circumstances that were never fully explained and never needed to be. Sitting Bull took his people into Canada and held out for four more years before hunger brought him back.

The Powder River country opened.

That was what Declan noticed. Not the surrender. Not the politics. The opening. The range that had been contested ground for twenty years, Crow against Lakota, Lakota against Army, Army against everyone, was suddenly, almost overnight, available. The hunters came in by the hundreds. Then the thousands. Men Declan had never seen before working ranges, he had worked alone for thirty years, their camps visible from ridges that used to be empty, their fires burning all night, as fires burned when men didn't care who saw them.

He worked around them.

He came in with less each season.

In the spring of 1877, he came to the Crow camp for the last time with Joker under him.

The horse was twenty-eight years old. He moved at his own pace now, careful, deliberate, the opinions still present but quieter, as if the effort of expressing them had become more than the satisfaction was worth. Declan had been checking him over more carefully each morning, running his hands along the legs and flanks with the attention of a man reading something he wasn't sure he wanted to finish reading.

The camp was smaller than it had been.

Daxpitcheehísshish was at the fire outside his lodge. He was always at the fire now, the lodge too warm in the mornings, the open air the thing that kept him present in the world. He sat with his hands in his lap and his eyes on the middle distance and the particular stillness of a man who had stopped measuring time in seasons and had started measuring it in days.

Ashkáale was working nearby. She looked up when Declan rode in. Their eyes met the way they met now. Directly, without the weather look, without the filing. Just two people who had stopped pretending they weren't looking.

He tied the mule at the picket line.

He unsaddled Joker slowly, running his hands along the horse's back as the saddle came off. Joker stood for it with his eyes half closed, leaning slightly into the pressure of Declan's hands. The old horse's ribs were visible in the spring light in a way they hadn't been two years ago.

Declan set the saddle on the mule's back. Cinched it. Transferred his kit, the Sharps, the saddlebags, the bedroll, from where it had always lived behind Joker's saddle to behind the mule's. The mule stood for this with the long-suffering resignation of an animal that had made its peace with its situation years ago.

Then Declan stood with Joker's lead rope in his hand and looked at the horse for a moment.

Joker looked back.

Declan walked him across the camp to where Daxpitcheehísshish sat at the fire.

The old chief looked up. He looked at Joker first, the long assessment of a man who had been reading horses his whole life and could read this one plainly. Then he looked at Declan.

Declan held out the lead rope.

Daxpitcheehísshish took it.

He looked at the horse again. Joker lowered his head slightly, and the old man put his hand on the horse's nose and held it there. Joker stood absolutely still, his eyes soft, his breathing slow and even.

"He is a good horse," Daxpitcheehísshish said.

Declan looked at the old chief. At the face that had been reading the plains for eighty years. At the hands that had signed papers and led war parties and built fires and held children and done everything a man's hands did across a long life on hard ground.

"You are a good chief," Declan said. "He was always more than that. But he's done with the range."

Daxpitcheehísshish looked at the horse.

"I am done with the range, too," he said.

They stood with that for a moment. The fire between them. The camp around them. The mountains behind it all, permanent and indifferent and entirely unconcerned with the moment passing at their feet.

Then Daxpitcheehísshish turned and said something to Ashkáale in Crow. Something short, something that carried the quality of an instruction and a blessing simultaneously. She looked at her father. Then at Declan. Then she went back to her work.

Declan walked back to the mule.

He swung up into the saddle.

The mule moved out of the camp at the mule's pace, which was not Joker's pace and never would be.

He didn't look back.

Ashkáale watched him ride out.

She had seen the whole of it, the unsaddling, the transfer of the kit, the walk across the camp. She had seen her father's hand on the horse's nose and the horse going still under it. She had heard the four short sentences that passed between the two men.

He was always more than that. But he's done with the range.

I am done with the range, too.

She worked her hide.

She understood what had just crossed the camp. Not just the horse. The thirty years behind the horse. The boy from County Clare who had come west on a flatboat up the Missouri in 1849 and learned to ride from a German liveryman and spent three decades becoming something the plains required. Hard and patient and cold and capable of things most men couldn't do. All of that had lived in the horse as much as in the man. Joker was the last witness. And Declan had given the last witness to her father to keep until neither of them needed keeping anymore.

She kept working.

Iichíilee sat beside her and said nothing.

Daxpitcheehísshish died in December of 1877.

Not suddenly. How he had done everything, with the particular economy of a man who had finished his accounting. He spent the last weeks at the fire in the mornings and in the lodge in the evenings, and he talked to whoever came and sat with him, which was everyone, and he said the things that needed to be said and left unsaid the things that didn't need saying.

To Ashkáale, he said: *Hold what is left. The reservation is what we kept. It is not enough. Hold it anyway.*

She held his hand and said nothing because there was nothing adequate to say, and he would have known that better than anyone.

He died in the night, quietly, in the manner of men who have decided about it.

Joker died three days later.

The horse was found at the picket line in the early morning, lying on his side in the frost, his eyes open, his expression no different from the expression he had carried through every morning of his twenty-eight years. The particular look of a horse that had opinions about the world and had expressed most of them, and was done now. He had eaten his hay. He had drunk his water. He had simply lain down at some point in the night and not gotten up again.

Ashkáale sat with him for a while, as she had sat with her father.

Then she went back to work.

Declan heard about both of them at the trading post.

A Crow man he knew by sight mentioned it in passing, the old chief in December, and the horse a few days after. Just information. The kind of thing that moved between camps and posts and fires, as all information moved on the plains, without ceremony, delivered to whoever it found.

Declan was sitting with his coffee.

He heard it.

He finished his coffee.

Went outside and stood in the cold for a moment, looking at the Bighorns.

Twenty-eight years, he thought. *Since Gruber's paddock. Since the dead grass along the fence.*

He didn't think anything else about it.

He went back inside, paid for his supplies, loaded the mule, and rode north toward the range.

1878, 1879, 1880.

Each year, the same pattern, the variation only in the numbers, further to ride, less to find, smaller loads coming back to the trading post. He adapted as he always had, adjusting his range, his expectations, filing the changes as they came, and working with what was left.

What was left kept getting smaller.

The Northern Pacific Railroad reached Miles City in 1881, and Declan saw the first train from a ridge six miles north of the tracks. Just a black line of smoke moving east across the plain with a sound he had heard described but not heard, the particular shriek of a thing that didn't belong to the landscape it was moving through. He watched it until it was gone.

Then he looked at the range around him.

The hunters had come in behind the railroad, as hunters always came in behind anything that made the work easier. Hundreds of them now. Camps visible in every direction, the smell of hides and woodsmoke, and the particular smell of a slaughter in numbers. The sweet rot of meat left to the plains because the hides were the thing, and the meat was nothing.

He worked around them.

He came in with a third of what he'd expected.

Ashkáale saw him regularly now.

Not just at the trading post. At the camp. He came to the camp, sat by the fire, and they talked. Iichíilee sat nearby doing her work without pretending she wasn't listening because there was nothing left to pretend about. He had been coming to this fire for years. He knew which log she sat on, and she knew where he put his hat. Iichíilee knew both of these things and had stopped remarking on them.

They talked about the range. About the reservation, the boundaries, the pressure from the government to reduce them further, the way the world kept finding new ways to take what had already been taken. They talked about Iichíilee, who now had a man. He was a young Crow warrior named after his father's horse, steady and capable, the kind of man who showed what he was through the quality of his work rather than the volume of his words. Declan had met him once and filed him under: *good enough.*

They talked about Ireland sometimes.

She asked questions, and he answered them. The island, the ocean, the cottage, the cold. The language that sounded like water over stones and meant things English couldn't quite reach. She told him about her mother, who had died when Iichíilee was small, who had been the one who taught Ashkáale to work hide how she worked it, who had told stories how stories needed to be told, not to explain but to carry.

Like Bíawacheeitchish, Ashkáale said once.

Like your mother, Declan said.

She looked at him.

He was looking at the fire.

She went back to her work.

He went out in the fall of 1883 as he had gone out every fall for thirty-four years.

The mule packed with supplies. The Sharps in its Cheyenne sheath. The Colt at his hip. The same kit in the same configuration he had been carrying since Fort Laramie in 1853, when he'd walked out with Bill's rifle and his own and headed north toward the range.

He rode two weeks north and west.

He found bones.

Not fresh, months old, some of them a year, the skulls bleached white in the autumn light, the bones scattered across the grass by wolves and weather. He rode further and found more bones. Then carcasses too old to have any smell left in them, just the dried hide and the collapsed ribs and the particular way an animal looked when everything useful had been taken from it and the rest left for whatever the plains sent next.

He rode further.

The silence was wrong.

He had known the silence of ranges between herds. The quiet that meant the animals had moved on, were somewhere to the north or south, would be findable if he rode far enough in the right direction. This was different. This was not the silence of something that had moved. This was the silence of something that wasn't there anymore.

He rode for another week.

He found a small band on the third day of the second week. Eleven animals, a bull, and some cows, moving slowly and separately from each other, how animals moved when there were not enough of them to move together. He sat on a low rise and looked at them.

Eleven animals.

He didn't raise the Sharps.

He sat for a long time.

The bull looked up at him once. The old flat eyes, the massive head, the breath rising white in the cold air. The same animal that had shaken the ground under sixty million feet in 1849 when he'd stood at the Powder River for the first time and understood what millions meant.

Eleven.

He turned the mule and rode back.

He came into the trading post with nothing.

No hides. No meat. Just the mule and his kit and the Sharps in its sheath and the particular expression of a man who has done the arithmetic and found the answer.

The trader looked at the empty mule.

"Nothing out there," Declan said.

The trader nodded. He had seen a dozen men come in the same way in the past two weeks. He poured coffee without being asked.

Declan sat with it.

Around him, the post had the particular quality of a place that had been built for a purpose that no longer existed. The hide racks empty. The scale unused. A few hunters at the far table were talking in the low voices of men discussing what came next, which was a conversation nobody had a good answer to.

He drank his coffee.

He thought about 1849. The Powder River. The smell of them coming over the ridge before you could see them, filling the air completely, the way the falls at Niagara had filled the air with mist. Joker trembling beneath him. The ground shaking. Two hours for the herd to pass.

He thought about Bill. The bottle tucked under his arm.

He thought about the Cheyenne sheath on his saddle, which was on the mule's saddle now, which was not the same thing but was what he had.

He set his cup down.

Rode to the Crow camp.

Ashkáale was at the fire.

She looked up when she heard the mule. She watched him dismount, tie the mule, walk to the fire, and sit across from her. She read his face as she had learned to read it over twenty-five years. Not what it showed but what it didn't show, the particular quality of the flatness when something had happened that he was processing.

She waited.

"The herd is gone," he said.

She looked at the fire.

She had known it was coming. Had been watching it come for years. Had watched the numbers in his loads getting smaller each season, had watched him ride further for less, had understood the mathematics of it long before he was ready to state them. But hearing him say it, the flat declarative weight of it, no drama, just the fact, was different from knowing it.

The fire moved between them.

"What will you do?" she said.

He looked at her.

The fire. The mountains going dark behind the camp. The plain stretching south toward where the range had been and wasn't anymore. Iichíilee somewhere nearby, very still, not pretending anything.

He looked at Ashkáale, and she looked back, and the thing that had been true for ten years and that both of them knew was true sat in the air between them in the particular way of things that are waiting to be said.

"I don't know yet," he said.

She looked at him for a moment longer.

Then the corners of her mouth moved. Just slightly. The smallest possible smile, the first he had ever seen on her face, the one she had been keeping back for years.

She went back to her work.

He rode back to his camp and lay on his back and looked at the stars over the Bighorns and didn't sleep for a long time.

I don't know yet, he had said.

But I know where I'll be while I'm figuring it out.

He didn't say that part.

He didn't have to.

29

Always Ashkáale

It was Iichíilee's idea.

She said it casually, as she said things she had thought about carefully, as if the thought had just arrived, as if she hadn't been watching them both for years and understanding what they needed better than either of them did.

"Take the ponies out," she said. "My uncle's ponies. The evening is good."

Ashkáale looked at her niece.

"I have work," she said.

"The work will be here," Iichíilee said. "The evening won't."

Declan was at the fire. He said nothing. He had learned years ago that the conversations between these two women operated on a frequency he could hear but not fully read, and that the wisest response to most of them was to wait and see what they produced.

What they produced, after a moment's silence in which Ashkáale looked at her work and then at the mountains and then at something that wasn't either of those things, was Ashkáale standing and setting her work down.

"Two horses," she said to Iichíilee.

"Already asked," Iichíilee said. "My uncle said yes."

The ponies were at the picket line. A gray and a roan, both good animals, the roan with the particular quality of attention in his eyes that meant he had opinions and intended to share them.

Ashkáale went straight to the roan.

"The gray is calmer," Declan said.

"Yes," she said. She was already checking the roan's feet, running her hand along his neck, reading him how she read everything, directly, without performance.

"He's going to give you trouble."

She looked up at him. That look. The one that had stopped being the weather look years ago and had become something else, something warmer, something that had his name in it even when she wasn't saying his name.

"I am the better rider," she said. Simply. As a fact.

He looked at the roan.

He looked at her.

"Yes," he said. "You are."

She swung up onto the roan without difficulty, settling him with her legs and her hands and something else. The particular authority of a woman who had been riding since she could walk and had never once been uncertain about it. The roan shifted, tested, found what he was dealing with, and went still.

Declan mounted the gray.

They rode west toward the mountains.

The light was going off the Bighorns as October came in, not quickly but completely, the peaks going from gold to orange to a particular deep rose that had no equivalent anywhere Declan had ever been. The plain below the mountains went purple in the shadow. The grass caught the last of it and held it briefly, each stem lit separately, the whole range glowing from the ground up.

They rode without talking for a while.

This was something they had learned over the years, that silence between them was not absence but presence, that it carried as much as the words did and sometimes more. Iichíilee had once said, not quite to either of them, that watching them sit together without speaking was like watching two rivers run alongside each other. He had filed that. He still had it.

"Tell me something about Ireland," Ashkáale said.

He thought about it.

"The light is different," he said. "It comes in low. Off the water. Everything is green from it." He paused. "Nothing like this."

"Better or worse."

"Different," he said. "Just different."

She looked at the mountains.

"I have never seen the ocean," she said.

"It's loud," he said. "Like the falls at Niagara, it doesn't stop. Ever. Day and night."

"Like the wind here."

He looked at the plain around them. The grass moving in long slow waves in the evening air.

"Yes," he said. "Like the wind here."

They rode.

The roan moved easily under her now, the early testing gone, the animal having made his assessment and decided she was worth carrying well. Declan watched her from the corner of his eye, the straight back, the easy hands, as she moved with the horse rather than against it. He had been watching her for twenty-five years, and he was still not done watching her.

Tell her, he thought.

He didn't.

He had not told her in the willow draw in 1849 when he cut the rawhide from her wrists and pointed west. He had not told her across a hundred fires in twenty-five years. He had not told her when she said *because he was right*, and Iichíilee had carried it back to him like a gift he hadn't known how to open. He had not told her when the herd was gone, and she smiled for the first time, and he lay awake all night thinking about what he meant by *I don't know yet.*

He had not told her.

He rode beside her in the last light of an October evening on the Crow reservation, and he did not tell her.

The roan stumbled on the uneven ground near the creek bed.

Not a bad stumble, the kind that happened on broken ground in failing light, the front foot finding the edge of a cut in the earth that wasn't visible until the foot was already in it. The roan went down on one knee and lurched sideways trying to recover. Ashkáale came off cleanly, like a good rider came off, not fighting it, just releasing, her body understanding before her mind did that the ground was coming.

She hit the creek bank.

The sound was wrong.

Declan was off the gray before the roan had finished recovering. He was on his knees beside her before the echo of it had cleared.

She was on her back. Her eyes were open. She looked at him with an expression he had never seen on her face before. Not pain, not fear, something quieter than either. The particular look of a person who has just understood something and is deciding whether to say it.

"Ashkáale."

"I'm here," she said.

Her voice was right. He ran his hands along her arms, her legs, checking her as he checked Joker, systematically, looking for what was wrong. Her arms were fine. Her legs were fine. He got to the back of her head. His hand came away dark.

He didn't let her see his face change.

"Don't move," he said.

"I know," she said.

He carefully put his hand under her head. She winced once and then was still. He felt the warmth of it spreading against his palm. He looked at the creek bank where she had landed and saw the rock there. Not large, just there, the way rocks were just there, the way bad luck was just there, without intention, without malice, simply present in the wrong place at the wrong moment.

She was looking at the mountains.

The last of the light was on them. Gold and rose, the particular deep blue of the sky above them going to dark.

"It's beautiful," she said.

"Yes," he said.

He was still holding her head. The warmth spreading. He didn't look at his hand.

Tell her, he thought.

He opened his mouth.

Nothing came out.

Twenty-five years of almost. Twenty-five years of the words sitting at the back of his throat like something he had swallowed wrong and never been able to clear. He looked at her face in the last light. The jaw set as it had always been set, the eyes direct as they had always been direct, the particular quality of her that had been catching him off guard since 1849, when he watched her argue a trader into a tin pot and a pouch of tobacco and walk away without looking back.

He couldn't say it.

He had never been able to say it.

She looked at him.

"Declan," she said.

He looked at her.

"Thank you," she said.

He shook his head. He didn't understand. He had not done enough. He had never done enough. He had come and gone for twenty-five years and never said the thing and never made the offer. Whatever accounting she was doing in her head was wrong; the numbers were wrong, and she was crediting him for things he hadn't done.

"I haven't—" he started.

"You did what you knew how to do," she said. "Every time." She paused. Her breathing had changed slightly. Shallower. "The willows. The Lakota. The horse. The fires." A pause. "You came back. You always came back."

He was still holding her head. The rock. The last light on the mountains.

"I should have—"

"Yes," she said. "You should have." And she smiled. The smile. The one from 1883 at the fire, the one he had been carrying ever since. "So should I."

She looked at the mountains.

"I love you, Declan Shea," she said. Simply. As a fact. The way she said everything.

He looked at her face.

He still couldn't say it.

But she knew. She had always known. That was the thing about Ashkáale: she had always known everything he couldn't say and had waited twenty-five years for him to find the words and had finally decided to say her part without waiting for his.

"I know," she said, reading his face as she had always read it. "I know."

Her eyes stayed on the mountains.

The light finished going off the peaks.

The stars came out over the Bighorns the way they always came out, all at once, enormous, indifferent, the same stars that had been there before any of this and would be there after.

Her breathing slowed.

Then stopped.

The blood was warm in his palm.

He sat with her.

He didn't move for a long time. He held her head in his lap, looked at her face in the starlight, and said nothing because there was nothing left to say and no one to say it to. The plain was quiet around him. The horses stood nearby. The mountains were dark.

She is gone, he thought.

That was all. Just that. The flattest, most final thought he had ever had. The thought that contained everything and explained nothing.

He kissed her gently on her forehead.

He sat with her until the cold came down off the mountains.

Then he gathered her up.

She weighed almost nothing. He had not known that. He had never held her before, not like this, not completely, and she weighed almost nothing. That fact hit him somewhere. Hit him in a place he hadn't used for 25 years. He stood with it for a moment before he could move.

He carried her to his horse.

He mounted with her across the saddle in front of him, his arms around her, holding her gently as he should have held her years ago when there was still something to be held. The gray moved out steady and careful in the dark, the roan following on its own, both of them understanding without being told that this was not the time for opinions.

He rode back toward the camp.

The stars moved overhead.

The plain was dark and vast and entirely silent.

Iichíilee was at the camp's edge.

She had been watching for them. She saw him come in from the dark, one horse, two shapes, and she understood before he reached her. She had understood the moment she saw his face.

She didn't make a sound.

He dismounted, lifted Ashkáale down, carried her into the lodge, laid her on her pallet, and covered her with the blanket she had made herself the previous winter, the one with the geometric pattern she had spent three months getting right. He smoothed it over her. He sat beside her.

Iichíilee came in and sat on the other side.

The fire burned down.

Neither of them moved to add wood.

When it was almost out, he stood.

He looked at Ashkáale's face one more time.

Then he walked out of the lodge.

Iichíilee came to the entrance.

She watched him cross the dark camp to where the mule was pick-eted. She watched him check the packs, systematically, methodically, the hands that had done everything doing this one more thing. She watched him mount.

She looked at his face.

It was the face she had feared she would see. The thing that had been opening in him for twenty years, slowly, reluctantly, the way a door opened in a house that had been shut too long, was shut now. Shut completely. The flatness back in the gray eyes, the jaw set, the particular quality of stillness that meant he had decided about something and was done deciding.

He didn't look at the lodge.

He didn't look at her.

He rode out of the camp without looking back, and the night closed around him, completely, without ceremony, without the courtesy of a shape to watch until it was gone.

She stood at the lodge entrance for a long time after the sound of the mule's hooves had faded into nothing.

Then she went back inside and sat beside her aunt, added wood to the fire, and watched the light come up on the face she had been watching her whole life.

Work your hides, she heard.

Work your corn.

Because he is right.

She sat with her until morning.

He rode until the dark took him, then the dawn, then the seasons.

The year turned.

He worked.

He didn't look back.

30

Wherever The Work Is

The mule died in the Black Hills foothills on a Tuesday morning in September of 1883.

No warning. No visible decline beyond the general decline of age that Declan had been watching for two years and adjusting for, shorter days, lighter loads, the careful mornings that had replaced the indifferent ones. He'd gotten up before light to break camp and found the animal lying on its side in the grass, breathing in the shallow, rapid way of something that had already decided.

He crouched beside it.

Ran his hands along the neck and flank as he had always run his hands along animals he was trying to read. The mule's eye found him. Not frightened. Just present. The particular look of an animal that has done its work and knows it.

He sat with him for a while.

The light came up over the hills. The grass around them caught it and held it briefly, going gold in the early morning, how grass did out here, briefly, completely, then settling back into its ordinary color as the sun climbed.

He took out the Colt.

One round.

Then he sat with the mule for a while longer.

Six years, he thought. *Since Joker.*

He didn't think anything else about it.

He sorted what he could carry from what he couldn't. The Sharps and the Colt and the Cheyenne sheath and his bedroll and the saddlebags with what money he had. He left the packsaddle and most of the camp gear. The vultures would find the rest.

He shouldered what he was carrying and walked east toward the sound of the stamp mills that had been audible since the previous evening, a low mechanical thunder that didn't stop, day or night, the sound of the Black Hills being reduced to their component parts.

* * *

He'd been reading the newspapers when he found them.

Not systematically. Just when one appeared, at a trading post counter, left on a table in a railroad town saloon, passed from hand to hand among men who had nothing else to read. He read them as he read everything, taking what was useful, filing what mattered, discarding what didn't.

What mattered was the accounting.

The papers had been running the numbers for a year now. The buffalo. How many had been there, how many were left. The figures were published plainly, without apology, as if the men who had done the killing and the men who had profited from the selling and the men who had written the policy that made it all possible had simply decided that what had happened was a fact of history now and facts of history didn't require apology.

Three hundred and twenty-five animals remaining.

He read that number at a table in a Miles City saloon in the spring of 1883. He had a cup of coffee in front of him. He had mostly finished the eggs. The paper was three weeks old.

Three hundred and twenty-five.

He'd stood at the Powder River in 1849 and watched sixty million of them come over a rise and shake the ground for two hours.

He finished his coffee.

He thought about Ashkáale on the ridge above the Bighorn, watching the survey column move through former Crow land. *When men measure ground, they have already decided it belongs to them.* Her father's words, her voice. He thought about what she had said at the fire in 1875, when the herd numbers were already bad. *There is nowhere further to go after the mountains.*

She had been right about everything.

He set the paper down.

Walked out.

* * *

The papers had other things in them, too.

Crazy Horse. He had read the account of it first at a trading post on the Yellowstone in the autumn of 1877, weeks after it happened. The newspaper version was brief and certain: the great war chief had been brought in peacefully and then had attempted to escape imprisonment and had been mortally wounded in the struggle. The Army regretted the incident. The Indian question in the Powder River country was effectively resolved.

He had read this account with the flat attention he brought to things he knew were wrong.

He had heard the real version at that same trading post, from a man who had been at Fort Robinson that September. Not a soldier, a civilian contractor, the kind of man who was present everywhere the Army went and who nobody paid attention to and who therefore heard everything.

What the man said was this.

Crazy Horse had surrendered in May to protect his people from starving. He had come in peacefully with eight hundred followers and given up his weapons and his horses and settled at the Red Cloud Agency. He had tried to cooperate. He had been sworn in as an Army officer in anticipation of going to Washington to meet the President. And then in August the Army had asked him to take up arms again and help fight the Nez Perce, who were themselves running to avoid being put on a reservation, and Crazy Horse had said he would fight until not a Nez Perce was left standing, meaning he would fight as hard as he could, and the interpreter who disliked him had told the Army he had said he would fight until not a white man was left, and the Army had decided to arrest him on the basis of a translation everyone who knew the language understood was wrong.

And then, at Fort Robinson, as he was being walked toward the guardhouse, Crazy Horse had understood what was happening and had struggled, and a soldier had put a bayonet in his side.

He has killed me now, Crazy Horse had said. Those were his last words.

The Army's official journal entry said: *mortally wounded in trying to escape.*

Declan had read that phrase, set the paper down, and looked at the wall of the trading post for a moment.

Trying to escape.

He knew what trying to escape looked like. He had seen men try to escape from situations that were going to kill them. What happened to Crazy Horse at Fort Robinson was not that. What happened was a man who had surrendered in good faith being walked into a jail on the basis of a lie told by a man who didn't like him, and a soldier putting a bayonet in him when he objected.

He had filed it.

It joined everything else he had filed across thirty-five years of the plains.

The Fetterman Fight. The Crow warning that the Army ignored because Bridger exaggerated about Indians. The treaty that gave the Lakota the Crow's Powder River country and called it peace. The survey column moving along the Yellowstone. The gold in the Black Hills reported from the grassroots up. The railroad pushing through in 1881. The hide hunters flooding in behind it.

All of it filed.

All of it adding up to the same account, written in the same hand, telling the same story in the same voice: *this land is available and we have decided to take it, and the people who were here before us will have to find somewhere else to be or cease to be entirely. Either is acceptable to us.*

He didn't feel anything about it.

That wasn't in him.

He just knew what it was.

* * *

He walked into Deadwood on a Wednesday morning in October of 1883, carrying what was left of his life on his back.

The town announced itself first by smell, the stamp mills processing ore around the clock, the smell of crushed rock and mercury, and the particular industrial sharpness of a place that had decided what it was and committed to it completely. Then the noise. Then the buildings coming up out of the gulch as the road descended, frame buildings mostly, some brick now, the rough camp of 1876 having become something more permanent without quite becoming respectable.

He took a room. Ate. Slept in a bed.

In the morning, he went looking for what remained to be done.

* * *

The gold was underground now.

That was the first thing he understood about Deadwood in 1883. The Homestake mine ran twenty-four hours a day, with the stamp mills processing ore that came out of the earth in the hard-rock country around Lead. George Hearst's operation. Capital, machinery, and men working in shifts in the dark. A different kind of work entirely from the placer gold of the early days, the men with pans in the creek beds, the individual proposition of a man and his luck.

But the creek beds were still there.

And men were still working them.

Not getting rich. The ground that had been rich was picked over. But a man alone with a pan and patience could still find color in the gulches above town, could still pull enough from a good day's work to justify the next day's work and the one after that.

Declan bought a pan, a short-handled pick, and a set of rubber boots.

He went to Bullock and Star's hardware store for the rest of what he needed.

* * *

The store sat on Main Street, a real establishment, well-stocked, the kind of place that had been doing serious business since 1876 and knew the difference between what men heading into the hills needed and what they thought they needed.

Sol Star was behind the counter. A compact, efficient man with the particular economy of movement of someone who had been selling things to optimistic people for seven years and had developed a precise assessment of what any given man was going to require and what he was going to waste his money on. He looked at Declan's list and began filling it without comment.

Seth Bullock came out of the back.

Not to serve. Just present in the way of a man who owned the place and moved through it on his own schedule. He looked at Declan as he looked at everyone who came through his door. The steady assessment of a former lawman who had been reading men his whole adult life and didn't bother to dress up what he saw.

He read Declan.

Declan read him back.

A big man. Direct eyes. The particular quality of stillness that Declan had seen in a handful of men across thirty-five years. The stillness of someone who was not afraid of what came next because they had thought through most of the possibilities and made their decisions about them in advance.

"You've been out here a while," Bullock said. Not a question.

"Thirty-five years," Declan said.

Bullock nodded once.

Nothing else needed saying. Bullock went back to what he'd been doing.

Sol Star set Declan's supplies on the counter.

Declan paid. Picked up what he'd bought. Walked out into the Deadwood street.

* * *

He worked the creeks for six weeks.

Found color three times. Not enough to matter. The ground was what it was, picked over by seven years of men who'd gotten there first, the easy gold long gone, whatever remained requiring either the capital and machinery of the Homestake operation or the kind of luck that didn't come to men who had been on the wrong side of luck their whole lives.

He filed this, too.

Packed his pan and his pick.

Went back to the cards.

* * *

The Gem had the best game in Deadwood.

He knew what the Gem was. Al Swearengen had been running it since 1877, and the town knew what Swearengen was and had decided to leave him to it, the arrangement between the badlands of lower Main Street and the rest of the town as clearly drawn as any treaty line, and about as reliably honored.

He sat at the table near the wall. Facing the door. The same way he always sat.

He played four nights a week.

He won more than he lost, which was the only mathematics that mattered.

He watched Swearengen move through his establishment with the particular efficiency of a man who had built something exactly how he intended and had no illusions about what it was. A broad man. Watchful. The eyes moving over every person in the room with the flat assessment of someone calculating value and risk simultaneously.

Swearengen's eyes stopped on Declan once.

Held there for a moment.

Declan held them back.

Something passed between them that wasn't communication exactly. More like the mutual registration of two men who had both been in enough rooms to know which men in any given room were worth watching. Swearengen's eyes moved on.

Declan played his cards.

* * *

He walked back to his room from the Gem on a Wednesday night in late October.

The stamp mills ran in the distance. Low and constant. The particular thunder of the Black Hills being reduced to their component parts, running day and night without pause or apology. He had been hearing it for weeks and had stopped noticing it as you stopped noticing anything that didn't change.

He climbed the stairs.

Lay on his back on the bed.

He thought about the mule in the foothills, the eye finding him in the early light, the one round, the sitting with it after in the grass while the light came up gold and indifferent over the hills. Six years since Joker.

He thought about three hundred and twenty-five animals.

He thought about the newspaper account of Crazy Horse. *Mortally wounded in trying to escape.* He had the real version filed somewhere in him. The interpreter who twisted the words, the general who condoned the arrest and left the post before it happened, the bayonet in the side, the last words spoken to nobody in particular in the dark outside the guardhouse at Fort Robinson. *He has killed me now.*

Six years ago. Already becoming the official version in the newspapers, the version that would get told in schools and written in books and passed down as fact by men who hadn't been there and hadn't known the people who had. The gap between what the newspaper said and what Declan knew widened every year and would keep widening until the newspaper version was the only one left standing.

He looked at the ceiling.

He thought about Goes Ahead's face in the draw after Little Bighorn. About the battle, the newspapers called a massacre. Custer heroically overwhelmed, the savages victorious, and what he knew of it from the scouts and the hunters and the men who had read that ground. Custer warned twice. Custer rode in anyway. The same pride that killed Fetterman. The same certainty that the people who had been living on that land for generations didn't understand it as well as the man who had been there for three days.

* * *

He thought, just once, briefly, about a smile at the corners of a mouth that had held it back for fifteen years. About the weight in his arms that was almost nothing. About a fire burning down, and two people not moving to add wood.

The stamp mills ran.

Deadwood went on being what it was outside the window, noise and mud and the smell of ambition gone sour, indifferent to the men it chewed through.

Tomorrow, he would need a horse.

31

Deadwood

Deadwood in the fall of 1884 was the kind of place that never quite slept and never quite woke up.

He came up the main thoroughfare on a Tuesday morning, moving through the crowd the way water moved around rocks. The mule trader's animal steady under him. The Sharps in its Cheyenne sheath. The Colt at his hip. The buffalo coat worn thin at the elbows, the hide stiff with old grease and something darker.

He passed the rope corral at the edge of town.

A man was working a roan mare at the far end. A wolf-dog lay near the gate with its head on its paws, watching the street.

The dog's head came up.

Declan felt the eyes on him without looking. The particular quality of attention that wasn't aggression and wasn't welcome. Just clarity. The dog knew exactly what he was.

He stopped, looking at the horses in the corral.

Historical Appendix

**A Historical Note and Appendix Empty Ground — Book Two of
The Long Reckoning**

The events and characters of this novel are fictional, but the history
surrounding them is not. What follows is a record of that history
— the people, the nations, the events, and the forces that shaped the
world Declan Shea moved through for thirty-five years. It is offered
not as a comprehensive account but as a foundation, a record of what
was real beneath the story.

The Apsáalooke — The Crow Nation

The people called themselves Apsáalooke — Children of the Large-
Beaked Bird. French interpreters translated the name as *gens du
corbeau*, people of the crow, and the name that stuck in English was
not their own.

They were not always Plains people. In the eighteenth century,
pressure from the Saulteaux and Cree peoples, who had earlier access
to firearms through the fur trade, pushed the Apsáalooke westward
from the Ohio Eastern Woodland area. From there, they moved
further west, eventually settling in the Yellowstone River valley and
its tributaries in what is now Montana and Wyoming — the country
that would become their homeland, the country they would spend the
next century defending.

The Crow Nation is divided into four main groups: the Mountain
Crow, the River Crow, the Kicked in the Bellies, and the Beaver Dries
Its Fur. Each group occupied different parts of the territory, moving

with the seasons and the buffalo, but all understood themselves as one people with one history.

They became renowned as horsemen. Among the plains nations, the Crow were known for breeding and trading the finest horses, developing herds that were the envy of neighboring tribes. Horses were wealth, horses were status, and horses were the instrument of everything the plains life required — hunting, raiding, warfare, migration. The Crow were masters of all of it.

Their greatest enemies became the tribes of the Blackfoot Confederacy to the north and the Lakota-Cheyenne-Arapaho alliance to the east and south. Both pressed against Crow territory from different directions across the entire nineteenth century. The Crow were never a large nation — never more than a few thousand people in any given generation — and they maintained their ground through skill, through their reputation as fighters, and eventually through a strategic alliance with the United States government that was not friendship but calculation.

In 1851, the Fort Laramie Treaty recognized a large Crow territory stretching across southwestern Montana and northern Wyoming. The treaty was supposed to hold. It did not. By the late 1850s, the Lakota had begun pushing west across the Powder River — the dividing line the treaty had established between Lakota and Crow territory — and the encroachment accelerated through the 1860s. The Oglala Lakota winter count records that in five out of eight years between 1857 and 1864, it refers either to Oglala triumphs over the Crow or to Crow triumphs over the Oglala. The year 1857 is remembered specifically for a battle in which the Sioux killed ten Crow warriors. The country from the Powder River to the Yellowstone, which had been Crow country as recently as 1851, was effectively lost to the Lakota by 1860.

Facing enemies on multiple fronts and a Lakota nation that was actively displacing them from their own treaty-guaranteed hunting grounds, the Crow made a decision that has been misunderstood ever since. They allied with the United States Army.

This was not a surrender. This was not naivety. This was the calculation of a people who understood that the Lakota were the immediate existential threat, that the Army was the only force capable of checking the Lakota, and that an alliance — however uncomfortable, however unequal — offered better odds of survival than fighting everyone at once. As one Crow historian has noted, the Crow allied with the Americans against their traditional enemies. They did not become Americans. They remained Crow.

The 1868 Fort Laramie Treaty formalized the terms of that alliance in ways the Crow had not fully anticipated. The treaty that ended Red Cloud's War — fought primarily between the Lakota and the United States over the Bozeman Trail — required the Crow to cede approximately thirty million acres of the territory the 1851 treaty had guaranteed them. The Powder River country. The Tongue River country. Everything east of the Bighorn Mountains. In exchange, the Crow received a reservation in the heart of the old territory — south of the Yellowstone, the Bighorn country, the mountains — and crucially, the right to hunt on the ceded lands as long as those lands remained unoccupied by white settlement.

The hunting rights provision was fought for and won by the Crow negotiators in two days of hard bargaining. It was written into the treaty. It has been litigated in American courts as recently as 2019, when the Supreme Court ruled in *Herrera v. Wyoming* that the Crow Tribe's off-reservation treaty hunting rights remain intact.

The Battle of the Little Bighorn — June 25-26, 1876 — was fought on the Crow reservation, on land the Crow had been promised and had not ceded. The Lakota and Cheyenne were there without Crow consent. The Crow scouts who guided Custer's Seventh Cavalry were fighting, among other things, to expel people who had been occupying

Crow territory for years. Six Crow scouts rode with Custer's column in the final days of the campaign. They warned him. He did not listen. They survived. He did not.

The Crow reservation in southeastern Montana is the fifth-largest in the United States — roughly 2.3 million acres. It is more land than most nations retained because the Crow had allied with the Army against their traditional enemies. Whether that alliance was the right choice is a question the Crow people have lived with ever since. There is no clean answer.

Kinship — Baáhpitche and the Crow Kinship System

The Apsáalooke kinship system is among the most studied in anthropological literature — distinctive enough that anthropologists named an entire category of kinship terminology after it. The Crow kinship system, as it is known in that literature, organizes family relationships differently from European kinship structures, with specific and socially significant terms for relationships that English collapses into single words like "aunt" or "cousin."

The term **Baáhpitche** designates the paternal aunt — the father's sister — a relationship that carries specific social weight in Crow culture. Iichíilee's use of this term when addressing Ashkáale throughout the novel reflects the precision of Apsáalooke kinship language and the particular importance of the father's sister in Crow family structure.

The author has made every effort to use accurate Crow kinship terminology, understanding that errors in its representation are the author's own and that correction from Crow speakers is welcome.

The Lakota and the Northern Cheyenne

The Lakota — the western branch of the Great Sioux Nation — were among the most powerful nations on the northern plains in the nineteenth century. By the early 1800s, they had expanded west across the Missouri River, pushing other nations before them, reaching as far as the Black Hills of what is now South Dakota, which they took from the Kiowa, and the Powder River country of Wyoming, which they took from the Crow.

The Northern Cheyenne allied with the Lakota through the middle of the nineteenth century, a partnership forged partly by proximity and partly by shared enemies. Together they controlled a vast swath of the northern plains — the Black Hills, the Powder River country, the Yellowstone drainage — and they were prepared to fight for it.

The Fort Laramie Treaty of 1851 attempted to establish territorial boundaries among the plains nations. For the Lakota and Cheyenne, it worked in their favor, as it recognized their control over territory that had recently belonged to other nations. The Crow, the Arikara, and the Pawnee — all had ceded ground to Lakota expansion before the treaty made that expansion official.

The discovery of gold in Colorado in 1858-59 set in motion a chain of events that would eventually destroy the Plains Indians' way of life. Settlers and miners flooded onto treaty-guaranteed land. The Army intervened on behalf of the settlers rather than the treaty holders. The Sand Creek Massacre of 1864 — in which Colorado militia attacked a peaceful Cheyenne and Arapaho encampment under a flag of truce, killing over one hundred people, the majority women and children — radicalized the southern plains nations and sent a clear message about the value of American treaty promises.

Red Cloud's War, fought from 1866 to 1868, was the Lakota and Cheyenne response to the Bozeman Trail — a wagon road that had been built through the heart of their hunting grounds to connect the Oregon Trail to the Montana gold fields. The Army built forts along the trail to protect emigrant traffic. The Lakota and Cheyenne besieged them. On December 21, 1866, Captain William J. Fetterman led eighty-one men out of Fort Phil Kearny in pursuit of a small decoy party led by Crazy Horse. They crossed Lodge Trail Ridge and rode into two thousand warriors waiting in the cold. Not one soldier survived. The Lakota called it the Battle of the Hundred Slain.

It was the worst military defeat the United States had suffered on the Great Plains, and it was won on land the Army had occupied without the consent of the Crow, who held the treaty right to that territory. Crow scouts had warned the Army of the gathering of warriors on the Tongue River. A major at Fort Laramie dismissed the warning. He did not believe Bridger exaggerated about Indians, he wrote, and did not believe much of what Bridger said.

The 1868 Fort Laramie Treaty ended Red Cloud's War on terms favorable to the Lakota. The Bozeman Trail forts were abandoned. Red Cloud signed only after the soldiers had marched out and the Lakota had burned the forts behind them. The Black Hills were recognized as part of the Great Sioux Reservation, held in perpetuity. The Lakota and Cheyenne retained unceded hunting territory north of the North Platte River.

Six years later, in 1874, Lieutenant Colonel George Armstrong Custer led an expedition into the Black Hills — Lakota sacred ground, guaranteed by treaty — ostensibly to find a location for a new fort but also to investigate reports of gold. His dispatches to the eastern newspapers reported gold from the grassroots up. The reports were exaggerated. The rush that followed was not. By 1875, miners were flooding into the Black Hills in violation of the treaty. The government attempted halfheartedly to keep them out, then stopped trying.

When Lakota leaders refused to sell the Black Hills, the government declared that any band not on a reservation by January 31, 1876, would be considered hostile and subject to military action. Most bands could not have received the order in time even if they had intended to comply. The Great Sioux War of 1876 began in March.

The Battle of the Little Bighorn was fought on June 25-26, 1876. Custer's column of approximately six hundred men was divided into three battalions and attacked the largest gathering of plains warriors in recorded history — estimates range from fifteen hundred to two thousand fighting men, representing the Lakota, Northern Cheyenne, and Arapaho nations, encamped in the valley of the Greasy Grass on the Crow reservation. Custer's scouts — six Crow and thirty-nine Arikara — had warned him the village was far larger than he understood. He attacked anyway. Two hundred and sixty-eight soldiers died. Among them was Custer.

The Army's response was to redouble its efforts. By the winter of 1876-77, the Lakota and Cheyenne were being pushed onto reservations by relentless military pressure, cold, and starvation. Crazy Horse surrendered in May 1877 with eight hundred followers to protect them from starvation. He was dead by September 5 of the same year.

The circumstances of Crazy Horse's death at Fort Robinson, Nebraska, remain contested. What is documented is this: he had surrendered peacefully and given up his weapons. In August 1877, the Army asked him to take up arms again to help subdue the Nez Perce. He agreed to fight as hard as he could. An interpreter who was hostile to him translated his words as a threat against white people. The Army moved to arrest him. Being walked toward the guardhouse on September 5, he struggled — whether he pulled a knife or was bayoneted from behind depends on which account you read and who was telling it. The Army's official journal recorded that he was mortally wounded trying to escape. His last words, reported by witnesses, were: *He has killed me now.*

His parents buried him in an unknown location. The exact site has never been established.

Sitting Bull held out in Canada until 1881, when hunger brought his people home. He surrendered at Fort Buford and was held as a prisoner of war for two years before being placed on the Standing Rock Reservation. He was killed there in December 1890 during an attempt by Indian police to arrest him, two weeks before the Wounded Knee Massacre.

The Buffalo — Before, During, and After

Before the hide hunters came, there were between thirty and sixty million bison on the North American plains. The number is difficult to establish with precision because no one had reason to count them. They were simply there — a fact of the landscape as permanent and fundamental as the grass and the sky, the engine of the plains economy and the plains cultures for thousands of years. The seasonal migrations of the herds had organized the lives of the plains peoples for longer than any record reached. The buffalo provided food, shelter, clothing, tools, and spiritual sustenance. Everything the Plains nations were was in relation to the buffalo.

The hide trade began in earnest after the Civil War. Eastern factories had discovered that buffalo hides could be tanned into excellent leather for industrial belts and machine parts — the mills running day and night across the northeast had an appetite for leather that appeared, to the men supplying it, essentially without limit. The completion of the Union Pacific Railroad in 1869 was the mechanical turning point. Before the railroad, hides had to be hauled overland to river transport — slow, expensive, limiting. After the railroad, a hide taken on the Powder River in the morning could be in a St. Louis processing facility within days. What followed was an industrial slaughter conducted at a scale and speed that no one had previously imagined possible.

The southern herd was destroyed first. Between 1871 and 1875, approximately four million southern plains bison were killed. By 1876, the southern herd was gone. The hunters moved north.

The railroad divided the herds. The Union Pacific cut across the ancient north-south migration routes and separated the buffalo into southern and northern populations. The Northern Pacific, which reached Miles City, Montana, in 1881, did the same to the northern herd — opening it to industrial-scale hunting just as the collapse of the southern herd was pushing thousands of hide hunters north in search of new ranges.

The northern plains — the Powder River country, the Yellowstone drainage, the ranges that had been contested ground between the Lakota and the Crow and the Army through the 1860s — opened fully after the 1868 Fort Laramie Treaty and drew hunters in the hundreds, then thousands, through the early 1870s. In 1872 alone, approximately 2,000 hunters were working the southern plains simultaneously, each killing an average of fifteen animals per day. A skilled hunter working alone with a Sharps rifle could take thirty to fifty animals in a single stand, a thousand or more in a season. Working in crews with skinners and camp tenders, the numbers were higher.

The hides went east. The meat was left to rot. The bones — the skulls, the ribs, the great curved horns — were left on the plains in quantities that staggered even the men who had made them. Within a decade, bone collectors were working the range behind the hunters, gathering what remained and shipping it east to be ground into fertilizer and bone char for sugar refining. The plains were stripped to nothing and then stripped again.

The ravens followed the hunters the way they had once followed the wolves — learning that the sound of the Sharps meant food, gathering at the report of the rifle before the animal had finished falling. This is documented behavior, not literary invention. The wolves, too, changed their patterns — abandoning the edges of the herds where they had always worked and moving instead to the hunters' wakes, where the meat lay in quantities beyond anything the wolf's understanding of the world had evolved to process.

The United States Army was aware of what the destruction of the buffalo meant for the plains nations and, in some cases, actively encouraged it. General Philip Sheridan opposed a Texas bill to protect the buffalo, suggesting instead that every hide hunter deserved a medal for doing more to settle the Indian question than the entire Army had managed in thirty years. He was not speaking metaphorically. The destruction of the buffalo was warfare by other means. The hide hunters were its instrument. Most of them did not know this. Some did not care. A few understood exactly what they were part of and kept working anyway because the money was there and the plains were vast and the animals seemed, until suddenly they didn't, inexhaustible.

The northern herd's collapse followed the southern herd's pattern but more quickly. In 1876, an estimated half million buffalo ranged within a hundred and fifty miles of Miles City. In 1882, approximately 200,000 hides were shipped from the Dakota Territory. In 1883, forty thousand. The following year, one carload. Hunters who outfitted in the fall of 1883, spending hundreds of dollars, expecting another season, rode out and found nothing. The animals had not moved. They had simply ceased to exist in numbers sufficient to find.

The last wild buffalo count in the continental United States, conducted in 1889, found 325 animals.

For the Plains nations, the destruction of the buffalo was not merely an economic catastrophe. It was the deliberate elimination of the material foundation of their entire world. When the buffalo were gone, the way of life that had depended on them was gone too — and the nations that had lived that way were left on reservations, dependent on government rations, with the knowledge that what had been taken from them had been taken deliberately, systematically, and without apology.

A Note on the Buffalo Hunters and Declan Shea

Declan Shea is a fictional man. The hide hunters he represents were real.

The fictional hide buyer in the 1872 chapter of this novel — Granger, with his ledger and his columns of numbers — represents the commercial infrastructure of the trade: the purchasing agents, the shipping contractors, the processing facilities, the eastern manufacturers who received the hides and turned them into goods and never asked and did not want to know what the supply chain looked like at its source end. These men were not unusual. They were doing ordinary commerce in a system that had decided, from the top down, that the destruction of the buffalo was not a tragedy but a policy.

Declan Shea worked the Powder River range from 1849 to 1883. He was fictional. The range he worked was real. The animals he took were real. The silence he found when he rode out in the fall of 1883, expecting another season, was real. Every hide hunter who rode out that fall found the same silence.

They had done the business so thoroughly that even they were surprised by how completely it was done.

Declan understood what he was part of. He filed it. He kept working.

That is the most honest thing this novel can say about the men who did what he did.

A Note on Violence Against Native Women and Children

The taking of Native women and children by white men was documented throughout the northern plains during the period this novel covers. It occurred in multiple forms — opportunistic violence by drifters and frontiersmen operating beyond any legal accountability, trafficking into mining camps and frontier towns, and predation by men who understood that the plains offered them impunity that settled territories would not. No formal records were kept. The women and children taken rarely appear in the historical record except in the accounts of the communities from which they were taken.

The incident depicted in this novel — two white men taking a Crow child from the edges of a camp before dawn — is fictional. The pattern it represents is not.

The Bozeman Trail and Red Cloud's War

In 1863, a frontier guide named John Bozeman blazed a trail north from the Oregon Trail through the Powder River country of Wyoming — through territory the Fort Laramie Treaty of 1851 had recognized as belonging to the Crow, through territory the Lakota had been occupying by force for a decade — to reach the Montana gold fields more directly than any existing route. Within two seasons, the trail was carrying thousands of wagons. The Crow watched the emigrant traffic from the ridges. The Lakota attacked it.

The Army responded by building three forts along the trail in 1866: Fort Reno, Fort Phil Kearny, and Fort C.F. Smith. All three sat on Crow treaty land. The Crow provided scouts and intelligence to the garrisons and were compensated with the protection of Army rifles against the Lakota — the same arrangement that had governed Crow-Army relations since the early 1860s.

The Lakota and Cheyenne under Red Cloud laid siege to the forts. Wood-cutting parties were attacked. Supply trains were picked apart. The soldiers inside the walls were effectively prisoners.

On December 21, 1866, Captain William J. Fetterman led the relief party out of Fort Phil Kearny with eighty men. He had been at the fort for seven weeks. He had famously boasted that with eighty men, he could ride through the Sioux Nation. He had come close to being ambushed earlier in December and had reportedly told his commanding officer afterward that he had learned his lesson about Indian fighting.

Crazy Horse led the decoy party. Ten warriors who showed themselves on Lodge Trail Ridge — taunting, retreating, showing their backs, drawing the soldiers forward. Fetterman followed them over the ridge. Two thousand warriors waited in the cold on the other side. The fight lasted perhaps twenty minutes.

Not one soldier survived.

Before the battle, Crow scouts had ridden through the Lakota encampment on the Tongue River and reported to Jim Bridger, the legendary mountain man and Army scout then stationed at Fort C.F. Smith, that the camp had taken half a day to ride through. Bridger reported this to the Army commander at Fort Laramie. The commander wrote in response that he did not believe much of what Bridger said. He exaggerated about Indians.

Eighty-one men died because one commander would not listen to the people who knew the ground.

The pattern had been established at the Fetterman Fight, and it held through the Little Bighorn. The Plains Nations understood the country they were fighting over. The Army repeatedly refused to believe them.

Red Cloud's War ended in 1868 with the second Fort Laramie Treaty. The Bozeman Trail forts were abandoned. Red Cloud signed the treaty only after the soldiers had marched out. The Lakota burned the forts behind them. It was the first and last time a plains nation fought the United States to a standstill and dictated the terms of peace.

The Little Bighorn, 1876

The Battle of the Little Bighorn was fought on June 25-26, 1876, in the valley of the Greasy Grass River — the Lakota name for the Little Bighorn — on the Crow reservation in what is now southeastern Montana. It was the most significant engagement of the Great Sioux War and the most famous battle of the American Indian Wars.

The immediate cause was the government's attempt to force the Lakota and Cheyenne onto reservations after the failure of negotiations over the Black Hills. The deeper causes stretched back through decades of broken treaties, stolen land, and the systematic destruction of the buffalo herds that had supported the plains nations.

Six Crow scouts guided Custer's Seventh Cavalry to the Little Bighorn: Half Yellow Face, the eldest and pipe carrier; Whiteman Runs Him; White Swan; Hairy Moccasin; Goes Ahead; and seventeen-year-old Curley. Before the battle, the scouts changed out of their Army uniforms and put on their own clothes. They told Custer they wanted to die as Crow warriors if they died that day. Custer sent them back before the final charge. All six survived.

The scouts had warned Custer at the Crow's Nest overlook on the morning of June 25 that the village in the valley was enormous — larger than he understood, larger than anything they had seen. He could not see it himself through the morning haze. He attacked anyway.

The village contained between eight thousand and fifteen thousand people, with an estimated fifteen hundred to two thousand warriors. Custer divided his regiment and led five companies of approximately two hundred and ten men toward the northern end of the village. Within an hour, they were dead. Every man. Custer among them.

The Crow called it a tragedy without winners. Their scouts had guided the soldiers. The soldiers had died. The battle had been fought on Crow land without Crow consent, against Crow enemies who had been occupying that land for years. The Crow had been on the right side and the losing side simultaneously — a position with no clean name and no easy accounting.

The Army's response to the defeat was total war. By the winter of 1876-77, the Lakota and Cheyenne resistance was broken. Crazy Horse surrendered in May 1877. Sitting Bull fled to Canada. The unceded territory became United States land. The reservation era had begun.

Bíawacheeitchish — Woman Chief

The woman the Crow named Bíawacheeitchish — Woman Chief — was born around 1806 into the Gros Ventre people of what is now Montana. When she was approximately ten years old, a Crow raiding party captured her, and a Crow warrior adopted her as his own, raising her among his people. She never returned to the Gros Ventre.

From an early age she was drawn to the activities that Crow

culture assigned to men — riding, hunting, warfare. Her adoptive father encouraged her. She became an expert markswoman and horsewoman, capable of field-dressing a buffalo with the skill of an experienced hunter. When her father died, she assumed leadership of his lodge.

She earned her place in Crow history during a Blackfoot raid on a fort sheltering Crow and white families. She stood and fought when others fled, killing two attackers and playing a decisive role in turning back the raid. Afterward, she organized her own war parties, raiding Blackfoot settlements and returning with horses and scalps. The Crow council of chiefs gave her a seat among them. She rose to third rank among the leaders of her band of one hundred and sixty lodges.

She wore women's clothing throughout her life while performing the roles the Crow assigned to chiefs — negotiating, leading war parties, and accumulating the honors of a warrior. She married four women who managed her lodge while she was in the field. The devices on her robe represented her own brave acts, each one.

Edwin Denig, a fur trader who knew her for twelve years and wrote the most detailed contemporary account of her life, said she compiled a war record so distinguished that it elevated her to a point of honor and respect not often reached by male warriors, certainly never before conferred upon a female of the Crow Nation.

In 1851, she represented the Crow at the Horse Creek Treaty negotiations. In the summer of 1854, she traveled north as a diplomatic envoy to make peace with the Gros Ventre, her birth people. They killed her.

She was approximately forty-eight years old.

Her story was kept alive in the Crow oral tradition. She is still regarded as one of the great figures of Apsáalooke history.

Other Historical Crow Women Warriors

Bíawacheeitchish was the most famous but not the only Crow

woman to earn recognition as a warrior and leader.

Akkeekaahuush — Comes Toward The Near Bank, approximately 1810 to 1880 — was an infamous war leader alongside her husband, Knife. She was captured by the Piegan in battle and later escaped.

Biliíche Héeleelash — Among The Willows, 1837 to 1912 — was a prominent war leader and pipe carrier known for riding into battle in her finest female clothing. She made no concession to male convention in dress or manner. She was a woman warrior who dressed entirely as a woman.

These were not anomalies in Crow culture. The Apsáalooke recognized and honored women who chose the warrior's path. Their names were kept.

Historical Figures in the Novel

Several historical figures appear in this novel, either directly or by reference. A note on each:

Daxpitcheehísshish — Red Bear was a documented Mountain Crow chief active in the mid-nineteenth century, approximately 1807 to the 1860s. He appears in the historical record as a leader of the Mountain Crow band during the period the novel covers.

Búahisshish — Red Fish was a historical Apsáalooke leader of the mid-1500s during whose time the Crow came to control obsidian sources in what is now Yellowstone Park. His name is used in the novel for a character set in the 1850s-1860s.

Bíawacheeitchish — Woman Chief is documented above. She died in 1854, three years before the novel's Crow storyline begins. Her legacy lives on in the story through Ashkáale's telling.

Biliíche Héeleelash — Among The Willows is documented above. She was alive during the novel's timeline and is referenced as such.

Ho'néheevǎhtóohe — Howling Wolf is a documented Cheyenne name meaning Howling Wolf, recorded in Cheyenne language materials. The character in the novel is fictional, but the name is real.

Jim Bridger — mountain man, scout, guide — was a historical figure present at Fort C.F. Smith in 1866, where he received and reported the Crow warning about the Lakota gathering that preceded the Fetterman Fight. The Army's dismissal of his intelligence contributed directly to the deaths of eighty-one men. Bridger retired from scouting in the early 1870s due to failing health and died in 1881 in Missouri.

Seth Bullock arrived in Deadwood in 1876, opened a hardware store with partner Sol Star, and became the town's first sheriff. He is documented as an imposing and effective lawman who helped bring order to one of the most violent camps in the American West.

Al Swearengen arrived in Deadwood in May 1876 and operated the Gem Theater — a saloon, dance hall, and brothel — for twenty-two years. He is documented as among the most brutal figures in Deadwood's history, controlling the lower end of Main Street through violence, political alliance, and the exploitation of vulnerable women. He left Deadwood penniless after the Gem's final fire in 1899 and died in Denver in 1904 under circumstances that remain unclear.

A Note on the Crow and Cheyenne Languages

The Crow names and words in this novel are drawn from documented sources, including the Crow Language Consortium dictionary, the fieldwork of Robert Lowie and Fred Voget, and the Little Bighorn College Library's Apsáalooke language resources. The author has made every effort to use accurate spellings and meanings, understanding that Crow is a living language spoken by approximately five thousand people today and that any errors in its representation are the author's own.

The term **Baáhpitche** — paternal aunt, the father's sister — is drawn from Apsáalooke language documentation. It is used by Iichíilee when addressing Ashkáale throughout the novel.

The Cheyenne names are drawn from documented sources, including the Behind the Name Cheyenne language submissions and official

Cheyenne language materials. The name **Heávohe** — meaning devil, derived from the Spanish *diablo* — appears in documented Cheyenne language sources.

The Onondaga name **Gahsóhda'gęh** — meaning Eel Moving or Eel in the Water — is drawn from Onondaga language documentation. The character who bears this name appears early in the novel and represents the Haudenosaunee presence in central New York that Declan encounters on his journey west.

The author acknowledges that working with living indigenous languages as an outsider is a responsibility that requires care, humility, and the acceptance that perfect accuracy may not be achievable. Any errors in the representation of these languages are unintentional, and the author welcomes correction.

A Note on Sources

The history in this novel draws on a wide range of published sources. Among those most useful to the author:

On the Crow Nation: *The Crow Indians* by Robert Lowie; *Crow Country* by Frederick Hoxie; the Little Bighorn College Library's Apsáalooke historical and language resources; the timeline of Apsáalooke chiefs compiled by Little Bighorn College.

On the Lakota and Cheyenne: *Bury My Heart at Wounded Knee* by Dee Brown; *The Killing of Crazy Horse* by Thomas Powers; *The Last Stand* by Nathaniel Philbrick; *Son of the Morning Star* by Evan S. Connell.

On the buffalo: *American Bison: A Natural History* by Dale Lott; Ken Burns's documentary *The American Buffalo* and its companion timeline; the All About Bison historical timeline.

On the Fetterman Fight: *Where a Hundred Soldiers Were Killed* by John H. Monnett; the Fort Phil Kearny historical records.

On the Little Bighorn: *Little Bighorn Remembered* by Herman J. Viola; the Little Bighorn Battlefield National Monument archives; *Crow Scouts at the Little Bighorn* — multiple sources, including the Billings

Gazette and True West Magazine.

On Deadwood: *Deadwood: The Golden Years* by Watson Parker; the Deadwood History timeline; the Adams Museum records.

On Woman Chief: the writings of Edwin Denig, particularly *Five Indian Tribes of the Upper Missouri*; the Distinctly Montana article on nineteenth-century women warriors of the Apsáalooke and Piikáni.

On the Cheyenne language: Behind the Name Cheyenne submissions; official Northern Cheyenne language materials.

On the Crow kinship system: the anthropological literature on Crow kinship terminology; the Crow Language Consortium dictionary; the fieldwork of Robert Lowie.

The photograph of a buffalo skull pile taken in Raines, Michigan, circa 1892 — two men dwarfed by a mountain of skulls awaiting shipment to eastern processing facilities — informed the 1872 chapter of this novel more than any written account. It is widely reproduced and available through the Burton Historical Collection at the Detroit Public Library.

The author visited the Crow Reservation and the Little Bighorn Battlefield, the Crazy Horse Memorial, the Black Hills, Deadwood, the Bighorn Mountains, and the Powder River country while researching this novel. The landscape is as described. The history is as recorded. The people who lived it deserve to have it told accurately.

ACKNOWLEDGMENTS OF LIMITATION

I am a white author writing about Native American experiences and histories. While I have tried to approach this work with respect, research, and humility, I acknowledge that I am writing from outside these communities and cultures.

Native peoples' own stories, told in their own voices, are essential and irreplaceable. This novel is not and cannot be a substitute for those voices. It is one white character's journey toward understanding the historical realities of dispossession and his role as witness to those events.

I encourage readers to seek out books, films, art, and scholarship created by Native authors and artists, whose perspectives and stories are central to understanding these histories and their contemporary legacies.

Any errors in this novel—historical, cultural, or linguistic—are mine alone. I welcome correction and continued learning.